Tempt the BOSS

NATASHA MADISON

Tempt The Boss ©2017 Natasha Madison

Cover Design: Melissa Gill with MGBookCovers & Designs
Book formatting: CP Smith
Editing: Julia Goda Diamond in the Rough Editing
Proofing Author Services by Julie Deaton

To Lisa, without you there would be no book!

Tempt the Boss

CHAPTER ONE

Lauren

Beep, Beep, Beep. My hand snakes out from underneath the warm cocoon of my blankets. Grabbing my phone from the side table, I shut it off and bring it under the blankets with me. Seven minutes later, I feel it vibrate under my pillow between my hands.

Pulling myself up and swinging my legs out of the bed, I walk downstairs, going straight for the coffee machine. Thank god for this programmed machine, because the coffee is ready for me to drink.

I blink my eyes a couple of times while I turn on the light over the stove. With it lightly dimmed, I lean against the counter and look at the clock. Five-thirty on the nose. Smelling the coffee, I slowly take a sip to not burn my tongue. My brain jolts awake as the hot, strong brew rolls over my tongue.

It's the calm before the storm. In thirty minutes, I will have to get the kids up and get them ready for the bus that is always here at exactly seven-ten.

I look into the dining room, taking in the hurricane that is my children. Opened backpacks linger on the floor near the chairs, papers are tossed on the table, homework they finished but haven't put away. No matter how much I tell them to clean up the table before they go to sleep, Gabriel, who is ten, and Rachel, who is six and a half going on twenty, always leave it until the last minute. Something they inherited from their father.

I look around the house—the open concept floor plan makes it easy to see into the rooms around me—taking in the changes that the house has gone through in the last six months. No more men's sneakers at the door. No more suit jackets hanging on the back of the chair at the table blending in with the backpacks.

Nope. Nothing. Nada. Taking another sip of the coffee, I let my mind wander to when it all changed.

Walking up to the children's school for the parent/teacher interview, I am running late, of course. I had to pick up Gabriel from soccer practice, while rushing Rachel to gymnastics, then we grabbed McDonald's in the car on the way home. Eating my cheeseburger in the car is why I now have a mustard stain on my shirt. Pulling a scarf that I find in my backseat, I throw it over my neck hoping it covers the stain.

Once in the school, I make my way to the classroom of Gabriel's teacher. I run down a list of things that I need to get done when I get home. Thinking about the birthday parties that the kids are invited to this weekend. The gifts are already sitting in the trunk waiting to be wrapped. I hope that Jake will at least be available on Sunday.

Stay-at-home mom. That is my job, and I love it. Sometimes. Most times. More days than not. My husband, Jake, is an ad executive in the biggest marketing firm in the city. He spent the last eight years working his way up the ladder. His long work hours are our sacrifice until he gets that corner office, then he can cut back a bit. At least, that's what he keeps saying. I still stand by my conclusion he is a workaholic.

We met when I was fresh out of college; I had just started working at the same agency he did. Not the one he's with now, but the first agency he worked at after college. I was hired as the office temp assistant. Since it was a small office of only five, it was normal that we spent all day together. Those long hours together resulted in us becoming good friends. Becoming a couple was the natural next step. I don't think it surprised anyone when we walked in on a Monday morning holding hands, both of us looking at each other with our hearts in our eyes.

Getting to Ms. Alvarez's door, I knock once and then walk in. Looking around, I'm shocked to see Jake sitting in one of the chairs in front of the desk, while Ms. Alvarez sits in hers.

Walking up to him, I lean down and kiss him on the lips. "Hey, I didn't know you would be here," I say, sitting down in the chair next to him.

He nods at me and then looks down at his shoes. I don't know how to describe what came next, except to say that my world crashed around me. It's like my heart knew it. It's like my body knew it had to go into protection mode.

"Lauren," he says, still looking at his shoes. I look down at them wondering what he is looking at exactly. I will never forget them. Brown, with light brown laces. Stain free, scuff free. Clean.

It is at this point I start to panic, start to think something is wrong. "What's the matter?" I ask him and then look over at Ms. Alvarez. She is gorgeous with beautiful thick, black curly hair that is always styled perfectly. Whether she wears it in a ponytail or loose, you can't help but envy her fantastic hair. She always looks so put together, but right now, she's looking at my husband nervously as she blinks away tears, and her hands clasped together in her lap are shaking.

"I've met someone." The breath I have been holding rushes from my lungs. My legs go so weak, I feel it so strongly even though I am sitting. My heart is beating so hard and fast, I hear it echo in my ears. My mouth gets dry, and my hands start to tremble as I feel that heart starting to break.

"What?" I look at him and then at Ms. Alvarez. "Jake, now is not a good time. Not here." It's like I'm begging him to not tell me. Like I'm begging him to take it back.

"I love her," he says with a whisper, and then all the pieces to the puzzle start coming together. Gabe's tutoring classes that Jake would always pick him up from—the ones they'd always be late getting home from. I look at my son's teacher and see a tear run out of the corner of her eye while she smiles at my husband. My fucking husband—the one who made vows to me. The one who promised to love, honor, and cherish me for the rest of his life.

"You?" I say to him and then look at her. "You slept with my husband?" I ask her while I feel Jake's hand on top of mine. I shake it off, not wanting to feel his touch right now. Not wanting him to try to comfort me.

"It was me. I started this. I did this, not Camilla." He tries to reach out and touch me again. Getting up from the chair, I start to pace the room. *Thoughts are running through my mind. How did I not know? How did I not suspect? Was it because I was too tired for sex? Was it because I still needed to lose the extra ten pounds that I had lingering on me? Was it because I was too tired at the end of the day to even talk to him?*

Stopping in my tracks, I look at them. He has now stood up and so has she. A desk still separates them. "We had sex last night," *I tell him, and he doesn't continue to look at me; instead, he looks at her.*

"It was the last time. Kind of a good-bye kind of thing," *he says, now looking at the floor.*

"A good-bye thing." *I now raise my voice.* "A good-bye thing?" *I shake my head.* "How long? How long has this been going on? How long have you been sleeping with your student's married father?" *My voice is firm, anger starting to rush through me.*

"Lauren, let's not—" *he tries to say, but I don't give him a chance. I yell, and this time loudly,* "How long? How long have you been sleeping with her and coming home to me? How long have you been telling me you love me and lying about it? How fucking long, Jake? How much of my life is a lie?"

They both look at each other. "Seven months," *he answers right before there is a knock on the door. The principal sticks his head inside* "Oh. Mr. and Mrs. Watson, is everything okay?" *The poor man doesn't see anything coming.*

"Oh, we are totally fine." *My voice starts to rise, while my hands start to shake.* "I've come to attend my son's parent/teacher conference only to be told his teacher is fucking my husband. Looks like in addition to tutoring her students in math, she also offers sex ed lessons to their fathers! She deserves a raise." *I laugh humorlessly. Maybe I'm having a stroke. Maybe, just maybe, this is all a dream.* "But other than that, I would say everything is perfect."

I walk to the chair that I have been sitting in, picking up the purse that fell off my shoulder while my life fell apart. Grabbing it, I turn to walk out as Jake grabs my wrist. "Lauren, wait."

I yank my wrist away from him, the force shocking both of us. "Don't fucking touch me," *I hiss before I walk past the principal and right into the hallway, where I'm greeted by the president of the PTA, Colleen.*

The tears have now started to freely fall down my cheeks. "Oh, *honey, I just heard." I look at this woman who I thought was actually my friend. I tilt my head to the side. "You knew?" I don't really need her to answer, since she puts her head down to look at her hands she is wringing together.*

I can't stop the angry laugh that bursts from my mouth. I'm that oblivious spouse who everyone makes fun of. I'm that wife who said it would never happen to me. I'm that woman who they all feel sorry for. I'm her. That poor, clueless woman who can't seem to keep her husband from falling dick first into a sexy, twenty-something woman. I look around to see who else is looking at us.

The secretary, the principal, Colleen, and four of her posse, who are there trying to get parents to join the PTA, Jake, and her. "Does everyone know he was having an affair? Was I the only one who didn't know?" I throw my hands out to the side, turning on my heel as I walk out of the school, vowing never to return.

I get in my car and make one phone call to Kaleigh, my sister. I don't know how much she understands between the sobs and the yelling, but ten minutes later when I pull up to the curb of my perfect house, she is there throwing Jake's clothes out of our bedroom window. They land right in the front of my house on the lawn.

It takes her a full five minutes to toss everything out. I stand here, still in shock, still in a daze, looking at the mountain of his clothes. Clothes I bought him. Clothes I picked out. Clothes I washed, ironed, and put away. I don't see Kaleigh come from the side of the house with the gasoline container in her hand. I just see her pouring it all over his clothes. She walks over to me, handing me the packet of matches. "Let's burn this motherfucker down."

And we do. Till one of the neighbors calls the fire department, who rush out, three full trucks, lights blaring in the night, an EMT, and one police cruiser. I sit here on my lawn, watching the flames rising up from the pile of everything that he owns before the whole mess is drenched in water.

The second alarm sounds, bringing me out of my trip back into that nightmare.

"Gabe! Rachel! Time to get up, guys! Mommy starts her new job today," I yell, hoping they hear me. I take another sip of my coffee before I make my way upstairs to get ready for my new job. Yay me.

CHAPTER TWO

Lauren

I look at myself in the mirror, smoothing the front of my skirt down. What a difference six months make. Gone is the extra weight that had been lingering on my petite frame for the last six years, thanks to some cardio at the gym and the fact that I stopped eating. You would think that your husband leaving you would have you drowning your sorrows in carbs, ice cream, and cheese, but it was actually quite the opposite for me. On the rare occasion I actually have a little bit of an appetite, the second I put something in my mouth, I feel sick. So, I am getting there slowly but surely. I have grown out my hair, adding layers into it instead of just the 'mom bob' I had been sporting. I also added some golden, honey-colored highlights.

I'm dressed in a tight, gray knee-length pencil skirt that I paired with a light pink silk shirt with a ruffled collar and cap sleeves. I've added my very favorite Manolo Blahnik black Mary Janes, a Mother's Day present from three years ago. If nothing else, he left me with two beautiful children and a closet full of designer heels.

I take a deep breath. This is it.

My phone beeps again. "Ten minutes, guys, let's go." I walk out of my room, heading down the stairs while watching my ten-year-old put his cereal bowl in the sink and grab all his papers from the table, shoving them in his backpack. "Rachel, don't forget to pack your reading log that's on the couch."

I look over at my sister, who is nursing her second cup of coffee. She sits with her legs crossed, watching it all. Dressed in her yoga pants that mold perfectly to her thin, five-foot-seven-inch body and a loose sweater that falls off one shoulder. "How do you remember this stuff?" she asks.

"It's magic. Once you become a parent, you'll get a brain," I tell her with a smirk.

"Then what happened to Jake?" She smiles back while taking a sip.

"Okay, I take that back. Once you become *a mother*, you get a brain. I mean, I don't think all men are dicks. Look at Dad," I tell her while I put the milk back in the fridge and pick up the cereal box, putting it back into the cupboard. My phone alarm sounds again. "Two minutes, guys!" I have my phone set to different times so I never run late. It's another thing I got when I became a mom.

I look over at Kaleigh, who is now reading the newspaper. "Aren't you going to be late?" I ask her while I grab the lunch boxes and walk to the door with the kids.

She folds the paper in half. "Nope, I have a client at ten-thirty. We are doing yoga in the park today. Become one with the earth and all that." She does the Namaste hands, while I walk out with the kids to go to the bus stop.

I hold Rachel's hand while we walk to the bus stop, her brown hair done in a side ponytail with a huge flower headband. "Don't forget, Auntie Kay will be there when you get off the bus this afternoon, because Mommy has the new job." She looks up and smiles at me, one tooth missing. "I know, Momma, you said it. Twice." I look in front and see that Gabe is talking to another kid who is waiting at the bus stop. Once the kids get on the bus, I wave to them and turn to go home.

Mrs. Flounder, who is my next-door neighbor, comes out with curlers in her hair and a cigarette hanging from her lips. "Hey there, Lauren, you look fantastic. Is today the day you finally become free of that scum bucket?" she asks while picking up her paper.

The news that Jake cheated on me spread faster than the flames did over the pile of his gasoline-soaked clothes. Of course, once it was confirmed that Camilla slept with a father of one of her students, she was quietly transferred. She is now teaching at another school a town over.

Telling the kids that we were getting a divorce was hard, but they didn't seem surprised by it. I guess half of their friends' parents were divorced, so it wasn't unusual to them. I, on the other hand, didn't have such an easy time with the idea. I honestly thought forever meant forever, not till someone sexier waves their ass in my face and shows me attention. Maybe if he'd come home and done the vacuuming once in a while, I would have showed him some attention. Fuck, maybe if he'd picked up his sweaty socks, I might have felt inclined to do even more for him.

Shaking my head no at Mrs. Flounder, I look at her. "I start my new temp position today."

"Oh, that's nice, dear. Time to earn the bacon." She shakes her hand and goes inside. Once I get back inside, I grab my lunch and my purse. I look at Kaleigh, who is now in the middle of my living room doing some crazy yoga pose. "I'm so fucking nervous. What if I fuck up or cry or, or... fuck up?" I look at her while she moves back to standing instead of balancing on her head.

"You are going to go in there and kill it. And if you don't"—she shrugs her shoulders—"then you don't. What's the worst that can happen? You fall face first in your boss's crotch?" I glare at her, throwing my hands in the air.

"Don't forget, the kids are off the bus at two forty-five. Did you set an alarm?" I ask her.

"Yup, on my internal clock." She rolls her eyes at me. "Stop stressing. It's going to be fine. You are going to be late if you don't leave now." She ushers me out the door. "Don't forget to play nice and make friends. Friends who are nice and hot and have big dicks!" she screams after me as I get into my car and close the door. Mrs. Flounder gives me the thumbs up, clearly in agreement with my sister. "Dear God," I mumble to myself as I start the car.

I shouldn't use the word 'car', because this isn't a car, it's a minivan. A big, safe, screams it's-for-a-family vehicle. I obviously got this in the divorce settlement, while he drives around in his new Mercedes, which is not for families. It's for cheating bastards who only get their kids every other weekend and once during the week.

Making my way to work, I'm stuck in a bit of light traffic. Nothing that is bumper-to-bumper, just flowing slowly. My eyes keep traveling between the clock and the GPS on the center console, as well as the occasional peek at the GPS on my phone, which just so happens to calculate the traffic between where I am and my destination.

I'm singing along to Maroon Five's "Don't Wanna Know" when a call comes in. Penelope's name flashes on the screen. Penelope is my friend from college, the only friend who I kept in touch with. She runs an HR firm that specializes in placing temps. She is the reason I have this job right now.

"Hello," I say while I wait for her voice to fill the car.

"Hey there, just checking in. You ready?" she asks me. I hear her rustling papers in the background, so I know she is already at her desk.

"Yup, I'm on my way there now. I'm so nervous, I may puke, though. But I'll be on time." I chuckle at the thought of me barfing all over my new boss. I brake for the traffic that is slowing to a crawl in front of me when I feel my van jerk forward slightly. My head flies forward and then snaps back. Looking in my mirror, I see that someone just hit me.

"Oh my god. Someone just ran into me. Fuck me, P. I have to call you back," I say, unlocking my seatbelt and climbing out of the car.

I put my Tory Burch sunglasses on top of my head, walking to the back to see the damage. I don't even have time to get there before I hear a raspy voice ask, "What the hell is wrong with you? You just stopped!" I put a hand over my eyes to block the sun and see him. And boy, do I see him. My heart skips a beat when he whips his aviator sunglasses off his face.

He's about six feet tall, maybe taller, with dark hair that's short on the sides and a bit longer at the top, which almost looks like it was combed back by his hands. His eyes are a mossy green with shimmery gold flecks in them that I can see thanks to the sun hitting them just right. A freshly-shaven face that shows off the strong angles of his jaw and hints at where I'm sure a five-o'clock shadow of delicious stubble will emerge in a few hours.

He's wearing a suit minus the jacket. His dark blue pants are a perfect fit, molding to him like they were made especially for him, and from the looks of them, they probably were. His crisp, white dress shirt is open at the collar and covers his broad chest and thick biceps. His sleeves are rolled up to his elbows and show off a big, masculine silver Rolex watch.

He throws his hand up as he angrily asks, "Is something wrong with you? Are you drunk?"

I take a step back, putting my hand to my stomach. "Are you talking to me?" I look around, wondering if there is someone else he could be talking to. "You hit me. You. Hit. Me." I storm to the back of the car to assess the damage. I see that my bumper is a bit scratched, but his Porsche is going to need some body work.

"I can't believe this. I can't flipping believe this! Now I'm going to be late because you were probably too busy on your phone texting to pay attention to the road." I walk to my car, opening the door and leaning across the seat to grab my purse. Cars pass us slowly, everyone taking a look to see what's going on.

Looking at the clock on the dash, I see that I have to be at my new job in twenty minutes. Grabbing my license, registration, and insurance ID card, I slam the door and walk over to see him leaning on the side of *my* car, watching me.

"I'm going to be late. Is there any way we can just exchange numbers and get all the information after?" I ask, looking through the papers.

I hear him huff. "You probably don't have insurance, which is why you want to call me later so you can get some while I drive around with a missing light." He walks over to his car, leans down, and grabs his phone from the driver's seat.

I look at him. "So, you weren't on the phone? Riiighhhhttt," I say, glaring at him.

"I don't have all day. Some of us have actual work to do. What do you want from me?" His tone is snarky.

"Actually, I don't want anything from you. My car has a scratch, yours is the one that is damaged. Besides, it wasn't even my fault. Maybe we should call the police to make a report so we can get it on the record that you were driving while texting." I lean my head to the side. "I'm not a police officer or anything, but I think that's against the law."

He snarls at me, "Just give me your number." I tell him my number, and when he asks my name, I gladly tell him. "The woman whose car you hit because you were texting while driving." He looks at me and his eyebrows pinch together. "Is that name already taken?" I ask him, waiting for his answer. When I realize he isn't going to reply, I ask him,

"Now, what's yours?" He shoots off his number, and I store it in my phone.

I turn around to walk away. "Aren't you going to ask me my name?" He puts his hands on his hips, his biceps bulging, and his chest looking impossibly broader.

"Nope, no need. I just put you under 'Asshat who texts while driving and hit my car.'" I smile at him. "Have a fabulous day," I grumble, turning around and getting back in the car.

Fuck. I see that I now have ten minutes to get there. I dial Penelope right after I buckle and take off, watching the asshole get into his car. "I think I might still make it," I tell her even before she says hello.

"It's okay. I called and told them there was an accident on the way, and they said not to worry, that Austin was going to be late, too. So, you're still good to go. How's the damage?" she asks.

"Minivan: 1 – Porsche: 0." I laugh and tell her I'll check back in with her at lunch.

When I finally make it to the office building, I check my face and apply lip gloss one more time before walking inside. I look at my phone and notice that I'm only seven minutes late. Not bad all things considered. I walk in and tell the security guard I am there for Barbara at Mackenzie Jacob Associates. When he calls up, he gets the all clear to send me up.

I make my way up to the forty-sixth floor and walk to the receptionist, who is smiling from ear-to-ear. "Hi. I'm here to see Barbara. My name is Lauren. I'm the temp," I explain as she gets up and comes around to shake my hand, introducing herself as Carmen. She then takes me back to meet Barbara.

Barbara is short with white hair, and her glasses are perched on her nose. "Hey there, Lauren. I'm so happy to finally meet you. I've heard great things from Penelope." She reaches out to shake my hand and motions for me to sit down.

"Thank you so much, and I'm so sorry I'm late. I was in a little fender bender, and I tried to finish as fast as I could," I tell her, sitting down in the chair in front of her desk.

"No worries. I heard Austin was going to be about ten minutes late, but he got here right before you did. Now, if you will fill out these papers here, I will get your elevator pass ready for you," she says while she goes to her cabinet in the corner.

Because this is just a temp job, I don't have to do much. Just an emergency contact form. "Now, I should warn you that this is the tenth temp we have hired for this position... this month," she finishes quickly.

I look at her, confused. "But it's only the seventeenth of November." My heart starts racing. What if he throws me out? What if he laughs at me since I haven't worked in ten years?

"Mr. Mackenzie is, um, well... special to work for," she murmurs while looking down at the papers in front of her and not even trying to make eye contact with me.

"Special? What does that mean?" I ask, my eyebrows pinching together.

"Let's just say that my money is on you." She gets up. "Shall we?" She points to the door. I nod at her, trying to get some saliva going in my mouth. It's dry, and my palms are sweating. I think my armpits are actually starting to sweat, too. Oh, boy. I can't do this. I should turn around and run away.

But before I can make my move, we reach a door that is closed. The big brown door is solid, and the windows that look out into the office have their shades drawn. I hear Barbara knock on the door before we enter.

I don't see much in front of her. I just look around the office at the view of the city, since there are wall-to-wall windows affording it an amazing view. I don't have a chance to look much further, because all I hear is a raspy voice asking, "Are you fucking stalking me? Did you follow me here?" I whip my head around to look at him.

Just my luck. It's the asshat from this morning, the one who hit me. Except now, the asshat is sitting behind the desk, the desk that, apparently, belongs to my new temporary boss.

CHAPTER THREE

Austin

I'm already having the shittiest day ever and it's only fucking eight o'clock. My alarm didn't wake me at five a.m. like it does every day, so I didn't have a chance to get my run in before I had to head to work.

Just a quick shower and a coffee before I hurried out. I walked out of my apartment, rushed to the elevator, and ran smack into my ex, who, according to her, 'just happened to be in the area.'

It took a lot for me not to roll my eyes at her. She wasn't in the area; she's fucking the dude who lives upstairs. Not that I care. I was the one who let her go. Whatever, I blew her off and headed to my car.

Right as I started up my car, my mother decided it was a great day to call and lay out everything that's wrong with my life. I'm nearing forty; all I have is my career, blah blah blah. Newsflash, Mom, that's all I want.

So, just when I thought it couldn't get any worse, I hit a mini bus, or a van, or whatever the hell it's called.

I expected a frumpy housewife to get out of the car, but instead I was greeted by a woman who could only be described as sex-on-a-stick, or I guess I should say two sticks, because those legs of hers aren't something I'll forget anytime soon. I couldn't even talk I was so stunned. Then she bent over her seat and presented me with the most perfect ass. I think I actually groaned.

My cock was getting ready to salute her right then and there as she walked back to me from her minivan. The thought that she was someone's wife and I was jonesing on her made my skin crawl. I may be an asshole, but I don't fuck with marriages or people in relationships. There are more than enough single people on earth to not get involved with someone who isn't.

I tried to see if she was wearing a ring, but I couldn't see anything. I took her number, and she rushed away.

The whole way to work, I replayed the scene in my head over and over again. I tried to think back on anything that I could have said that would have had her reacting so hostilely.

I got to the office just four minutes late. I absolutely loathe tardiness; people who are late drive me nuts. I built this company from the ground up. I am now the most sought-after commercial contract developer in the city, especially when it comes to entertainment establishments. If you want to open a restaurant or nightclub in this city, let's just say I am known widely as the best choice to make sure it happens.

There is never a dull moment in this business. If I have to get in there and swing a hammer or wash the damn glasses myself, I do it. There is nothing I won't do to protect my and my company's reputation. If you are opening a restaurant or a nightclub and you attach it to the name Mackenzie Jacob, chances are it'll be a hit from day one.

So now, here I am walking into my office a few minutes late. The cute new receptionist, Carmen, is batting her eyes at me as I walk in, dragging out her greeting. "Good Morning, Mr. Mackenzie." She's new here, so she mustn't have heard the news yet, but I don't fuck where I eat. Ever.

"Morning. Is my new temp here yet?" I ask her, getting right to the point as she hands me my messages. A new temp who is yet another thing I didn't need today.

Since my secretary retired last month, I've gone through six or seven temps…okay, maybe ten. But it's not all my fault. I can't take it if they're stupid and I have to sit there and spell things out for them. I need someone who can take direction, get it right the first time, and just do what I ask the first time I ask it. It's simple, really.

When I ask you to get me coffee, I'm not asking you to join me for a cup. When I tell you to scan and email something, I don't need reporting of the task as if you're waiting for a sticker on your paper. When you have a caller on hold, I don't need you announcing them to me through the intercom in a singsong voice. I also don't need you knocking on my door every few minutes to ask me if I need anything. Trust me, when I need something, you'll be the first one to know.

"Can you tell Barbara I'm in now?" I prompt her, walking away while I pull the collar from my neck, making my way down the hall toward my corner office.

I walk into my office, taking in the view of the city. We are on the forty-sixth floor, so I can see the skyline perfectly, and at night, it's even better. I eat, sleep, and breathe my work. There aren't set hours for my work. So, if I have to be at the office for fifteen hours a day, then that's what it takes. Which is why I don't need, or want, a wife at this point. I'd just let them down.

I've lost count of how many relationships I've had that have ended because I wasn't there when I said I would be. I'm married to my work, and she is my first priority.

Sitting in my chair, I start going through the messages. I flip through them, seeing two messages from Vegas. I'm thinking of branching out and opening an office there, but something is stopping me. I like to stay local. I like to show up during construction. I like to pop in when you least expect it, and I wouldn't be able to do that if I branched out to Vegas.

I'm about to call them back when there is a knock on the door. I don't even have to tell them to come in before Barbara opens the door. I look over at her. She's been here from day one, but she isn't what I'm looking at this morning; it's the girl behind her.

Fucking unbelievable! This crazy chick followed me to my work. She is probably coming to sue me. I'll show her. "Are you fucking stalking me? Did you follow me here?" I growl at her while I stand up behind my desk.

Barbara's face pales and her mouth hangs open, but not the sassy one behind her. "Follow you? Are you insane?" She looks at Barbara. "I can't do this. I totally understand why you've gone through so many temps. Who would work for him?" She shakes her head. "Not only did he hit my car"—she looks at me—"while texting. The first thing he asked was if I was drunk!" She looks back at Barbara, who then glares at me. Great, just great, she's on crazy chick's side. "You would think he would ask me if I'm *okay*, right? Nope, not this guy. He wanted to know if I was drunk at eight a.m. Who the hell drinks at eight a.m. anyway?" She folds her arms under her breasts, unnecessarily pushing them up. Fuck. I can't stop the mental image of her standing there, arms crossed under her tits, in nothing but her shoes. I shake that thought from my head.

"Wait." I throw the messages on my desk. "You, you're my temp?"

"No, sir," she says, and fuck me, but does that ever make me want to hold her hands behind her back as I bend her over my desk and pound into her while she calls me sir. "I *was* your temp." She looks at Barbara. "I wish you well." Then she turns and starts walking out the door.

Barbara's raised voice stops her. "Wait a second!" She looks at me. "Austin Montgomery Mackenzie, is Lauren telling me that you hit her car and then asked her if *she* was drunk? I raised you better than that, young man," she chides in that sharp tone I remember from my childhood. Okay, so Barbara was also my nanny growing up. That was to be expected when you're the child of world-renowned doctors who jetted around the globe saving lives. One is a cardiologist, and the other is a brain surgeon. They had very little time to raise a child. So, that's where Barbara came in, and she stayed until I was eighteen. She retired, but when I opened this firm, she was the first one I thought of to handle the HR side of the company, something I knew she would handle far better than me. "Apologize right this second, Austin," she demands, and I scoff at her. I will not do any such thing.

"She braked suddenly for no reason! There was no one in front of her," I defend myself. Barbara's eyebrows pinch together, and she takes her glasses off so they hang on the chain around her neck. I know that if I don't say sorry, this will just end in her quitting again. Last time, it cost me a month-long Mediterranean cruise. "Fine," I huff out, "I'm sorry I accused you of being drunk. I should have just called you what you are—a reckless, clueless female driver."

Lauren stands there glaring at me as Barbara yells, "I quit!" This must shock Lauren, because she immediately goes to Barbara and strokes her back. "Oh, no. No, no, no. Please, really, it's fine. It's totally okay. I accept his apology." She aims a glare at me. "I understand now why so many women left, he's a..." She leans in and whispers in Barbara's ear.

I don't know what she says, but they both snicker. Great, just great.

"Yup, my money is on Lauren." She looks at me. "You're lucky she saved you this time." She smiles at Lauren. "Let's do lunch tomorrow. Austin's treat."

She leaves the room, leaving us all alone. "Fine. I guess I'll try and work with you, for Barbara." She walks out to the desk facing my office. She puts her purse on it. Turning the computer on, she grabs a pen and notepad and comes back in. "No time like the present to get this out of the way, so why don't we start with your expectations of me?"

I look at her while she sits in the chair in front of me, crossing her legs at her ankles. I sit down, leaning back in my chair, and start rocking. "Okay, fine. I expect you to be on time. Every day. No exceptions."

She doesn't write it down. "That isn't a problem. I hate when people are late, so you don't have to worry about that. Unless, of course, irresponsible people hit my car while I'm innocently driving, I'll be here on time."

"There is a list on your desk of routine tasks required of this position that you can read. If it's not clear enough, then come ask me questions. How's that?"

She gets up. "That sounds like a plan." She turns to walk away, and I watch her. Every fucking step she takes she swings her hips; the best thing is, she has no idea she's doing it. She has no idea that I'm sitting here negotiating with myself about my own rule. I'm not sure how I'm going to get anything done, because fucking her on my desk is the only thing I can think of that needs to be done right now.

CHAPTER FOUR

Lauren

I walk out of the office on shaky legs but manage to make it to my desk. I look up, letting out a slow breath.

I look down at the list that sits on my desk of tasks to be done during the day.

Looking over the list, I realize it looks pretty straightforward. Storing my purse under the desk, I take out my phone, sending a quick text to Penelope.

Get me the fuck out of this job. STAT.

I turn and start going through the emails. I forward most of them to Austin, since I have no idea which ones are important or not.

When the phone on the desk rings, I look down to see if they wrote down how to answer it. When I notice that there are no instructions on the paper, I just answer with, "Hello."

"Can you tell me why I have fifty extra emails that you forwarded to me?" His snarky voice makes me close my eyes and count to ten. It's like dealing with my children.

"I didn't know which one is important or not, so I forwarded them to you for handling or direction," I respond, looking at the list, checking to see if I missed something.

"It defeats the purpose of having an assistant if I have to answer my own emails," he huffs into the phone. "Come in here. I'll show you how it's done," he growls before he slams the phone down in my ear.

I take the phone from my ear and look at it. Did he just hang up on me? Without saying 'please' or fucking 'thank you?' I put the phone back down in the cradle, slamming it a little forcefully. There are a couple of things I just won't tolerate. Being called a bitch is one of those things, and the other is when you don't say fucking 'please' and 'thank you.' Three words. Very easily said, and they make a world of difference in any interaction.

I get up and walk over to the door, knocking once. I walk in and sit down in front of him. "How are you going to see what to do if you aren't over here so I can explain it to you?" he asks.

"Okay, now, just a minute. We may have started out on the wrong foot here." I watch him watching me. "But I'm not your slave. I'm your assistant. While I am paid to do things for you, I also haven't even been here an hour yet, an hour that we've spent arguing, by the way, and not going over things. I'm learning as I go, and while I'm learning, I'm going to make mistakes. I get you don't know how to socialize with people." He starts to sit up straight, trying to talk, but I hold up my hand. "But I will not tolerate rudeness. You want something done, you say 'please'; I do something for you regardless of whether you pay me or not, you say 'thank you.'"

He nods at me. "Please," he says through his clenched teeth. "Come over here so you can see." He is clenching his teeth together so hard I think they might shatter.

"See, was that hard?" I get up and walk over to his side of the desk. The moment I get close to him, I realize my mistake.

Before, I didn't feel his presence next to me, I couldn't smell the woodsy, spicy scent of him. So, I make a mental note to not get this close to him again.

We go over all the fifty emails I sent him, and I take notes as we go along. It lasts maybe an hour. Right before I walk out the door, I turn and ask him, "How do I answer the phone? There is nothing in the notes." I have one hand on the door knob, ready to walk out.

"What do you mean?" He looks up at me with a raised brow. "I thought you were calling me Asshat?"

"Fine, then, that is exactly how I'll answer," I say, walking out of the room, fighting the temptation to slam the door behind me.

I walk over to my desk, drop the pad on it, and throw myself into the chair.

I look at my phone and see that there are five messages from Penelope.

What happened?
Are you still there?
Are you okay?
I don't know what you did, but Barbara just called and extended your contract. What do I say?
Whatever you do, don't kill him!

I answer her right away.

He's an asshat, and he's rude. He's a jerk, and he's a dick.

Her response is immediate.

I've been told, but you are the best person for the job.

I roll my eyes.

How am I the right person? I have killed him a million times in my head since I've gotten here, and it's only been an hour. I want out.

I answer the emails that came in. My stomach rumbles, and I automatically look at the clock, seeing it's almost noon.

I pick my phone back up, and there is a final text from Penelope.

They doubled your salary. Why don't you see how you feel tomorrow?

Ugh, I'll deal with Penelope later. I get up and bend over to grab my purse from under the desk.

"Holy mother of God," I hear said loudly behind me. I go to straighten myself up too fast and knock my head on the desk, the bang echoing in the vast office space.

"Oh my god, are you okay?" I hear behind me as I feel hands trying to help me up. "Are you okay? I'm so sorry. I didn't mean to scare you."

He is holding my hand while my hand is rubbing the back of my head. "It's okay. You startled me," I start to say and then look at him.

Crystal-clear blue eyes crinkled with laugh lines greet me. His blond hair is falling onto his forehead. He is almost on top of me at this point, my back pressed into the desk.

"What the hell is going on here?" The roar comes from behind me. I push this stranger away from me and look over at Austin. He stands there with his hands on his hips, the vein in his neck twitching.

"It's my fault, Austin," the stranger says, dropping my hand. "I came in and was surprised to see her. I startled her, and she knocked her head under the desk. I was just helping her up," he says as he walks around my desk, right up to Austin, and slaps him on the shoulder. "I was wondering if you wanted to get lunch?"

Even though his 'friend' is standing next to me, he hasn't taken his eyes off me. "No, I'm eating in. I have to go over the Grey Stone Park file. Lauren, can you get me lunch? Go to the deli at the corner; we have an account there. Just tell them it's for me. They know what I like."

I put my hand on my hip, glaring at him, waiting for it. When he doesn't say anything, I cross my hands over my chest. "Please," he hisses out.

"Fine." I grab my bag and walk out, holding my breath till I get inside the elevator. I grab my phone and text Kaleigh.

Please get me three bottles of wine for dinner.

I put the phone back in my purse and make my way to the deli on the corner, where I get my boss his lunch, all the while praying that I will actually get through the day without poisoning him.

CHAPTER FIVE

Austin

When I opened the door and saw my childhood best friend, Noah's, hands all over Lauren, I wanted to rip out his jugular and then spit down his throat. I have no fucking idea why. She is my assistant, making her the definition of off limits.

We both watch Lauren walk away, her ass swinging from side to side with each step. I'm so intent on watching her, I don't even notice Noah push me aside and walk into my office.

He throws himself on the couch I have in the office, while I open the shade to see out into the office space.

"Jesus Christ, who was that sex kitten in heels? I nearly had a heart attack when I walked up to find her bending over," he says, looking in the direction of her desk.

"My new stay-away-from-her assistant," I grumble as I sit down on the other side of the couch.

He throws his head back and laughs. "Oh, what happened to the 'don't fuck where you eat, Noah' speech that you always give me?"

Noah and I have been best friends since we were in kindergarten. His parents were both criminal lawyers, so we were always with our nannies. Of course, no one could top Barbara, while he kept getting different nannies every week. Until he was old enough to fire them himself and hire whoever he wanted. By the ripe old age of fifteen, he had gone through thirty nannies, and at that point, he was hiring them to teach him everything they knew about sex. That was until his parents found him fucking his last nanny bent over the pool table, while she was wearing his mother's shoes. We still laugh about it today; well, at least I do. He just sits there and groans.

"She's crazy," I say. "I hit her car this morning, and then she shows up in the office. I thought she was fucking stalking me."

That just pushes him over the edge, and now he is laughing so hard the couch is shaking. "You hit her car and then thought she was following you? Holy shit. Were you an asshole to her?"

I smirk at him. "She named me Asshat in her phone." That set us both off. I figure if I laugh I'll notice how stupid the idea of getting her under me is. Getting her naked and sweaty and wet under me. Fuck, I need to do something about this.

"You know you're fucked, right?" He finally stops laughing and throws his hand over the couch. "When you saw me touch her, I thought you would charge at me like one of those bulls running toward the red sheet."

"She's nothing more than a crazy chick with a tight ass. Who will get me coffee daily."

"Oh, really?" Her voice cuts through the air, and just when I thought I could turn her opinion of me as an asshat into that of a nice guy, I'm caught again. "Well, then, I'm happy I could assist you in your day," she snorts, coming in and dumping the bags on the table in front of us. "I also got something for your friend," she huffs and then walks away. This time slamming the door on her way out.

"Oh fuck, you are in so much fucking trouble. Dude, she is going to fucking string you up by the balls. Remember that chick you played in college? The one you promised to bring home during spring break? She turned around and cancelled all your tickets. Then she put that ad all over Craigslist 'Lonely man searching another lonely man.'" I shake my head thinking about it.

"She was fucking crazy! I had to change my number four times. Four! Then I had to start wearing beanies so she wouldn't recognize me." I shake my head, while Noah laughs so hard he falls over. I look over at him "It was fucking May! I had to take three showers a day. I had no idea the head could sweat so much."

He finally stops laughing and looks in the bag that Lauren just dumped on the table in front of us. "If I were you, I'd enjoy this. It's probably going to be the last meal she hasn't had the time to spit in." I open the box that has my name on it. It's pastrami on rye, touch of mustard and a pickle. The other box has a ham and cheese on brown.

We spend the next thirty minutes eating our lunch while shooting the shit about everything else.

"Are you going out this weekend with Deborah?" he asks me. Deborah is a family friend who I turn to when I have nothing else going on. We both have jobs that keep us busy; she is in real estate law, so we touch base from time to time. I shrug my shoulder. "Not sure what my weekend plans are. What do you have planned?"

He takes out his phone, scrolling. "Andrea, that is who I plan to do. I met her at Starbucks. She has the longest legs I've ever seen. I plan to have them wrapped around my neck, and not in a wrestling move, either." He raises his eyebrows. "If you know what I mean."

I chuckle at him. I don't think I've ever seen him with someone more than twice. He gets up, putting the garbage in the bag. "This has been a hoot, but sadly, I must run."

He takes the bag while he walks out. I follow him out and see him stop at Lauren's desk. She is busy typing something, so she only turns her head. "Thank you so much for lunch, Lauren. You were a life saver." I roll my eyes at the bullshit he's spewing, but it's the sweet smile that Lauren is giving him that really gets to me. I'm about to scoff when he walks away, leaving her with a wink.

"He is so nice," she says while she continues typing. I don't know why I feel like I want to rip the keyboard out from in front of her just so she will look at me, just so I can see her face.

"Yeah, well, looks can be deceiving," I comment while leaning into the door jamb.

She finally stops typing and looks over at me. "Don't I know it." Her eyes roam from my head to my toes. It makes my spine stand straight.

"I'll have you know that I'm the nicest guy here." I have no idea why I'm trying to convince her of this. I couldn't care less if she likes me or not. I'm her boss, she is my temp. The fact that I want to see her smile at me is not the point right now. Nor is the fact that I'm also wondering if she is wearing a thong under her skirt or going commando? Does she wax or shave? Landing strip or bare? All these thoughts are running through my mind, so I don't hear her talking to me right away. "I'm sorry, what did you say?" I ask her again.

"I said Denis sent over the files and plans that you asked him about. He said if you want, he can meet you there so you can go over it. He also said the loft that you were asking about has a roof top terrace that would be great for a restaurant during the day and a bar at night."

She has been here less than six hours, and she is a million times better than the last ten temps I threw out of here. "Also, I've gone over your schedule and color coded all your meetings, so that when you click on the color, all files that correspond to that meeting will pop up as well."

She organized my whole schedule in three hours. "I didn't touch Saturday or Sunday, since it's not my job. Unless there was a note in there that said it's a work-related event or meeting."

I run through my schedule in my head and wonder if I wrote anything private down. She must see that I'm thinking this, because she laughs. "Don't worry, I didn't find your little black book notes." She shakes her head, picking up her Starbucks drink that is red with berries in it. "Is there anything else you need from me?" she asks, looking down at the notes in front of her.

I don't say anything; I just walk back to my desk to go through the notes she just sent me. I also check my calendar and see that everything is organized not only by color, but alphabetically. Jesus, where has she been all my life?

I spend the next three hours going over the plans with Denis, making sure everything is set for us to visit the site of the new nightclub that is set to open in a couple of weeks.

When I hear a knock on my door, I yell for whomever it is to come in. Once the door opens, I see Lauren poke her head in.

"I'm heading out. Just thought you should know." I look at my watch and see that it is already four p.m.

I lean back in my chair, putting my hands together. "I guess for the first day, that's okay, but there might be times when you may have to stay late." I don't even finish before she cuts me off. She opens the door and walks inside my office. She stops right in front of my desk, cocks her hips to the side, and places her hands on them.

"No go. I have two kids. My hours are eight to four. Not one minute later. I don't care about eating lunch at my desk, but I made it crystal clear that my hours were non-negotiable when I took this position."

"Why can't your husband get them?" I hold my breath as I wait for her answer. My stomach starts to burn, my chest tightening at the thought of her going home to someone. Then, just like the she-devil she is, she glares at me.

"I'm divorced, and I have full custody of them, so if you can't accommodate my limitations, it's better we find out now and part ways." She starts to turn around and walk away. I clear my throat, watching her fling her hair around. It's almost like she is doing it in slow motion, just like the commercials for shampoo.

"Fine, okay," I concede against my better judgment. "We'll work around it." I tilt my head and smile. "You're welcome."

She nods her head, but I see her pressing her lips together. I'm sure if I weren't her boss, she would tell me to go fuck myself, and I don't know why just the thought that she would fight me on this makes me want to belly laugh. She turns and walks out, closing the door softly behind her, which I know is the opposite of what she really wants to do.

I pick up the phone and dial Barbara, who answers on the second ring. "Yes, Austin."

"What is the story with Lauren?" I ask her, looking out into the office space, watching her pack up her things, pick up her phone, and scroll through it. I see her put the phone to her ear and smile at whoever answers. The thought that it's her boyfriend, or any man for that matter, makes me want to snatch that phone away from her and smash it.

"I don't have a 'story.' She's a temp. All I have is her emergency contact form that she filled out this morning. And I'll have you know, I've already called Penelope and gave her a raise."

"What?" I shout at her, and by the time I look up, Lauren is gone.

"You called her a drunk, and she didn't even kick you in the balls, which is what you deserved, by the way. I raised you better than that."

"I don't even know why I try with you." I slam the phone down, but not before I hear her laughing.

I turn to my computer and try to Google her name, except all I have is her first name. I search the company directory to find her full name: Lauren Harrison. With that, I turn back to Google and go on my search.

I see that she has a Facebook account, but I can't access anything because she has it set to private. The only thing I can see is the profile

26

picture that she has of her two kids. She is in the middle with her son on her side, hugging her, and her daughter on her lap. You can't see her hands, but you know she is holding both of them. Her son looks nothing like her, but her daughter is her clone. I try to look through her friends, but I can't get anything. When a knock on my door startles me, I close down the page and yell out.

My partner, John, comes walking in. "Hey," he says while he makes his way to the chair in front of my desk, throwing himself down in it. "Just saw your new temp." He whistles. "If I weren't married, I think she might be worth bending the rules for." John has been married to his wife, Dani, for twelve years now. 'College sweethearts till the end' is their motto. She works at a big marketing firm downtown. We often use her when promoting our brand.

I shake my head at him and say, "Dani would skin you alive and leave you with nothing but your two balls hanging all the way to the floor. Right before she sets you on fire." I know full well she would do that and so much more.

He laughs out, folding one leg over the other. "She pretty much would leave me with maybe the hair on my head. Other than that, it will all be gone."

"If you're lucky. How was Vegas?" He just got back from Vegas. He went to see if he thought branching out there was doable for us. I'm still unsure about it.

"It was what you expected. It's hard to get your foot in the door anywhere. They all 'have their own people.' Dani and I checked around, but I'm leaning more toward shelving this for a later date." I nod, agreeing with everything he is saying.

We spend about thirty minutes talking about the projects we have going on. He has four restaurants that are opening up in the next three months. All different cuisines and atmospheres, so he's excited for what is to come. We discuss the nightclub/restaurant project that I have taken on. It's more of a challenge, because everything has to work for both purposes.

After that, he tells me he's leaving. I look at the clock, seeing it's only six-thirty. I haven't been out of the office this early in forever. I decide I'm going to hit up the gym.

I close up everything, making my way outside. I walk by Lauren's desk, where her scent of berries lingers lightly. I see that she has Post-its all over her computer screen.

I walk over and can't stop myself from moving a few around. It's childish, I know, but I can't help it. This is what she does to me.

CHAPTER SIX

Lauren

He asked me to stay late—as if. I was very specific about that when I filled out the form. I pick up the phone right before I head out, dialing Kaleigh. I'm surprised when I hear Rachel's voice, "Hiya, Mommasita." I smile just thinking of her standing there in the kitchen with her curls bouncing.

I walk out to the car telling them I'll be home in twenty minutes. I pull into my driveway, put the car in park, and rest my head on the steering wheel, clearing the stress of the day away by drawing in a few breaths and letting them out. I think it's the first time all day that I finally breathe normally.

I don't have much time to myself before I hear Gabe running out of the house. "Mom, you have to come in quick." The tone of his voice snaps me back to reality.

I sling my seatbelt off, getting ready to run inside. "What's the matter?" I look at him.

"Aunt Kay is making supper." He looks at me nervously, his big, brown eyes open wide in dismay.

"Oh, crap," I say and quickly head into the house. The last time she attempted cooking us dinner, we ate sticky peanut cauliflower wings. There was nothing good about that concoction. Hell, it was barely edible. I won't even talk about the aftertaste it left in my mouth, either.

I hurry in the door just as I hear the smoke detector go off. "Oh, dear Christ, Kay, what the hell are you doing?" I grab a broom out of the closet and position myself beneath the smoke detector, using the broom to fan the smoke away. "Jesus, Jesus, Jesus," I chant while looking over to the kitchen in time to see Kaleigh pulling a tray of charred, smoking cauliflower out of the oven.

"Oh my god, oh my god, oh my god! I'm so sorry! We went outside to do some kid yoga, and I totally forgot," she explains while she walks with the pan to the sink, turns on the water, and soaks the smoking remains of what was once cauliflower. The sizzling sound of water hitting a hot metal pan fills the quiet room, along with a burnt, smelly, steamy smoke that has the potential to set off the now silent smoke detector again. I do the only thing I really can do, which is to continue fanning.

"Oh, Auntie Kay, what are we going to eat now?" Rachel asks. She would have been the only one of us to attempt to eat one of Kaleigh's creations.

Kaleigh slaps her hands together. "Oh! I have some tofu we can cut up and…" Before she can even finish that sentence, Gabe and I both yell a combined firm yet panicky, "No!"

I look over the mess that is my kitchen and begin a mental count to ten. "Okay, I'm going to change. Gabe, start your homework. Rachel, go start studying your spelling words. You"—I point at my sister—"clean up this mess. I'll find something to throw together for pasta."

She groans. "I don't have any gluten-free pasta here."

I look at her. "Okay, so you'll be going home. Got it." I point to the kitchen. "Clean this mess up before you leave."

I head upstairs and change out of my work clothes, throwing on some yoga pants and a sweatshirt. I'm in mom mode now. I get back downstairs and see that Gabe is sitting at the table doing his homework, while Rachel is in the living room writing her words, and Kaleigh is putting things in the dishwasher. "Oh, good news," she informs me. "I found some rice, so I'll throw whatever sauce you make on there. Yumm-O."

I shake my head, laughing at her as I start prepping the veggies to go into my pasta primavera. After I've sautéed everything and added the pasta, I toss it with a bit more olive oil and some parmesan. "Kay, set the table," I call over to her.

She looks over my shoulder and complains, "I can't eat that. You put cheese in it."

"It's okay," I whisper to her. "I won't turn you in to the vegan police. We'll pretend it never happened." I serve up some pasta onto plates for the kids.

I hear the fridge open, followed by a squeal from behind me. "Score," she squeals, taking out one of her frozen meals from the freezer. "Look! Tofu ravioli! Saved!" She does a little dance on her way over to the microwave, raising her hands in the air and shaking her ass as she pops it in. "Oh yeah, oh yeah, oh yeah!" She continues dancing till the microwave beeps.

She pulls it out, peeling off the filmy plastic cover, and waves it under my nose. "Smells so good, right?"

I raise my eyebrows and nod yes, but I'm totally lying. Throughout the meal, the kids tell me about their day. Rachel tells me that today someone threw up in class because someone else farted. Apparently, this is hilarious to her, since she is in stitches about it as she retells the story.

By the time eight o'clock rolls around, I've got the kids bathed and tucked into their beds. I'm ready to pass out, but I come down the stairs to lit candles and a full glass of a crisp, perfectly chilled white wine. "Aww, if you weren't my sister—and I were into chicks—I'd make you my woman," I swoon, grabbing my glass and curling up on the couch with my feet under me.

"So, tell me about this boss of yours?" she prompts as she sips her own wine.

"Oh, where do I start?" I close my eyes as I try not to picture him staring at me. Trying even harder to not picture him looming over me. Definitely trying really, *really* hard to not picture him taking off his clothes while he looms over me and stares.

"Good-looking?" she asks.

I nod my head yes and finish off my glass of wine in one long, satisfying drink. I pick up the bottle, pulling the cork out with a pop, and pour myself another glass. "Too good-looking."

"Fit or chunky?" she asks, and now I know what she's doing. Small questions now, big discussion later.

"Fit," I answer, pausing to sip another glass that's already half drained. "Very fit." I think the wine is hitting me pretty fast, because I look around next before I whisper, "I think he has a six pack." Then I finish the remaining wine in my glass.

"Hair color? Eye color?" She fills up my glass again.

"Brown and hazel-green with gold specks." I drink a little more.

"Facial hair? Would you get a burn from his beard or not?"

I look up and think I blush a bit. "Depends on the time of the day. He was clean-shaven this morning, but he had a good five-o'clock shadow going by three o'clock." I drop my head back on the back of the couch and close my eyes. Seeing his eyes right away, the smirk he gave me, the way he asked about my husband, not swallowing before I answered. Then his eyes suddenly lighting up with mischief.

"You like him?"

My eyes snap open as I turn to her. "No! No, I don't. Absolutely not. I don't like him at all."

She giggles as she takes another sip. "He hit my freaking car, Kay, and then the asshat asked me if I was drunk," I plead my case. "Drunk at *fucking* eight a.m."

"He's gotten under your skin! There hasn't been anyone who's pushed you this far. Well, there was Pacey from Dawson's Creek…"

"Hey!" I point at her. "Joey went sailing with him all summer! Just because Dawson is there and crying, she thinks she should be with Pacey. He was always her choice." I pour myself another glass, spilling a bit as I do it.

"Do you think he manscapes?" she asks, putting her glass down on the table, while I just down another one.

"I have no idea, but I would guess it's probably manscaped. I mean, who doesn't manscape these days?" I look over and wonder.

"Some like to be free and let things be natural; there is nothing wrong with that. Don't judge. Well, unless you have to suck his dick, then by all means, you put your foot down. You don't need to be choking on long pubic hair. In fact, if you think it isn't, then just run. Run fast, like he's waving a bomb in front of you."

I nod at her. I should probably be taking notes. I feel like I should be taking notes so I can remember this.

"Shoes?"

"Nice. Black ones." I look at her, my eyes opening wide. "And clean. Very nice." I hate when guys don't have clean shoes; it's like having dirty feet. Ewww.

"Teeth? Straight? Crooked? White? Stained? Stinky breath?"

I tilt my head to the side and remember if he smiled today. I saw him smirk, I saw him glare, I saw his jaw muscle tic, but I'm not sure I saw his teeth. "I don't know."

"Big hands?"

"Oh yeah, so big." I open my hands wide to make her see how big, but I shake them a bit "This big." I motion with my hands, making big circles.

"You think he has a big dick?" I stop moving.

"He would have to. You can't be that good-looking and have a small penis. Actually, maybe that's why he's such an asshole! His penis is small. He has small penis syndrome." I look at her, waiting for her input. "I mean, why else would he be smoking hot and an asshole, unless... "—I giggle—"unless it's so big it hurts when he walks." I put my hand over my mouth and laugh out loud. "I can't sleep with him. He's my boss and besides, he doesn't even like me."

I rise from the couch, picking up my glass of wine and spilling whatever was left in it on the floor. "I need a dog, so if I spill something, he can lick it up." I look over at Kaleigh, and she is silently laughing. "You think we can get a dog and train him to bite my boss?"

"Yes, I think you just need to bring a picture and a sweater with you to training school so they can use his scent. They'll train the dog to attack your boss as soon as he gets close."

My mouth forms an O. "Oooh, we need to look into that," I say. And that is the last thing she says to me.

The next thing I know, I'm lying in my bed with her on the other side. "You think he doesn't like me because I'm old? Or ugly? Or is it because I'm fat?"

She leans over and strokes my cheek. "You are not old. You are the opposite of ugly, and you are definitely not fat. He acts like he doesn't like you, because he probably likes you too much. Remember Ricky in the third grade who chased you with a frog because he loved you? This is just the adult version."

"No way would he go for someone like me. He did say I had a tight ass, though. That means he was looking at it, right?"

She tucks a strand of hair behind my ear. "He was definitely checking you out."

I close my eyes. The room is spinning as the day replays in my head. I fall asleep to the sound of Kaleigh talking about a beef vegan soup that she is going to try to make, minus the beef, of course.

Her voice lulls me while I'm brought back to the day, sitting at my desk, knowing he was watching, feeling he was watching me.

CHAPTER SEVEN

Lauren

The next day, I make it to work without incident, clocking in at seven fifty-five. I make my way into the break room, where I get the coffee going.

I'm leaning against the counter, waiting for the coffee to finish brewing, when a tall man with glasses walks in. He is lanky, his tan pants are perfectly ironed with a crease down the front of the legs. His plaid shirt completes the look. I smile at him and say a polite "Hello."

He nods his head at me and goes to the fridge, where he stores his lunch.

"You must be Austin's new PA?" His voice is quiet as he waits for the coffee to finish also.

"I am." I reach out my hand to him to introduce myself. "I'm Lauren." He grips my hand, and his palm is just a tad sweaty, but not enough for me to wipe it on my navy skirt.

Today, I'm dressed in almost the same skirt as yesterday's, except that it's a dark navy blue and has some pleating at the sides. I've paired it with a plain white cotton button-down. It's simple, but professional. I've gone with my tan peep-toe pumps that give me an extra four inches.

"My name is Steven. I'm in the accounting department," he says while pushing his glasses up on his nose. "Are you enjoying your time so far?" he asks right as the machine lets out a gust of steam, letting us know that it's done brewing.

I grab the handle. "I am. I thought it would be harder at the beginning, since I haven't really worked in over ten years, but it's just like riding a bike." I smile over at him while I pour my coffee. He places his coffee mug on the counter and waits for me to hand him the pot. But I'm going to be friendly. "Please, let me, tell me when to stop." He smiles at me.

"When you're done flirting, you can fix me one, too. And we need to go over a couple of things." Austin's voice bursts into the room, startling me and causing me to spill a bit.

"Jesus, you scared me," I say while I put down the pot in the holder and quickly grab a napkin, cleaning up the spilt coffee. Steven quickly grabs his cup and heads out with a smile to me, a nod to Austin, and a mumbled, "Good morning."

"I know you're a temp and you don't know the company policies, but we have a no-fraternizing policy." He eyes me while putting his hands in his pockets.

I throw the napkin out and turn around to face him. He is dressed in a simple black suit, another crisp white dress shirt, looking sharp, and as if they were custom-fit for him.

He didn't shave this morning, so he's got more stubble than he did last night when I left, and I can't help but think to myself that I'd definitely get beard burn from that. "I'll have Barbara send over the policies so you don't get confused."

"I wasn't flirting with him. I just met him. I was merely being polite. Although I'm sure that concept is foreign to you." I pick up my mug and start to walk away.

"I asked for a coffee," He stops me, and my head turns and I snap.

"No. You didn't ask, you demanded. After you insulted me. Again. And for the record, when someone asks another person for something, it is customary that they follow the request with the word 'please.' The coffee's done. Help yourself." I glare at him.

I don't have time to say anything else before Barbara comes into the room. "Good morning, you two. Lauren, I love that skirt. Very, very nice," she compliments me while she grabs two mugs and goes about pouring her coffee.

"Barbara," I address her, "Austin was just going over the company policies that are included in the employee handbook. If it's not too much trouble, would you please send that to me? There is a non-fraternization policy Austin seems to believe I need to check out." I hold my mug in front of my mouth to hide my smile.

Barbara looks up at me with a surprised look on her face and then looks at Austin. "I will send it right over to you. It seems I don't have the right copy, since I don't remember that particular policy. Austin, if you've amended the handbook, perhaps you should send it to me so I can make sure those changes are noted and emailed to everyone," she suggests while she finishes making two cups of coffee, handing Austin one of the cups she prepared.

I look at Austin to see that his mouth is closed and he is swallowing, since he hasn't said anything else. "We just finalized it last week. I'll send it over," he says and walks away, leaving me and Barbara by ourselves.

I look at her and see her smiling as she raises her cup to her lips. "I hope you know that I won't be staying here long," I inform her. "I've already informed Penelope to look for a suitable replacement for me here, as well as another position for me somewhere else." I watch her sip her coffee and ask, "Does he always take half a sugar and no milk in his coffee?"

She looks at me with a surprised look. "I'm very observant." I smile at her and head to my desk. I turn on my computer, noticing that some of my Post-its have been moved.

I get up, heading into Austin's office. The door isn't closed, so I walk in. I check and see if he's on the phone before I ask him, "Do we have a cleaning crew come in here?"

He looks up from his paper, and his eyes slowly eye me from toe to head. "Excuse me?" he asks.

"My Post-its have been moved." His Adam's apple moves like he's swallowing. "I'm assuming someone was cleaning and moved them. So, my question is, do we have a cleaning crew?"

He leans back in his chair. "How do you know they've been moved? What do you do? Memorize them before you leave?" He laughs, but it comes out shaky.

"I don't have to memorize them. I post them alphabetically, which is why I know they've been moved."

His face turns a nice shade of white. Yup, asshat moved my shit. But instead he says, "Must be the cleaning crew."

I glare at him for a second. "If you could please let them know that I'll be cleaning my own desk from now on. Or you know what, I'll see if I can find their number and get in touch with them my—" I don't have time to finish before he pipes in.

"No"—he shakes his head—"I'll call Hector now and mention it." I nod yes at him. "Now, if that's all, I have a busy schedule and discussing your filing system isn't on it."

I turn around and head out the door, but right before I'm out of the door, he informs me, "I'm having a business lunch in my office with a friend. If you could make sure we both have lunch ready for noon. It will also be a private lunch. She eats light. So, a salad for her is good. I'll have my usual," he says.

My back is still facing him, so he doesn't see me close my eyes slowly and open my mouth in shock. It takes me a second to turn around, putting a mask on my face. "Considering I've been here for twenty-four hours, I don't know what your usual is. If you want me to order your lunch for you and your booty call"—I let out a little forced laugh—"oh, sorry, your 'private lunch,' I'm going to need to know exactly what you want for lunch. Send me the details via email." I turn and walk out of the room, not giving him a chance to reply.

I open my email and start a message to Penelope.

To: Penelope Barns
From: Lauren Harrison
Subject: GET ME THE FUCK OUT OF HERE

If you don't want to be responsible for my children being raised by Jake and his side slut, you will make sure I'm out of this job by Friday. Or better yet, tomorrow. Because I may kill him.

Sincerely,
Lauren
MY BOSS IS THE MAYOR OF DOUCHEVILLE

I hit send and then continue going through the emails. I forward the necessary ones and start making notes on what has to be done with the ones that I can handle. Within three minutes, there is a reply from Penelope.

To: Lauren Harrison
From: Penelope Barns
Subject: Re: GET ME THE FUCK OUT OF HERE

I'm working on it, but it doesn't help that Barbara is blowing up my phone to get you in there permanently. She isn't caving. PLEASE DON'T KILL HIM, HE'S MY BIGGEST CLIENT.

Sincerely,
Your friend Penelope, who is so fucking sorry and knows she owes you big time.

Ugh. What the hell am I supposed to do now?

To: Penelope Barns
From: Lauren Harrison
Subject: Re: GET ME THE FUCK OUT OF HERE

I don't know how you are going to repay me for this. There isn't enough wine in all of Italy to call this even.
I won't kill him, but I may poison him slowly.

Sincerely,
Your friend Lauren, who is already plotting how she will be getting you back one day.

I quickly reply and then take out my phone to text Kaleigh.

I've thought about it, he has a pencil dick and doesn't manscape.

She replies right away.

Fuck me, what did he do in ten minutes?
Besides the fact he fucked with my Post-its, he asked me to order

lunch for him and his fuck buddy.

Whoa, he touched your Post-its!

Really? That is all you got from the text? Did you not read he wants me to order lunch for him and his date?

I'm sorry, that was rude of him. You should make him pay. I mean, the last time I touched your Post-its, you switched my almond milk for cow's and I drank the whole thing.

I giggle to myself at the reminder. It was really funny watching her drink the whole carton in ten minutes. She was oohing and aahing about how great it tasted.

I continue with my task, trying to organize all the items that have been scanned, placing them in the correct files and relabeling everything so it actually makes sense.

The phone buzzes on my desk. I pick it up, but I don't say hello till I hear his voice bark into the phone.

"We have a conference with Denis and his team at three. I need all documents printed and labeled so we can see what is going on."

"Isn't it better if I just do a slide show with PowerPoint? That way, you can display it bigger instead of on the table," I suggest, smiling to myself.

"I wasn't sure if you knew how to do that, since you haven't been in an office environment in a while. I didn't want to expect anything."

I take the phone from my ear, ready to smash it on the desk. "I think I can manage it. If not, I can always use YouTube; they have tutorials."

I look into the office and see him staring straight at me. All I see is his jaw getting tight. "I hope you can manage that one." And he slams the phone down.

I quickly place it down in its cradle, smiling to myself. Score one for me.

But my mood doesn't last long. He sends me an email.

To: Lauren (Latest PA)
From: Austin Mackenzie
Subject: Lunch Order

Please order me a pastrami on rye and a grilled chicken salad, dressing on the side.

I want this by noon. Try not to mess this up. She's expecting it to be perfect.

Austin Mackenzie

My eyes glare at the screen, thinking if she wants it to be perfect, she's starting with the wrong date. I don't have time to answer when another email comes through.

To: Lauren (Latest PA)
From: Austin Mackenzie
Subject: Conference with Denis

Although I don't think you can bring anything to this meeting, you need to be there to take notes.
Try not to flirt, since he is also considered a co-worker.

Austin Mackenzie

My blood is boiling. I want to reply with a simple 'fuck off,' but instead I think of something better. Oh yeah, I'm going to give him something better, alright.

I place the order at the deli on the corner. At eleven-thirty, I start to get up, but I'm stopped by a woman walking down the hall.

She is wearing a brown trench coat tied at the waist. The trench coat falls to her mid-thigh. Her short blond bob of loose curls bounces with every step she takes. Her blue eyes shine. Her black Louboutins click-clack against the floor as she approaches.

"May I help you?" I ask while walking around my desk. She gives me the once-over.

"No, thank you," she huffs and continues walking straight into Austin's office. "Darling," I hear her purr. "It's been forever."

I look into the office, seeing her walk around the desk and sit on his lap. I don't know what he says, but I hear giggling that has me rolling my eyes.

I hear my phone ring. "Hello?"

"I'm going to need that lunch later. And would you close my door?" he says and then hangs up before I can answer.

I'll close his fucking door. I walk in and hear them whispering, the bottom half of the desk covering whatever he is doing. So gross. It's the middle of the day! My heart is beating so fast. I try not to look up, but he looks up right before I close the door. Something flashes in his features, but I don't get a chance to figure out what it is before the door closes. I hear the blinds start to shut. I'm not sitting out here while he fucks in his office.

I walk around the desk, grabbing my purse, and leave to go to lunch. I guess I'll be having the grilled chicken salad, dressing on the side.

I pull my phone out of my purse and shoot Kaleigh a text.

He's fucking some woman in his office!
Your boss?
No, the fucking tooth fairy! Who else would I be talking about?
Barf. Make sure you use Lysol wipes on the surfaces you sit on.
You don't want to be catching cooties.
Do people still use the word cooties?
Ummm. Yes.

I walk out of the building to the hustle and bustle of lunchtime. Once I make it to the deli, I pick up the order and eat the salad there.

I'm almost done when my phone buzzes. When I pick it up, I see 'Asshat who hit…'

Where are you?

I look at the clock and notice that it's only been twenty minutes since I've been gone. Wow, I guess he's a wham bam thank you ma'am kinda guy.

I'm at the deli having lunch. I didn't think you would be finished so soon. My bad.
I don't pay you to think. Bring me my lunch.

I smash my phone down on the table. That's it. I've fucking had it.

I walk over to the Walgreens across the street. I pick up a bottle of Dulcolax. "You don't pay me to get your lunch either, asshole," I grumble to myself while I walk back to the office. Once I make it there, I go the other route, picking up a water bottle from the kitchen.

I take a quick look around the kitchen, checking to see if anyone is coming this direction. When I see no one is there, I take out the Dulcolax and open the package.

I start reading the dosage instructions on the package when I hear someone coming. I shove the box and the bottle into my purse. When I turn around, I see Steven walking in.

"Hey. Are you having lunch?" he asks, going to the fridge and grabbing his bag.

"Nope, just finished. I'm picking up a water bottle for Austin. I just got his lunch." The fact I'm lying and that I might be caught is too much.

My neck starts to burn, and I'm pretty sure he can hear my heart beating it's so loud.

"Oh, he hates water. Bring him a Coke instead," Steven suggests while he smiles and walks out.

Fuck. I walk back in and grab a Coke can out of the fridge. Looking for a glass, I finally find a red solo cup in one of the cupboards.

I open my purse, scan the package, and see that the dose is five ml. I have no idea how much five ml is, so I use the cap to measure, hoping for the best. What's the worst that can happen? I can't control the snicker that bursts from my mouth.

Pouring the Coke into the cup, I grab a spoon and stir it. There you go, Asshat. Take that!

I walk back to my desk, depositing my purse on it.

His door is open and so are the shades. When I peek my head inside, he is sitting alone on the couch, his jacket still on. Jesus, he had sex and still looks the same.

I dump the bag on top of the table in front of him, placing the cup of laxative-laced Coke next to it.

"What took you so long?" he growls, grabbing the bag and opening it to take out his sandwich.

"How was I supposed to know it would take you ten minutes to seal the deal?" I cross my arms under my boobs while I lean on one leg.

He takes two bites of his sandwich and then drinks a long gulp of Coke. "You going to watch me eat?" He looks at me from the corner of his eye.

I don't reply to him. Instead, I turn on my heel and walk out, taking a seat at my desk as I watch him eat his lunch and drink the Coke. When he's finished, he throws everything out, including the cup.

He doesn't buzz me or talk to me until five minutes to three, when he gets up and walks out of his office.

"Let's go, Denis is here."

I grab everything I need and follow him to the conference room. Right before he opens the door, I hear his stomach start gurgling.

He looks up to see if I heard it, but I keep my head down, pretending I didn't. It's all I can do not to laugh out loud.

I'm introduced to Denis, who is a short, older man with that bald-on-top-hair-wrapped-around-the-sides thing going on.

I don't say anything else to him as I put my things down and start to set up the PowerPoint presentation.

Denis and Austin start talking, but his stomach gurgles again, this time louder.

I look over at him and notice that his forehead is starting to get shiny and beads of sweat are forming on his temples.

He takes off his jacket, unbuttons his cuffs, and rolls up his sleeves. He walks to the end of the table where water bottles are set up.

Opening one, he drinks half of it, then sits down at the head of the table.

I start the presentation and Denis starts speaking. "We have a great setup with the tables for the day crowd and the dinner rush. The good news is that once they're cleared away after the dinner service, the space has a good-sized dance floor." I look at the display, seeing what he is saying.

Austin's stomach grumbles very loudly. So loudly that Denis stops talking and we both look over at him. I see sweat is now pouring down the sides of his face, which is flushed and looks pained.

Denis looks over at him, his eyebrows raised in question. "Are you okay, Austin?"

He doesn't answer, but his stomach lets out another loud grumble before he shoots out of his chair, running for the door.

Denis looks over at me, unsure of what to do. I shrug my shoulders and feign bewilderment. "I guess he has some indigestion."

Denis nods his head in agreement. We wait about twenty minutes before I tell him that I'm going to go check on Austin.

He's been emailing and texting since Austin left. Walking into Austin's office, I hear moaning coming from the corner where the bathroom door is closed.

I walk over and knock on the door. "Are you okay?" I ask. He doesn't say anything, but I hear him groaning.

"I think I'm dying," he moans in between pants. "Call 9-1-1."

I giggle to myself. "I don't think you're dying. Maybe it's food poisoning." I try to keep my voice even so I don't give anything away.

I hear him moan one more time, followed by his pained reply. "No, I'm pretty sure I'm dying."

"I'll reschedule Denis," I say, turning and walking out while I hear him cursing God and everyone else.

Score one for me.

CHAPTER EIGHT

Austin

I walk out of my private bathroom and see that night has fallen outside. The moon shining its light into my office. The outside office is empty and the lights are off out there, with just the lights in my office on and dimmed.

I walk slightly hunched over to the couch, where I throw myself down and put a hand on my forehead. I have nothing on but my pants, and they're not even buttoned. I ripped my shirt off when I thought I was dying on that toilet. *Dying.*

The minute my stomach started gurgling, I knew something was wrong. Then the cramps started, followed by the sweats. The longer I sat at that conference table, the more certain I was that I might actually shit myself. Literally.

I am not exaggerating when I tell you I was dying. I thought for sure it was God's way of punishing me for calling in Danielle.

The minute she sat in my lap, I knew I made the mistake for two reasons. First, the look on Lauren's face made my stomach clench, and second, at the sight of the woman in my lap, my dick shriveled up. Even when I closed the blinds and she took off her coat, revealing her semi-naked form to me —encased in garters and all—my dick just lay there, not rising to the bait.

I tried to think of something to get him up, but he was just not interested.

I got up from my desk and closed her coat, telling her that it really wasn't the best time, I had a surprise meeting I had to get to.

She pouted and even stomped her foot. I made a mental note to block her number. She tried to claw at my chest, thinking it was sexy. Newsflash, pretending you're a cat is not sexy. At least not to me.

She walked out five minutes after she got here, and I sat there on the couch as I stared out at Lauren's desk. After about half an hour passed and I realized that she wasn't back, I texted her. Okay, so I was a dick, but seriously, where was she? Was she having lunch with Steven? With someone else?

But then she came in and dumped my lunch on the coffee table in front of me and put my Coke down next to it.

I sat up straight at that recollection. She fucking drugged me!

I text Noah right away.

My assistant put a laxative in my Coke.

I don't have to wait long before he sends me back a text filled with nothing but laughing and crying emoticons.

I send him back the middle finger.

She drugged me. I thought I was dying. I almost called 9-1-1.
You almost called 9-1-1 because you had the shits?

Which he follows with a text of shit emojis.

I shake my head, this isn't a joke. I almost died. The stuff that came out of me... I didn't think it was humanly possible to be full of that much shit.

I have to get her back.
Whoa there, you don't even know if she did anything.
I know it in my gut.
BAHAHA!!! Is there anything left in your gut? Maybe what you think you're feeling is just emptiness.

I don't even bother answering him at this point. I throw my phone down and get up slowly. I reach for a bottle of water. I look at it carefully to make sure it wasn't tampered with before I open it up and start drinking it.

I walk over to her desk and see it spotless. I rip all her Post-its down and crumple them up. I pull out her chair and sit down at her computer, then open it up, and start going through her emails.

She thinks I'm an asshole. I find emails to Penelope and see she's really thinking about quitting. Over my dead body. I'm going to fire her before she can quit on me.

I then think over last year when I got a virus from a porn site. Oh, don't sit there shaking your head; we all watch porn. I know you do, too.

I open up the porn site and start flipping on all the links that pop up. I click girl porn, anal porn, BBW porn, big tit porn, gay porn, lesbian porn, MILF porn; you name the porn, I open all the links and put her volume to the max. Take that, you little minx.

I close down her screen, rubbing my hands together in evil glee. The minute I do that, my stomach starts up again, and I barely make it to the bathroom, where I am, once again, sitting there thinking I'm dying.

It's almost three a.m. when I finally make it out of the bathroom. I decide to just spend the night in my office. Making sure I set my alarm for seven so I can get up and shower before she comes in.

I fall asleep with a smile on my face and at least five pounds lighter.

By seven-thirty, I am showered and changed. I opt for warm water with honey this morning instead of coffee. I rinse out the cup before using it just in case she's tampered with everything in the kitchen. Who knows, maybe she's trying to kill everyone in the office.

I'm sitting at my desk when she walks in. When she walks past my office, I see that her skirt today falls to right above her knees and is not as tight as the others.

Of course, my dick starts to stir right away. I look down and mumble, "Traitor" at him.

She takes off her scarf and jacket, and I see that her shirt is a V-neck today. Finally showing off some skin and a hint of her nice, full C-cups. Her cream sweater molds to her, and my traitorous dick has risen to fully salute her. I give him a firm squeeze as I picture Danielle from yesterday. He shrivels right up in response, leaving me shaking my head.

I watch her sit down and touch the mouse to bring her computer screen to life.

The second her computer fires up, the normally quiet office is filled with the sounds of loud sexual moaning.

"Oh my god! Oh my god! OH MY GOD!" she squeals, getting more and more flustered.

I get up from my chair and walk to my door. I lean against it as I say, "Watching porn at work. Real nice."

She throws a panicky look over her shoulder at me but doesn't have time to reply before she turns back to the screen, where a woman with the biggest tits I have ever seen in my life bounces on a guy reverse-cowgirl style as her voice echoes through the office. "Oh yeah, I like that. Play with my tits, give it to me harder! Ooohhhhh yeah, oh right there! Fuck me like that right there!"

She clicks that screen closed, but another one pops right up in its place. Two guys this time. "I'm going to fuck that ass hard, and you're going to take it all, baby."

When nothing else happens, she starts to freak out. "What the heck is happening?"

She tries to close it down but to no avail. The screen is frozen on the image of one of the guys' dicks entering the other guy's ass. His face looks pained—and not in a good way. The screen may be frozen, but the sound is still coming through loud and clear.

"Fuck that virgin ass, tear it up. I'm going to cream you so good." At this point, people are starting to arrive. They're looking over at Lauren, who now has her hands covering her face.

Barbara comes out of her office, walking with purpose right over to us. The moaning starts again, and the screen flickers to life. The first guy is now pounding into the second guy while ordering him to "jerk that cock while I fuck your ass."

"Lauren, dear, I don't think this is the time or place for this. Perhaps you should do this in your own place." She pushes her glasses up higher on her nose, "Oh, that is some scene, right?" She giggles a little.

Lauren turns around, her cheeks blazing pink with embarrassment. "I don't watch this. It was on my screen when I turned it on, and I can't seem to shut it down. I closed the screen." She clicks the X in the corner, but another screen pops up, titled 'Please Cum On My Face' with a girl on her knees surrounded by ten hard dicks all shooting off their loads at the same time on her face.

"See? I can't shut it down," she says as she places her hands strategically over the computer screen in an effort to block out the video. "It won't stop!" I see some tears in her eyes.

She looks over at me, and for just one second, I feel bad, but then I remember that I almost died yesterday in my bathroom, and I just smirk at her. The tears are blinked away, clearing to show a murderous rage in her eyes that is aimed at me.

"I'm going to call JP in tech support to come over here and get this situation taken care of," Barbara says while she picks up Lauren's phone.

"JP, can you come to Lauren's desk? She seems to have been watching porn, and it's taking over her system."

"I was NOT watching porn! It was already on when I got here," she insists adamantly.

Barbara puts her hand over the phone. "Sure, sure, dear, whatever you say." Then she turns back to her conversation with JP. "Oh, she has tried clicking everything, but it seems she must have stumbled onto the wrong site."

I don't know what JP is saying, but Barbara nods her head and laughs. "See you soon."

She hangs up the phone. "He'll be right over." She looks at me then Lauren. "But for now, he says to not click on anything else."

"I didn't click on anything to begin with," she says, throwing her hands in the air, her tits bouncing with her movements.

She stands up and walks around her desk, and I finally see the full effect of today's outfit. Her skirt isn't tight, it's loose, almost flowing, and whenever she moves, it brushes against her thighs. Her creamy, perfectly toned thighs. *She almost killed me*, I quickly remind myself.

"Well, this is awkward, knowing what your assistant's sexual proclivities are. You really shouldn't view that type of material during working hours, though. I should probably sit down with you and discus this." I shake my head and look down. "I don't think I can let this slide. I'm so sorry, but I'm going to have to let you go." I don't even finish saying what I want to say.

"What the hell are you talking about? You can't fire her for that. It's discrimination! You can't tell her what not to do on her own time," Barbara says.

"It's not her time, she is on the clock." I put my hands on my hips, glaring at her.

"Austin, it's not even eight yet. Technically, you aren't paying her yet."

I look at my watch and see that it is just a couple of minutes before eight. "Oh, please, she doesn't even want to be here."

I look at Lauren and see that her head is tilted to the side. She looks back at her computer and then back at me. "Where are all my Post-it notes?" She turns and looks me straight in the eyes.

I shrug my shoulders with what I hope is my best 'I don't know what you're talking about' expression. "Maybe the cleaning staff threw them out."

"What are you talking about? You know the cleaning staff only comes in on the weekend, Austin. I mean, they come and empty garbage cans, but they don't do the full cleaning until the weekend," Barbara puts in her two cents.

"Really," I hear Lauren say, putting her own hands on her hips. "Fascinating, since someone touched my desk two days ago."

I don't have time to answer before JP shows up with a briefcase. "Okay, where is the porn monster located?"

Lauren points to her computer, where she goes to tell him that she hasn't touched anything. It takes him a few minutes to get everything cleared up. "There, that should do the trick. It really wasn't that bad." He chuckles and looks at me. "Remember last year when I had to totally reconfigure your hard drive when the same thing happened to you?"

I look at Barbara and Lauren, who are both looking at me now. Barbara is smiling, while Lauren is glaring. "Thank you for all your help, JP. Now that the problem is fixed, perhaps you can start your day," I say to Lauren.

"Oh, I'm going to start my day, alright," she tells me with a twinkle in her eye, and I somehow know that she's just upped the ante.

CHAPTER NINE

Lauren

The rest of the day goes by without anything happening. That night before I leave, I take out four pieces of tape, folding them in half, and stick them under my mouse.

Take that, Asshat. I glare at him through his blinds, but he doesn't see me.

I send him an email before I go home, just letting him know I'm leaving.

I'm still so fucking embarrassed. The whole office was talking about the new PA watching porn at her desk before the start of the workday.

Steven didn't even say hello to me when I saw him in the kitchen; he just waved and looked down as he hurried out.

By the time I make it home, I'm almost in tears. The only thing keeping them at bay is the rage I feel. I slam my car door a lot harder than intended. I storm into the house, slamming that door behind me, too.

Kaleigh is the first one to come out of the kitchen to greet me. The look on my face has her rushing back into the kitchen and returning with a full glass of wine. It sloshes over the rim as she hurries it to me.

She quickly hands it over with a smile. "Should I ask?"

I drink half the glass before I answer her. "He gave my computer a porn virus," I say while I walk over to the couch and throw myself down on it.

She sits next to me. "What do you mean, a porn virus?"

"I mean that when I turned on my computer this morning, porn was just popping up on my computer." Kaleigh starts to laugh, but I turn and glare at her. "Don't you dare laugh! I was mortified. As if that wasn't bad enough, the screen was freezing up, but the sound was blasting. Before I could even do anything, all of this moaning and groaning was blaring all through the office. 'Oh, fuck me harder!' Ugh!" I put my empty glass down after I drain it. My arms are flailing around me as I continue my story. "Oh, and let's not forget the gay porn. Yeah, of course that's when the screen froze, just as one of the guys had his dick halfway in the other guy's ass!"

"Was it big?"

I look over at her incredulously. "What the hell does it matter?" I throw my hands up in the air. "And where are my kids?"

Her hand waves through the air. "At a playdate next door. You have soccer in an hour, so go get yourself changed. Unless you want to show up like that, make a statement."

"Fucking porn all over my computer. I can't believe he would do that."

"You did put a laxative in his Coke." I don't let her finish before I point at her and hiss out, "You cannot tell anyone about that. You promised."

She takes her fingers, zipping her lips closed. "Fine. Now, I'm going to go change and head to soccer where I'm hoping nothing else goes wrong."

"What could top your co-workers thinking you are flicking the bean while at work? I hope you washed your hand after."

"I didn't flick the bean at fucking work, jackass! He played with my computer and the asshole threw out all my Post-its."

Kaleigh shakes her head. "That asshat," she agrees just as the door opens and the kids run in.

"Who's an asshat, Auntie Kay?" Rachel asks while she climbs on my lap, rubbing her nose to mine. I grab her tiny face in my hand, kissing her on the nose. "Don't say asshat."

Gabe walks up to me, kissing me on the cheek. "Mom, we have to leave in thirty. Dad says he might make tonight's game," he says, jogging upstairs to change.

"Okay, change of plans, no changing for you," Kaleigh says. "Show him what he's missing."

I'm almost feeling better when my phone bings with a notification.

I see that it's a text from Austin.

Tomorrow when you come in, before you start with your porn surfing, I need you to pick up my dry cleaning. I'll share the address with you. I need those shirts for the conference I'm having with the marketing firm tomorrow afternoon.

I don't watch porn at work.

I beg to differ. Actually, JP begs to differ.

It's times like these when I want to take my phone and run it over. Actually, I want to run *him* over. Front and back. Just for fun.

I don't have a chance to answer, since Gabe runs down the stairs with his shoes slung over his shoulder, his chin pads on but not velcroed on the top. His uniform is almost on.

"We need to go if we are going to be there on time," he urges, going to the fridge and taking a cheese stick and an apple from the counter.

I look at Kaleigh. "Are you coming?" I get up and grab another apple and a cheese stick for Rachel.

"I wouldn't miss his game for the world," Kaleigh says while grabbing her yoga mat. "I could do yoga while he plays." Rachel comes into the room and claps her hands excitedly.

"I'm going to bring my mat, too, Auntie Kay. Can we do it doggie style?" I spew water all over the counter.

Kaleigh laughs at me and bends down, squatting in front of Rachel. "Downward facing dog, honey, not doggie style. That's for when you get older."

I slam the glass down in exasperation. "Kaleigh, I will not only make you drink cow's milk, I'll throw a burger at you."

Rachel giggles. "Gabe, when we get older, we can do it doggie style!" she sing-songs while walking out of the door to go to the car.

I glare at Kaleigh, who is laughing so hard she's hunched over in the corner, holding her stomach. "If she repeats that to Jake, I will kill you." I point at her while I walk out of the door. She follows me to the car still laughing.

When I get in the car, Rachel asks for me to put *Frozen* on, followed by Gabe, who is begging me to put on anything else but *Frozen*. He groans and moans the whole way, which is ten minutes past the point I almost jumped out of the car into oncoming traffic.

When we pull into the parking lot by the field, I see that Jake is already there. I look over at Kaleigh and mutter under my breath that it's a cold, cold day in hell, I suppose. We all get out of the car and Rachel runs over to him, her arms flinging all over the place. "Daddy, Daddy, Daddy," she screeches right before he leans down and swings her in his arms.

Gabe runs over to them, also hugging him on the side. Jake wraps one hand around his shoulder, squeezing him and kissing his forehead.

I don't stand around to hear their conversation; instead, I open the trunk, taking out our two soccer chairs. I walk over to the side of the field where the bleachers are. I say hello to a couple of people but not really making eye contact with anyone. I'm just not in the mood for small talk today.

The phone buzzes in my hand once more while I open the chair, and then one more time when I sit down.

Did you get the address?
Did you get the message?
Where are you? Why haven't you answered?

I don't have time to respond before another one comes in.

Are you watching porn?

I put my head back and type back.

Yes, and you're disturbing me.

I press send and look over to see that Jake is leaning against his car, typing away on his phone. Then my phone buzzes again.

Jesus, do you ever stop?

I roll my eyes, crossing my legs, looking over to see Kaleigh and Rachel bending down.

Nope! Leave me alone. I got the memo. I'll get your clothes. I think I can handle it.

I put the phone in the cup holder once the game starts. I clap when the kids run onto the field, yelling, "Go, Gabe, go!"

I'm not alone for long before Jake sits down in the empty chair beside me.

"You're looking good, Laur," he says, using his nickname for me from when we were married.

"Yup," is all I say, because my phone buzzes again. Three times, then four. I pick it up, reading it quickly.

What time will you be in?
I need it for noon!!!
I have a meeting with the developer from the club that will be opening in three weeks.
Are you there?

I groan and type back.

I'm not on the clock, therefore it doesn't matter where I am or what I'm doing or who I'm doing it with, for that matter. See you tomorrow at 8!

I look at the phone, seeing the bubble come up with the three dots. I wait. It goes off then comes back, then goes off again. Then the text comes through.

Who you're doing? I thought you were divorced?

I turn the phone off, so I won't answer or know if he answers.

"So, how is it being back in the job force?" Jake asks, opening a bottle of water and drinking it.

"Jake, I have to be nice to you in front of the kids so they don't think I'm a bitter bitch. But when it's just the two of us"—I point to him then me—"I don't have to be nice to you. So, if you don't mind, I'll dispense with small talk. I don't want to talk about my day, my job, if I'm doing okay, if I have a date, or really anything at all with you. So, if you'll excuse me, I want to watch Gabe's game." I look to the field. "In peace."

Jake doesn't say anything else to me for the rest of the game. We sit in silence as we watch Gabe's team win. When the three whistles ring at the end, I see Kaleigh roll up her mat and walk over to us.

Jake kisses both kids and promises to see them next weekend. It's his weekend, which means I get very familiar with my wine glass, my Kindle, and my couch. Netflix is also on deck for a big ol' marathon!

I'm so excited to do absolutely nothing that whole weekend, I almost skip to the car.

By the time the baths are over and everyone is tucked in, I turn my phone on to set the alarm. I have five messages, all from Asshat.

Hello???

Did you get my messages?

Why aren't you answering me?

Your professionalism is laughable. I don't even know why I still have you as my PA. Do you even know what PA stands for?

Unbelievable! Just get my clothes.

I want to write him back to go fuck himself, him and his pencil dick, if he can even find it.

I whip the covers off and march to the hall closet, where I take out Gabe's practical joke box he got for his birthday last year.

I open it, tossing aside the mustache glasses, Chinese finger traps, whoopee cushion, squirting ring, nail through finger, and electric shock buzzer, coming up with the itching powder. I take it out and close the box, replacing it on the top shelf.

I'll show that asshat professionalism!

The next day, I get up, shower, and dress in a gorgeous royal blue wrap dress that I pair with a slim-fitting, tailored white blazer, since the dress is sleeveless. I quickly tuck the itching powder into my purse before the kids see it.

I make my way over to his dry cleaners, which is on the other side of town. Once I walk in, I give them his name and phone number, and collect his clothes.

There are about five suit jackets, ten pants, and twenty-five shirts. I have to walk to the car twice.

Once I'm inside the car, I open my purse and climb into the backseat.

I grab all his pants, taking one at a time, unfolding them neatly, and opening and sprinkling some powder in the crotch area, then pressing the legs together to rub it in a bit. I repeat this until all his pants are done.

I smile to myself, but then my phone rings, startling me as the sound fills the car, causing me to jump as I bobble the bottle. It goes flying, landing on the floor near my foot. I let out a little yelp as I kick it away.

I peek at my phone and see that it's him.

"Hello?"

"Where are you? Why aren't you here?"

"Where am I? Did you not tell me to go get your clothes from the cleaners this morning? The cleaners that, mind you, is half way to Guatemala," I return tartly while climbing back into the front seat and starting up the car. "I'm on my way. What do I do with your clothes?" I ask him as I start making my way to work.

"What do you think you do with them? You bring them up!" he replies smartly.

"Bring them up? It took me two trips to get them all in the car. Are you even dressed?" I ask, merging on the highway. "What do you need for the meeting? I can bring up what you need, and then when I leave later, you can come down and get them from my car."

"Ugh," I hear him groan. "Okay, fine. Bring me up my black suit," he says and hangs up. He doesn't have to say anything, because the car lets me know, "Phone call disconnected."

Asshole.

Once I get to work, I slide open the back door and look for his black suit, except almost all the suits are some shade of black. Fuck. Grabbing what I hope is a matching jacket and pants, I walk into my office building.

Looking at my watch, I see that it's already nine a.m. Once I get to the floor and the door opens, I see Steven at the reception desk talking to Carmen.

"Good morning, guys," I say, smiling to them while I fold Asshat's suit over my arm.

Steven smiles at me shyly. "Morning. You're late this morning. Is everything okay?" he asks.

"Oh yeah." I point to the dry cleaning. "Had to get his laundry."

"Right. Are you staying in for lunch?" Steven asks. I shake my head no.

"I'm actually thinking of going to this restaurant around the corner. They have little tables outside. And it's beautiful today," I say.

"That sounds delightful," Steven says "What time are you going?"

"Probably around noonish."

"Would you like some company?" He puts his hands in his pockets. It's the same move that Austin uses, except with Steven it doesn't fit.

"I would love some company. I'll call you when I'm ready," I say to him and then walk down the hall to my desk, dumping my purse on it before I walk to his office.

Seeing that the door is closed, I knock and wait for him to tell me to come in.

I open the door and see him behind his desk, eyes on the computer while he types away.

"Here is your dry cleaning. Where do you want it?" I ask him.

"Just put it over the back of the couch and check your email. There are a couple of things that need scheduling; also, we have the grand opening for the club in three weeks. You need to attend with me."

"Which day?" I ask, trying to pull up my calendar in my head, hoping that I don't have anything.

"You have all of that in your emails. Now, if you're done asking me insignificant questions, you can go," he dismisses me, not once looking at me. "And because you were late today, you are going to have to eat lunch here."

"I wasn't late. I was running an errand for you. Besides, I have plans at lunch."

"Don't care. Change them." I'm about to tell him to suck a dick when Barbara knocks on the door and walks in.

"Good morning, you two. Austin, we are ready for you," she says, and he gets up and walks out.

I'm stuck watching his back while he walks away. He never once makes eye contact with me.

I take in the jeans he's wearing today. They hang low on his hips but are tight on his ass. And what an ass it is. The kind that makes you want to grab it and bite it.

Wait, what?! What the hell was that? I don't like him. I really don't like him! Not at all. Not even a little bit. In my head, he's my sworn enemy. Now, if only someone would send that memo to the rest of my body!

CHAPTER TEN

Austin

All night, I tossed and turned. The fact that I texted her and she didn't answer me pissed me off. Again and again, I waited for her answer but got nothing. The thought of her with someone else irked me. I tossed, I turned, I got up, I looked outside.

I kept my phone near me all night, just in case she answered. Finally, around two a.m., I fell asleep, and when my alarm rang, I rushed, thinking the phone was ringing.

So here I am, still pissed off that she didn't answer, mingling with the fact that I'm grumpy because I'm tired. And to top it all off, I have to go into a marketing meeting with Dani about the club that is opening in three weeks.

I also have to talk to John about the Christmas party that is coming up. I walk into the meeting with John and Steven, pissed off, because not only did Lauren just walk in, but she also looks hotter than she ever has. That dress wrapped around her catches every curve she has, and when she walks, you get a glimpse of her inner thighs.

So, now I'm sitting in this meeting with a hard-on. "Are we disturbing you, Austin?" I hear John ask.

I shake my head, leaning back in my chair, rocking. "Nope, I'm all ears." He looks over at me, eyes narrowed speculatively as if he's trying to figure me out.

"I think that's all for now, Steven. You're good to go," John says while still looking at me.

"Perfect. If you guys need me, I'm headed out to lunch with Lauren, so I'll be back after that," he says, gathering his things and getting up from the table.

"No, you're not," I almost shout, and he stops picking his things up to look at me. "She needs to set up for my meeting with Dani." I grab my phone, sending her a message, telling her that I need her to set up for my meeting with Dani.

"Oh, okay," he says, turning and walking out of the room.

"Want to tell me how she's going to set up for your meeting with Dani when Dani is the one bringing everything for the meeting?"

I shrug my shoulders. "She needs to make sure we have water and shit."

He slaps his hand down on the table and bursts out laughing. "You have it so bad for her, and you don't even know it yet."

"I don't have anything bad. She almost killed me! I have to make her life a living hell." But he doesn't say anything; he just continues laughing. "She fucking put something in my Coke, and I thought I was shitting out my organs."

He wipes the tears from the corners of his eyes. But just then the door is thrown open, and Noah saunters in. "What are you guys laughing about?" he asks, plopping himself down in the chair that Steven just vacated.

"Austin's PA put something in his Coke, and he had the shits all night long," John says between fits of laughter.

"It wasn't all night long; it was till there was nothing left inside of me," I correct him while Noah chuckles.

"Wow. I thought my PA hated me," Noah says.

"She caught you fucking her mother on your desk," I remind him.

"She didn't knock. It wasn't my fault." He points at me.

"You had sex with her the day before," I also point out.

He shrugs his shoulders, thinking nothing more of it. "At least she didn't try to kill me."

"She put your face on a billboard with your home address and open invitation for free lodging for the homeless," John comments, still laughing.

"We don't know if it was her," I tell him. "I know that Lauren gave me something, that's the difference here."

"And didn't you infect her computer with porn viruses?" John asks. "Barbara says you're paying JP for that visit yourself, by the way."

"You got her computer infected with porn? Oh, my fuck, you like her!" Noah accuses.

"How can I like someone who almost killed me? She also hates the fact of my very existence on this earth. Not to mention that she didn't even answer my texts last night."

"You texted her after hours?" Noah asks, confused.

"I needed her to pick up my dry cleaning." I'm making excuses right now that are so lame not even I'm buying them. "Besides, you text your PA at night."

"Yes," Noah confirms. "For sex."

I throw my hands up when they both laugh at me, then I look at my watch. "I'm not doing this. I have to get ready for Dani's meeting."

"Oh, yes, that's right. The meeting Lauren has to 'prepare' for." John even uses his hands to make air quotations. Noah continues laughing. Those bastards.

"Fuck off, the both of you." I storm out of the conference room and run straight into Lauren. I wrap my arms around her so she doesn't fall; one arm wraps around her waist easily, while the other brings her closer to me.

Her body fits mine perfectly. Her head tilts back, and I look into her eyes. They are startled at first, but then they turn softer. "Sorry," she says, and I get a whiff of her berry scent. If I bent just a bit, my lips would touch hers. I would be able to find out if that shiny, pink lip gloss of hers tastes like strawberries. I'd find out how those plump lips feel against mine and if I could get her to light up for me. Maybe then I'd finally figure out how she really feels.

All these thoughts are running through my mind, and I decide I'm going to go for it, to finally scratch this itch that has been taunting me since the moment she got out of her car on the side of that road. Before I can do it, though, the conference room door opens and Noah and John both come walking out. Their laughter stops the second they take in the scene before them.

"Hey," John says. Lauren pushes herself away from me.

"Hi, John. I wasn't watching where I was going and slammed into Austin. He caught me before I fell." She's babbling so fast and nervously, I don't think she realizes that it just makes us look even guiltier. "I've got to set up for the meeting. Excuse me," She rushes out, walking past them.

"Dude, cover that shit up." Noah points to my crotch, where it's plain to see that I'm, once again, at full mast. They both start laughing at me.

I walk away from them, shaking my head while I attempt to cover my hard-on.

Walking into my office, I slam the door. Fuck me, I can still feel her full tits pressed to my chest. I rub my hands on my face. Shit!

I stay in my office and out of sight until I change into my black suit. I tuck my white shirt in and thread my black leather belt through the belt loops of my pants.

I grab the file and walk to the conference room where I hear Lauren's laughter.

I open the door and see that she is talking to Dani. "Well, I'm glad I could help," she says then looks at me. "If you need me, you can call me." She gets ready to leave.

"Why don't you stay and take notes?" I ask while I go to the head of the table and take a seat.

"Sure," she replies and takes the seat to my left, leaving Dani to sit on my right.

Dani opens the plans for the restaurant first. "Now, if you look here, you can see that we added some booths upstairs that can be used for lunch or supper."

I look at the plans, but then I feel a prickle in my balls. So I adjust myself in the seat while she continues. "One thing I was thinking was that for supper, we can do a Tapas menu upstairs and at the bar, and stop serving at eleven. Which is good, since we won't have to move anything. We can also use the booths for a VIP section." She continues talking, but I'm having trouble focusing on her words, because my balls are starting to burn.

So, I pull my pants away from them, thinking that they are squeezing them.

"That sounds like a good plan. Can we also do some couples' booths?" I ask her right before I feel another prickle and then another.

Fuck, is there a mosquito stuck in my pants?

"That's a great idea! I'll look into that right away and get back to you with specifics," Dani says.

"I'd love to go out to a club with my friends and not have to deal with drunk, aggressive guys all night," Lauren puts in.

"I hear you. I'd love to do a girls' section," Dani says. "With booths all the way around the perimeter and comfy seating clusters, so you can sit down when your feet hurt."

"Yes! That's a really great idea. I love that!" Lauren answers enthusiastically.

I'm trying to concentrate, but my pants are starting to suffocate my balls. Jesus, did the cleaners shrink my fucking pants? What the hell?

"Excuse me." I get up and walk quickly to the bathroom in my office.

The minute I pull my pants down, I start scratching. It feels like my balls are on fire. I yank down my boxers and gasp out loud.

My balls have ballooned to three times their normal size. Well, one looks like it's twice its normal size, while the other is even bigger than that. Oh my god! What the hell?! I start to panic and pull my phone out of my pocket to call John.

"You need to come to my office right now," I demand and then hang up. I take a picture of my balls with my phone to inspect them closer.

I grimace at what I see. Holy fuck, they are huge and red, and are those bumps?

I hear John call my name. I open the door just enough to pop my head out. "Come here!"

"Ummm, no way. What the fuck, man? I thought you were in trouble," he says and turns to walk out.

"John! Get the fuck in here," I whisper-yell angrily through my clenched teeth.

He walks in, and I close the door as he looks down and gasps, taking in the state of my balls. "What the fuck, dude?!"

"I don't know what's going on! I was sitting in the meeting when I felt a prickling sensation. I thought my pants were just tight. Dude." I look down. "My balls."

I look up again to see that John is standing there, a hand over his mouth, his eyes wide. "You need to go to the doctor. Jesus, do you think they'll explode?" he wonders as he crouches down—a little too close considering our relationship—to get a better look.

"Get the fuck away from my balls, please," I snap while I take my phone out and call Noah. "If anyone knows anything about this kind of thing, it's Noah. Didn't he get crabs from some chick in the Hamptons once?"

He answers on the first ring, "Yo," and I put him on speaker.

"When you got crabs, did your balls swell?" I ask, closing my eyes. I haven't had sex in about a month, so I have no idea if this is some sort of a delayed reaction.

"You have crabs?" he asks instead of answering my question.

"I have no idea. My balls are on fire and have swelled up to the size of a baseball," I explain while I continue to scratch them.

"Don't touch them," John says from his side on the phone. "I'm Googling this. Can I take a picture?" he asks right before he looks up and sees the glare on my face.

"Oh, send me a picture, too," Noah says while John continues to mess with his phone.

"It says something might have ruptured or you could have a hernia. Did you lift something heavy?" he asks while continuing to read.

"I was in a fucking meeting! I lifted a goddamn water bottle!" I look down at my balls, which seem to have gotten even bigger. "Oh my god, I think they're getting bigger."

"Can someone please send me a picture?" Noah begs through his laughing.

"I'm not sending you a picture of my balls, man," I say.

"You really need to get that checked out," John says. "I'll call Phil, maybe he's on duty."

"What color are they?" Noah is still chuckling.

"Fuck you." The itch is so bad I can't stop scratching.

"Phil says he's at Mercy Hospital now. If you get there in the next thirty, he can see you," John says while he's on the phone with Phil.

"I'll meet you there," Noah says, and I hang up on him.

"Will they fit back in your pants?" John is now laughing at me, too.

"Fuck you, this isn't funny. What if they exploded inside?" I question as panic sets in, and my heart starts to beat faster. Jesus, what if I broke my dick?

I pull up my boxers then my pants, my balls protesting the constriction of my pants.

"Fuck, oh god, it hurts now," I groan as I head out of the bathroom. I'm walking like I'm severely constipated, or worse, like I just had anal sex with a telephone pole. "Someone needs to tell Dani that I'm leaving."

"On it," John says, typing on his phone.

"Let's go before someone else sees you." We walk to the elevator as fast as we can, given my condition. When we get to Mercy, Noah is outside with a wheelchair waiting for us.

"Is this curbside service, or what!" he says, laughing at us. "Come on, big nuts, let's get this taken care of."

I sit down and get wheeled inside, where Phil is waiting for us. When he ushers us to a room, I expect Noah and John to wait outside. But I'm not that lucky, and I shouldn't be at all surprised when they follow us into the exam room.

"Seriously? You guys really need to be in here?" I ask them both.

"I've already seen it," John mutters, while Noah says, "I wouldn't miss this for the world. Can I film this? Maybe do a Snap story? Oh! I know, it can be my Instagram story!" I glare at him. "We could do that Facebook Live thing, you know, for medical purposes, of course."

"No one is filming shit," I grumble while Phil tells me to lower my pants. I pull my pants and boxers off at the same time, and male gasps fill the quiet room.

"Jesus, fuck me, your balls are the size of a miniature poodle's head!" Noah exclaims, and I start scratching again.

"Fuck! They got bigger," John comments. "I didn't think it was possible. Phil, can they explode?"

Phil grabs a pair of exam gloves, pulls them on, and rubs them together. "I'm warming them up," he says and then proceeds to put his ice-cold, latex-covered hands on my poor burning, itching, swollen balls. He starts inspecting them, bringing them up to look at the underside of my scrotum and moving them to the side to inspect the area where my leg meets my groin. "I don't see any puncture marks, so it's not a bite. A small rash is forming on your scrotum, however."

I put my head back and let out a breath I have been holding. "It looks like you're having an allergic reaction to something. Did you eat anything different? Change soaps? Anything at all?"

I shake my head no. "I don't think so. I don't wash my clothes, and my pants just came back from the dry cleaners. Lauren picked them up this morning."

I look at Noah and John, who are now folded over laughing. "Dude! She fucking hates you! And obviously, she hates your dick!" Noah says.

"Good news is that it will be back to normal in about twenty-four hours, maybe forty-eight, tops. I wouldn't put the pants or boxers back on," Phil says. "The swelling should go down, but if it doesn't, call me and I'll give you some meds. I'm going to have the nurse administer some Benadryl, and I'm going to have you stay for a couple of hours to make sure they don't swell any further," Phil says while writing on a paper. "I'll be back." He walks out.

"If you sit down, do you think your balls will crowd your dick?" John asks while he types on the phone.

"Who are you texting?" I ask.

"Dani and Barbara. You want me to text Lauren?" he snickers.

Noah is now sitting in the only chair in the room while he types. "I'm sending flowers to everyone I fucked over as a thank you for not giving me swollen balls."

I have no comeback. I just close my eyes and lie down on the table to wait for the swelling in my balls to go down. It's five hours later when I'm finally discharged. I leave the hospital dressed in a pair of blue scrubs.

When I finally get home and settled, I take my phone out and see that I missed a text from Lauren.

I hope you're okay?

Oh, I'm going to be more than okay. I sit down to plot and plan. The stakes just went up.

CHAPTER ELEVEN

Lauren

Fuck, fuck, fuckity fuck! I fucked up this time and took it too far. I'm headed back to his cleaners where I picked up his pants this morning to have them recleaned.

I saw him shifting in his chair during the meeting, and I laughed inside until I saw his face change a little right before he took off and didn't come back.

I was still discussing with Dani how to place tables when she got the text from John telling her they were taking Austin to the hospital.

When I heard he was going to the hospital, my heart lurched in my chest. I debated whether I should go after him or hide, hoping and praying that he wouldn't find out it was me and one of my pranks. It was supposed to be a harmless joke, like the porn virus on my computer. I never, ever intended to actually hurt him.

By the time I left for the day, the word around the office was that he had an allergic reaction to something.

I practically ran to my car, calling Kaleigh the minute I was inside and the door was closed.

"I think I almost killed my boss!" I yell into the phone as I speed to his dry cleaners.

"What do you mean, almost? Does he know? Did you wear gloves?" She peppers me with questions, and I hear banging in the background.

"Kaleigh, please, just this once, can you try to be fucking normal?" I ask, thumping the steering wheel in exasperation as I start freaking out.

"Okay, fine. What exactly happened?"

"I put fucking itching powder in his pants. And I think his dick or his ass, or I don't fucking know, maybe his balls, was allergic to it, and he had to go to the fucking hospital!" I finish on a shrill yell.

"You put what?"

"Itching powder I took from Gabe's prank box! It was just supposed to be a stupid joke. A payback for the porn bombing he pulled on my computer," I say as my eyes start filling with tears.

"You mean after you put a laxative in his Coke?"

"Kaleigh, not now, for the love of God. You are on my side always. Blood thicker than asshat boss," I remind her. "The minute he ran into me and I almost fell but he caught me instead, I regretted doing it. Oh, god. Do you think he's going to know it's me?"

"I don't know. Does anyone else in the office hate him?" she asks me.

"I have no idea if anyone hates him. It's not something I can bring up, you know? I mean, I'm his PA; I can't go around asking people 'Hey, how are you? Isn't Austin an asshole?' Oh my god!" I pull up to the cleaners. "I gotta call you back. I'm at the cleaners. I'm bringing his clothes to be recleaned."

I hang up even though she is still talking. I rush into the cleaners, my arms full of all his clothes.

"Hi, there. I need all of these recleaned, twice please." I put the clothes down on the counter.

"Ma'am, you just picked these up this morning," the lady says while she picks up the clean clothes that are still in the plastic covers.

"Yes, I think something spilt on them, and he wants them cleaned again," I say, smiling "Twice."

"Twice?" she asks, confused.

"Yes, just in case. He wants them run through the cleaning process twice," I repeat to her, and she puts my special request on the card. I turn and rush out of there. I climb back into my car, toss my purse onto the passenger seat, and head for home.

While I brake at a stop sign, the empty bottle of itching powder rolls to the front floorboard at the same time as my phone rings. I see that it's

Kaleigh calling.

"Are you okay?" she whispers.

"No. I'm not okay. I caused my boss to end up in the ER with an allergic reaction and swollen balls because I was trying to get back at him." I feel the sob creeping up my throat.

"Did you get rid of all of the evidence?" she asks me.

"I still have the empty bottle here in the car." I look down at it, and it's almost as if it's taunting me.

"Throw it out of the car right now," she instructs me. "Open the window and toss it as far as you can."

I pick up the bottle and hold it in my hand. "Should I wipe it down?" I look around for a rag.

"Lauren, do you honestly think he is calling CSI to come and find the bottle? Just throw the fucking thing out the window and come home."

Just as I'm about to throw the bottle out of the window, I hear a honk, startling me. "Fuck," I say while the bottle falls into my lap.

"I'm on my way," I say while I drive on, and when I'm all alone on the street, I toss that bottle as far as I can while driving.

Once I park my car in the driveway, I text Austin.

I hope you're okay?

I wait a couple of seconds, but nothing comes in. So, I walk into the house, where I'm greeted with hugs and kisses.

When I finally tumble into bed, my phone beeps with a text from Austin.

I'm not coming in tomorrow, so you can take the day off.
Oh, are you okay? I heard you had an allergic reaction.
You could say that.
Well, I'll be here all weekend if you need anything. I'm hosting my parents and a couple of their friends for their anniversary brunch on Sunday morning, but if you need anything, please let me know.
Sure thing.

This is really weird. He's usually sarcastic and an asshole, but now he's all soft and not at all snarky.

The next couple of days are pretty much the same as usual. On Saturday night, after putting the kids to bed, I start preparing the dishes and everything for tomorrow's brunch.

Mom is having a caterer come in, since I'm hosting their anniversary brunch. We plan to set up outside and have a beautiful outdoor celebration with twenty of their closest friends.

My phone rings, letting me know that it's my mom calling.

"Hey, Mom."

"How did you know it was me?" she asks, all confused.

"Mom, the phone has caller ID." My mom isn't a tech friendly person. Last time she tried to FaceTime the kids, her screen was facing the other way and all we saw was her finger on the camera.

"Are you ready for tomorrow, dear? You didn't really have to do this, but we are so excited about it." Her voice is pitching higher with her excitement.

"It's my pleasure, Mom. You know I would do anything for you two." And I would. Mom and Dad have been married for thirty-nine years.

They met while Dad was visiting a friend from college. All it took was one look, and he was hooked. The minute he finished his residency, he came and proposed to Mom, promising to love, honor, and cherish her, and he actually kept those promises.

Mom stayed home with us girls, while Dad grew his practice. He's retired now, and the practice is in Josh's hands.

"You know, Josh is coming, and he's single again," Mom reminds me, interrupting my thoughts.

"Mom, please don't. We went on one date, and that was only because I was guilted into it."

My mother heaves out a huge sigh. "Oh, please, he's perfect for you! Single and a doctor."

"Mom, he's shorter than me, by almost a foot, and he's balding," I tell her.

"It's what's inside, Lauren, not what's outside."

"Mom, he's thirty!" I yell out.

"So he aged early, there is nothing wrong with that. He's a total catch," she says. "Oh, honey, I have to go. The Robinsons just got here. See you Sunday!" She adds, "Oh, and tell Kaleigh that a bra is mandatory!" I laugh and hang up the phone just as Kaleigh walks in.

"That was Mom." I point to the phone. "She said that a bra is mandatory this time."

She waves her hand like she isn't paying attention. "Oh, please, it was one time. How was I supposed to know that you could see my nipples through that pink sundress?" she says while grabbing her almond milk and drinking straight from the carton.

Right when I'm about to scold her to use a glass, the phone rings again. This time I see it's Austin.

"Hello?" I say tentatively, since he's never called me.

"I have an eight a.m. meeting Monday morning with Dani to finalize things, since I had to leave yesterday."

"Okay, I can get in a bit early and get things set up again," I confirm, looking at Kaleigh, who is looking at me, making the blowjob motion with her tongue poking her cheek.

"I need my dry cleaning. Is it still in your car?" he questions me, and my head snaps up as I wave my arms to get my sister to stop distracting me.

"Um, yeah, I still have it. How about I bring it to you on Monday morning, is that okay?" I'm freaking out and pacing the kitchen floor, while my sister pretends to be humping the counter. I mute the phone and look at her. "Would you be serious? He wants his dry cleaning." I unmute it while he grunts his okay.

"If that's all, I have to go. I have to run errands for my Sunday brunch."

"Yeah, that's all," he says and hangs up.

"Oh my god." I run to my purse, searching for where I put the dry-cleaning bill. Once I find it, I call the number at the top. They answer after one ring.

"Rinse and Clean, how may I help you?" the lady says right before I stutter out.

"Hi, hi, I was in a couple of days ago. I don't know if you remember me. I needed an order washed twice." I sit on the stairs. "The number is 076453."

"Oh, the one who brought back the clothes still in the wrapping. Yes, ma'am, I put a rush on it, and they should be ready in about an hour."

I look at my watch and see that it's already almost four. "Okay, thank you. Are you open tomorrow?" I ask her, knowing I won't be able to get there and back before I have to get Gabe to his soccer game.

"We are open until four on Saturday and noon on Sunday," she says and hangs up after we say good-bye.

"Fuck! I have to add a stop to our growing list of things to do tomorrow. Next time I offer to host a brunch, kick me in the ass, please," I tell Kaleigh. The day flies by in a flurry of errands and preparations, and before I know it, it's Sunday morning.

I set my alarm for eight, since the caterers will be arriving at eight-thirty.

I make my way downstairs just in time to see Kaleigh walk in the door still wearing last night's outfit.

"Oh, the walk of shame. Nice. Very Nice," I say while I sip my coffee and she sits down at the counter.

"What's a walk of shame?" Rachel asks, and I look over at Kaleigh.

"It's when you are still wearing last night's clothes," Kaleigh discloses to her and then whispers to me, "After they were on the floor of the hot guy whose cock you rode all night." And then she throws her fist, pumping.

I smack her arm and pick up Rachel in my arms. "You get to wear the pretty dress today. Are you excited?" I ask her.

"So excited! We get to go get our hair fixed?" She throws up her hands, mimicking Kaleigh.

The doorbell rings, and I let the caterer in while we go upstairs to get dressed so we can leave the caterers to do their thing while we get pampered.

Even Gabe comes along for the fun. Well, not fun for him, but he pretends.

Once we get home, we all rush upstairs to change with only twenty minutes to spare.

I hurry into my room and pull out my white skirt that is tight to the knees with pleats all the way around. I pair it with a tight brown spaghetti-strapped camisole that molds to my boobs, and my brown strappy wedges.

"Umm, Lauren? I think you should see this," I hear Kaleigh say at the same time the doorbell rings. I spray my perfume on and rush downstairs, where my parents have just walked in with all of their friends arriving at the same time.

"Happy Anniversary, Mom and Dad." I greet them with a hug.

"Thank you, dear," Mom says, hugging me in return.

"Please, everyone, come in. I had the backyard set up for our brunch." I point the way to the backyard. Kaleigh, who has changed and is now wearing a pretty, pink sundress—with a bra, I might add—rushes over to me.

"I think you need to see outside before everyone else does." she says with her teeth clenched, which confuses me.

"What are you talking about?" I ask and then the doorbell rings again. I go to answer it before Kaleigh does. I open the door to be greeted by a guy holding a huge chocolate bouquet.

I gasp out in shock when I see that all of the chocolates are made of penises and the pail holding them is adorned with a huge pink bow. "I have a delivery for Lauren," he announces, looking at the clipboard in his hand.

"I…" I stutter while he pushes the pail into my hands. "I didn't order these." I look down and see that there are both white chocolate ones and milk chocolate ones, all on white sticks. I shake my head, my throat getting dry. He walks to his truck that is parked in the driveway and comes back with two more pails. "I don't want this," I say to him, but he's just a delivery guy, so he just smiles and leaves.

"Oh my god," Kaleigh says from beside me. "Don't freak out." She looks at me.

"Why would I freak out?" I ask right when my mother yells from outside.

I walk past the caterers, who are still preparing. When I walk into the backyard, my eyes survey the scene as my mouth hangs open at what I see.

I look at the white tables I ordered that are all set up with the turquoise tablecloths I requested. The little glass vases holding the white flowers in them just like I ordered in the center of each table. Except there are also bouquets of balloons—all white and turquoise, each one stamped with a penis.

Now, as if that isn't bad enough, there are also approximately fifty two-foot tall pink, penis-shaped helium balloons. The penis has a smile on the head and a blue bow around the shaft. They are all floating around the yard.

"Oh my god, oh my god!" I cry, looking over to see that there are penis straws in all the glasses. The table in the corner that I set up for the cake is now filled with cupcakes with little penis cake toppers.

"Dear, what is this?" my mother asks me with a forced smile on her face. My father is holding a glass of scotch, which he is sipping, mind you, through a penis straw.

"I didn't order this. They made a mistake." I look around, making sure everyone hears me.

One of the servers walks by with the chocolate penises. Of course, my mother grabs one before she even realizes what it is.

"Grammy, why are you eating a chocolate willy?" Rachel asks. "Look, Momma! It's just like Gabe's willy!" She grabs a balloon and runs over with it.

I look over at the guests, who are all snickering at this point. "Surprise!" Kaleigh yells. "You guys are in for a treat!"

Mom's best friend, Sarah, comes up to me. "I love it, it's very liberating. And fun," she giggles as she takes a sip of her drink through her own penis straw.

I am completely and utterly humiliated, and I'm about two seconds away from sobbing in the middle of my backyard. The song "It's My Party And I Can Cry If I Want To" is playing on repeat in my head. Tears well up in my eyes.

I'm about to have an epic meltdown, and we didn't even serve the meal yet. I hear a knock on the side gate and in walk, or should I say saunter, Austin and his friend Noah.

Austin looks like sin on a stick. He's dressed in blue jeans and a linen button-down shirt rolled up at the sleeves. His silver Rolex on his wrist, and his gold aviator glasses on his face. A dusting of two days' worth of stubble gives him an edge. "Oh, I'm sorry. I don't mean to crash your party," he says with a megawatt smile on his face.

I look over at Noah, who is looking around at all the penises, his eyes bulging out of his head. He turns and looks at Austin and covers his mouth with his hand. It is in this moment that I know I've been played.

"You." I point at Austin.

He walks up to me, turning his smile at Mom. "You must be Lauren's sister," he says, kissing her hand. She smiles and throws her head back and laughs.

"Oh, you silly boy. I'm Deidra, Lauren's mother. You can call me Dede," she invites while she smiles at him.

"You can call her nothing, because you're leaving. Now. And"—I turn to him—"how did you know where I live?"

"Lauren, stop being rude to the guests," my mother scolds while my father walks over and introduces himself. "Hello, son, I'm Frank, Lauren's father."

"No," I say, shaking my head. "He isn't a guest. This is my former boss." I look at him. "I quit. Done. Finished. Finito. I'm out," I snap with my hands on my hips.

"Who is the other one?" Kaleigh asks with a chin lift in Noah's direction.

"That's Noah," I answer. "Gabe, can you go inside and get my car keys? Mr. Mackenzie was coming to get his dry cleaning," I say to Gabe, who runs inside to get my keys.

"Mom, can I have a willy chocolate?" Rachel tugs at my skirt while she asks me the question.

"No, you cannot have a willy chocolate. We are going to eat in a minute." I turn and storm inside, walking past the kitchen to the bathroom, where I try to slam the door shut, but a brown shoe blocks it from closing.

"Seriously, what do you want?" I look at him. He pushes the glasses to the top of his head. I blink away the tears that have formed in my eyes and look away from him so he doesn't see. "Didn't you get your revenge already?" I throw my hands up. "You penis-bombed my parents' anniversary party!"

He leans against the closed door, folding his arms across his chest. His scent fills the room, making it feel small all of a sudden.

"You made my balls swell to the size of fucking grapefruits. I thought they were going to explode," he fires back at me.

"I did no such thing." I look at my shoes and then look up. "But this, this... You pushed it too far."

"How about we call a truce?" Austin asks. "I don't think I can take any more. I almost died, and my testicles almost exploded."

"Fine," I agree, putting out my hand to shake his. He grabs my hand in his, and the minute he touches me, my breath hitches and I try to pull my hand away, but he holds it firmly.

"Truce," he promises, his thumb stroking my hand. I look down where our hands meet. The room is getting smaller and smaller.

Right as I start to lean into him, there is a loud knock. "Hey, I don't mean to interrupt, but, um, Jake is here."

CHAPTER TWELVE

Austin

The minute she told me she was having a brunch at her house, I set a plan in motion. This was after I called the dry cleaners and asked them if they changed soaps.

I was told that my clothes had been brought back with the very odd request that they be recleaned—twice. That little shit.

It took about thirty hours for the swelling in my balls to go down. Thirty hours of praying to every god I could think of that they would return to normal. I just didn't want to have big balls anymore.

So when I finally calmed down, I put my plan in motion. I found her address in the company directory that only HR and higher management can access.

From there, I set out to find local businesses who sold party materials in the shape of a penis. I called in the event planner that I usually use, and she was nothing but professional. I was really surprised that she didn't even bat an eye at my strange requests.

"Isn't this a weird request?"

"Austin, you would be surprised the stuff I have had to find. Penises? Please. That's like trying to find princesses nowadays."

After telling her what I wanted, she set it all up to be delivered before noon. I called Noah and asked if he wanted to do brunch with me, but not telling him anything further in case he tried to talk me out of it.

When we show up in front of Lauren's house, that is when I fill in Noah.

"Where the fuck are we? I thought you said we were going to brunch." He looks over at all the white-picket-fenced houses.

"Yeah, pit stop first. I have to pick up my dry cleaning at Lauren's," I tell him, getting out of the car.

Once I make my way around her house, he asks me. "Why are we at her house?"

"She's having a brunch." I shrug. "I may have sent her some penis decorations," I say before walking to the side of the gate.

The first thing I see are all the balloons. Fuck, the event planner wasn't kidding when she said she could get anything.

"Holy shit, she is going to cut your dick off with dental floss," I hear Noah say before I knock and walk into the backyard.

I stop in my tracks, mid-step, when I see that it isn't just her parents, but there are about fifteen or so people scattered around the yard. Noah, of course, bumps into me, his mouth flopping open and closed in shock.

"Holy shit," he whispers. "Dude, I think she's going to cry," he says, and my eyes snap straight to Lauren.

When I put this plan into motion, I assumed she would probably intercept the decorations before her guests saw them. I thought she would spend her morning trying to hide and/or dispose of them before they arrived, and then spend the party looking over her shoulder, fearful of another delivery.

I head over to her and the women who are obviously her sister and mother. Her mother, who is right then biting into a chocolate penis. I'm introduced to Lauren's mother and father, and I'm pulling out all the charm. I'm not exactly sure why. I usually run away from parents.

I know she is seconds from slipping into meltdown mode, because she abruptly turns her back on her daughter and mother and hurries toward the house.

"Excuse me," I tell her parents, walking right into her house after her. She walks into the bathroom, slamming the door behind her, but not before I can wedge my shoe in there to block it from closing.

"Seriously, what do you want?" She looks straight at me. I move the sunglasses that I'm still wearing off my face to the top of my head. I stare at her valiantly trying to hold it together, noticing the tears that are welling in her eyes. She blinks repeatedly and stands tall to face me down.

"Didn't you get your revenge already?" She throws up her hands, and that's when I notice how what she is wearing hugs all of her curves. The tank top that molds to her full breasts perfectly, and the skirt that skims her body in all the right places.

"You penis-bombed my parents' anniversary party!"

I lean against the closed door, folding my arms across my chest. "You made my balls swell to the size of fucking grapefruits. I thought they were going to explode," I fire at her.

"I did no such thing," She tries to deny weakly. She breaks eye contact, looking down at her shoes for a moment, before she squares her shoulders and looks me in the eye. "But this, this... You pushed it too far."

"How about we call a truce?" I ask. I have no idea why I'm even trying to get on her good side. "I don't think I can take any more. I almost died, and my testicles almost exploded," I tell her the truth.

"Fine," she complies, putting out her hand to shake mine. I raise my hand to grab hers. The fit is perfect. As I take in the feeling of her hand in mine, I notice that they are soft, delicate yet strong. As soon as her hand slipped against mine, I felt my heart rate kick up. I rub my thumb along the soft skin of her hand, trying to find a reason why I shouldn't just pull her into me and plant my lips on hers. The memory of her body pressed against mine at work the other day still lingers in my mind.

"Truce," I whisper, my thumb still stroking her hand. She looks down at our hands that are still connected. It looks like she's not even breathing.

I can feel her getting closer and closer to me. Then, right before I feel her start to lean into me, there is a loud knock. "Hey, I don't mean to interrupt, but, um, Jake is here."

She drops my hand like it's a hot potato, pushing me aside and opening the door. Her sister greets us with a huge smile, Noah standing right behind her. "What do you mean, Jake is here? Why is Jake here?" I hear her asking, her voice rising with each question.

"Hi"—the sister pushes Lauren aside—"I'm Kaleigh, her favorite sister," she introduces herself.

"She's my *only* sister, and she will be homeless in a second if she doesn't get out of my way." Lauren's voice is angry.

I hear Noah chuckle behind her. Lauren turns and points at him. "You, if I find out you helped him, it's going to be on," she hisses and leans in closer to him when she continues, "like Donkey Kong." And then she walks away.

"What the fuck does she mean, like Donkey Kong?" Noah turns to Kaleigh, looking for an answer.

"Oh, I was only on that list once"—she leans in closer to Noah—"and I begged and cried to get off of it." She looks at me then back at Noah. "It was like living in that movie *The Shining*, but worse." Noah's face pales at that little tidbit of information. Yeah, welcome to my world, buddy.

He points at me. "If I get it like Donkey Kong, I'm going to put the pictures of your swollen, abnormally large testicles on a billboard in Times Square," he threatens, while Kaleigh just watches us.

"Who the fuck is Jake?" I ask her.

"Her ex. This should be fun," she claims, walking away from us.

"You took a picture of my nuts?" I ask him.

He shakes his head at me. "No, I took a burst of shots of your nuts." Then he walks out, following Kaleigh.

"What are you doing here?" I hear Lauren ask a guy who I assume is Jake.

"I forgot that today was going to be the brunch. I was going to see if Gabe wanted to hang out at the park." He looks over at a boy who is standing in the corner of the yard, taking a picture of a penis balloon. That must be Lauren's son.

"Why didn't you call first?" she questions then shakes her head. "You know what, it doesn't matter. He can't go with you, so—"

"Daddy, look at all the willies," Lauren's miniature clone says as she walks over to him, two chocolate penises in her little hands. "You want to eat a willy?" She extends her hand to offer him one.

"No, honey, that's okay, you can have them." He looks around. "I should go," he adds, nodding at everyone and then leaving the backyard.

"Hey, Mister." The little girl looks up at me. "Who are you?" She is biting off the tip of the chocolate penis in her little hand.

"I'm your mom's boss," I explain to her, squatting down in front of her.

"Oh, you're the Asshat?" she wonders, and Lauren's hand flies to cover her daughter's mouth in an effort to muffle whatever else she was going to say.

I look up at Lauren to see her shrug her shoulders. "This is Rachel and that is my son, Gabe." She points back to the kid in the corner, who just raises his hand in a little wave.

"Are we eating or not?" Frank asks.

"Yes," Lauren answers. "Everyone, please grab a seat wherever you feel comfortable. I'm going to tell Edward we are ready."

"You two can sit at my table," Kaleigh invites, while Lauren walks away.

She doesn't make it inside before she turns around. "They aren't staying."

"Oh, come now, Lauren. That would be rude," Dede chides. "You can sit at our table." She turns to Frank. "Let's go sit down, honey."

Once everyone is seated, I look around at our table. Noah, Kaleigh, Frank, Dede, Lauren, and Josh, who I found out is a doctor and bears a striking resemblance to Newman from *Seinfeld*.

He sits next to Lauren, standing up when she gets to the table and pushing her chair in. She looks over at him and smiles.

What the fuck is that smile all about? I wonder as I grab my glass of wine and down it in one gulp. "Slow down there, slugger. We don't want you flying off on one of those penis balloons," Noah whispers in my ear.

"So," Josh starts, looking at Lauren. "I hear congratulations are in order. You're back in the work force now." He continues in that annoyingly nasal voice of his, "How does this weekend sound?" He blushes and looks down to his hands. What a putz.

"Oh, um, she can't do it this weekend," Kaleigh answers for Lauren. "She's having her bikini area waxed and styled," she explains, nodding her head.

"What?" He looks confused.

"Well,"—Kaleigh leans in and whispers—"it's like the Amazon down there."

Noah spits water from his mouth, while their mother puts her hand to her mouth and Lauren throws her fork down on the plate, the clatter hushing the whispers at our table. "Kaleigh," she grates out, her jaw ticking.

"What?" she asks. "Was it a secret?" She shrugs. "So sorry." She brings her glass of wine to her mouth in an attempt to hide her smirk.

"Dear," Lauren's mother questions, "are you okay? Is this procedure normal?" She gives her daughter a look filled with concern.

"Mom—" Lauren starts before she is cut off by her father.

"Lauren, it's been a while since Jake left. Maybe if you—" he gestures with his hand in a circle and his finger sliding in and out—"you won't be so stressed."

I look over at Lauren, whose face is red with embarrassment and looks like she is going to lunge right over the table and throttle Kaleigh. She slams her hands on the table, the glasses clinking and rocking with the force of it. "I'm not having any hair removal procedures done, because it is not necessary. Can we please just—" This time, she is cut off by her mother.

"So, you've had sex since Jake?" Dede asks her, a smile on her face. "This is so good to hear." She claps her hands together then leans over and puts her hand on Lauren's. "I thought you had that glow about you."

"I'm going to the bathroom," Lauren excuses herself as she gets up and points to Kaleigh. "You"—she growls—"come with me."

"Oh," Kaleigh replies, completely unperturbed, "I'm good. I don't need to go. I'll just wait here. Keep the guests entertained."

"Not a word. Or else Donkey Kong," she promises before she storms off.

"So," Dede starts, turning to me. "How long have you two been dating?" She looks at me and then at the door that Lauren just walked through.

Kaleigh laughs. "Oh, they aren't dating, Mom. He's her boss," she helpfully points out. "He sent all these penis balloons."

Frank looks over at me. "You sent all these balloons and ruined all her hard work?" he asks.

"Um, sir, if I could just explain?" I start as my heart beats fast. Before I can say anything else, he puts up his hand to stop me.

"I like you," he declares right before someone clinks their glass and the speeches start.

I look around at the yard, taking in Lauren's family and friends. I sip my glass of wine and look over at Noah, who has his arm draped around

Kaleigh's chair and is whispering in her ear. Whatever he's saying is causing her cheeks to turn pink.

The seat next to me gets pulled out when Lauren's daughter sits down next to me. "Hey, Asshat, can I have your strawberries?" I look over her head to the door where Lauren disappeared a few moments before and see her walking back outside. With an angry scowl on her face. Oh, shit, the naked strippers must have arrived.

CHAPTER THIRTEEN

Lauren

I am in hell. Something or someone out there is driving the karma bus right into me. What I want to know is, what the fuck did I do wrong and to whom?

Not only is my boss, the bane of my existence, sitting at a table in my backyard with my parents at their anniversary brunch—after he sent me a yard-full of penis balloons, every single penis-themed party decoration known to man, and more penis-shaped chocolates on a stick than one woman could ever possibly eat— but as if that weren't enough, I'm now face-to-face with what appears to be the entire cast of the Australian all-male revue *Thunder From Down Under*.

"Hey there, mate, we are here to party," he taunts with a thrust of his hips.

"Please, you obviously aren't even from Australia. That accent sounds Jamaican." I put my hands on my hips, and I'm pretty sure that this is the straw that broke the camel's back. Visions of me picking up a knife and stabbing him in the fucking heart in a fit of rage dance through my head.

"Party was cancelled. But you can charge the card twice for your trouble," I tell them before slamming the door. I head back out to the backyard and look right at the man who has set this particular nightmare in motion.

I see Rachel in the chair next to him and watch as his head lifts, eyes seeking mine. I see it, the moment his eyes recognize the fury in mine and he realizes that I'm onto him.

"Okay, folks,"—he gets up—"I hate to cut out early, but…" he stammers, "but, but…" He looks to Noah for help, but Noah is too focused on whatever Kaleigh is saying. Austin kicks Noah's chair to get his attention.

His eyebrows shoot up when Austin says urgently, "Gotta go," then glances over at me and continues, "now would be good."

I don't know if Noah knows what is happening or not, but he throws his napkin on the plate in front of him "This has been fun," he murmurs, trying to escape while keeping an eye on me at the same time.

"Running off so early, guys?" I sing-song as I come up behind them.

"We intruded," Austin says. "Thank you for having us. Dede, Frank, I wish you many more years of happiness," he rushes out on a wave as he hurries out the side gate.

Kaleigh gets up. "What did I miss?"

"The entire cast of *Thunder From Down Under* just arrived." I look around to see if the guests are okay. I can't wait for this party to be over.

She looks around excitedly, pulling her skirt up a bit. "Where? Are they inside? Shit, do I look okay?" She fluffs her hair.

"Kaleigh," I whisper-hiss, "they aren't here anymore. I sent them away."

She groans. "Why? Why would you do that?" She runs to the side gate to see if they're still in the driveway. "Buzz kill." She calls me as she picks up Rachel. "Can you protect me from Mommy?" she whispers in her ear before blowing kisses in her neck.

I sit down in my chair and immediately start drinking another glass of wine as I try to calm myself by counting down from ten. It takes four times before I no longer feel like I am a danger to myself or others.

The rest of the afternoon goes by without any further penis-related incidents. All cupcakes have been consumed, minus the penis cake toppers that I removed before serving them.

Once everyone has left, I plop down into my chair and throw my feet up on the one Austin sat in. "That was fun, right?" Kaleigh asks.

"You told people I had a strange excessive hair issue on my hoo-ha that required a complicated bikini wax and styling." I glare at her.

"I was trying to get Josh to imagine that you're a woman with a hairy bush so he doesn't ask you out again!" She drinks from the wine glass she is holding in her hand. "You're welcome." She smirks.

"What the hell are we going to do with all those penis balloons?" I look around, hoping to see that some of them are deflating. Sadly, they are all still fully erect and happily smiling at me. "Asshole," I grumble under my breath.

"What's the story with Noah?" Kaleigh tries to be casual so I don't pick up on her curiosity over him.

"No idea. He's Austin's best friend from what I gathered today," I tell her while looking at Rachel, who is running in circles with, unfortunately, a penis balloon in her hand. "Ten minutes to bath time!" I call out, hoping she acknowledges me, but she just continues her one-girl—with a penis balloon—parade.

"Mom," I hear Gabe call from behind me. "Can I go to Jesse's house to kick around the ball?"

I check my watch and see it's almost seven. "Only for thirty minutes, okay?" I know he'll be forty-five minutes.

"So, what are you going to do to Austin for all of this?" Kaleigh asks, pointing to the balloons.

"Nothing." I smirk. "We called a truce."

"I know that smirk. I've been on the receiving end of that smirk!" She sits up.

"I mean, we called truce today, right? We didn't call truce on Wednesday when he made me run back out for a fucking crisp kosher pickle, because the one that came with his sandwich was limp, right?" I ask her with a perplexed smile on my face.

"What did you do now? From the pictures, his balls were almost the size of Gabe's soccer ball."

I slap the table. "You saw pictures?" My mouth hangs open.

She nods her head yes. "I did. Not the actual frank, though, just the beans. But they were ginormous." She motions with her hands, forming them into huge round objects in the air. "Now, what did you do!"

"Nothing that will make any part of him swell. I will never, ever do something like that again." The guilt still runs through me. "I may have shred one of his parking tickets that had to be paid by yesterday so he could avoid his car getting booted," I confess quietly, looking into the glass I picked up from the table.

"Holy shit. I hope you kept the photocopies, because you can't not pay that. He is going to know it was you," Kaleigh warns

"I know, I know. I kept them, so just relax." I put my hands on my hips and state defensively, "I'm going to pay them."

"When?" she asks, earning her an eye roll from me.

"Next week," I reply as I get up and ignore any further commentary from her. "Rach, bath time." I walk to the back door. "Don't you dare sit there and judge me, missy." I point at Kaleigh. "By the way, the potatoes had butter in them. That's for the bikini wax," I say before I turn my back to her and walk inside with the sound of her curses filling my ears.

The next week goes by without any more incidents. It seems we are both on our best behavior. Well, I am. He's still a Neanderthal, and I'm almost tempted to not pay his tickets, but I promised Kaleigh I'd be the better person. Apparently though, I was one day too late on that, because at around one o'clock, he storms out of the office without a word, running down the stairs instead of taking the elevator.

Twenty minutes later, he comes storming back in, huffing and puffing as he stops at my desk.

"Did you pay my tickets?" he asks as I pretend I'm shuffling around papers and hoping that he can't see my heart practically beating out of my chest.

"Um, yeah, I did. I have it here somewhere. Why?" I glance up and see the vein in his forehead is twitching and some sweat is gathering at the side of his face, obviously from running down the stairs.

He puts his hands on my desk, leaning into me as I lean back in my chair. I know I should be pissed that he's in my space, but I only feel a trickle of excitement. "Why, you ask? Because Trent just called from downstairs. They booted my car and towed it."

"No!" I say, trying to force a look of shock onto my face instead of laughing in his and saying, 'HA, in your face, sukkah!'

"Yes, Lauren, they towed me." He is leaning even further into me. "Now, you are going to lend me your car for the meeting I have to go to downtown."

"Um, I can't lend you my car. What if my kids get sick at school and I have to leave? What if—" I start but think the better of it as I take in the murderous look on his face. "Okay, fine." I duck under his arm to reach into my purse and grab the keys. "But if anything happens to it, you'll pay for it," I warn, dangling the keys in front of him.

He snatches the keys from my hand and turns to head into his office, slamming the door behind him, causing the shades to rattle on his side of the room. I pick up my phone to send Kaleigh a text.

Oopsie. I waited too long to pay the tickets.

I wait for her reply, hoping for some words of wisdom, which is not at all what I get.

Play with the devil, you're gonna get burned.

I look at my phone in confusion, because really, what the hell does that even mean? Before I can question her, Austin's door opens and he comes back out. He has changed out of his suit, which was probably all sweaty anyway.

The suit he's wearing now is navy blue and molds to him perfectly. He swings the jacket around, putting it on in one fluid motion, then grabs his cuffs, pulling them out of the sleeves of the jacket. He's not wearing a tie, but the top two buttons of his bright white shirt are undone, giving me a slight peek at his bronzed chest. The image of my fingers playing with that third button pops into my head, and I have to blink to clear it.

Having inappropriate thoughts about my boss is the biggest no-no in my life; that and there's the fact that I hate him. Well, maybe not hate, hate is a strong word. But I do dislike him, like a lot.

"You think Kaleigh can come get you if I don't get back on time?" he asks almost like he's worried about how I'm going to get home.

I nod my head yes and then tell him, "Listen, there are a couple of things you should know about the car," I try to explain, but I'm quickly hushed by him instead.

"Seriously, I think I got it. It's a minivan. How different can it possibly be from any other vehicle?" He heads to the elevator.

"Okay, but just so you know how t—" I continue from right behind him.

"Lauren, I got it. It's not brain surgery. I'm good." Then he gets onto the elevator and the doors close.

I look to Carmen. "Oh, well, I tried to warn him that *Frozen* is stuck in the DVD player and "Let it Go" is on repeat." I give a little shrug before I turn and walk back to my desk. Oh, to be a fly in that car right now!

CHAPTER FOURTEEN

Austin

The minute I got that phone call, I knew this had to do with Lauren. Ever since she came into my life, it's been one crazy, fucked-up episode after another. There has never been a time when I've frowned more than I have lately, but I can also admit that I've laughed more than I ever have as well. She brings out not only this insane, absurd awfulness in me, but also a fun, silly, playful side I didn't even know I had.

A month ago, I would have had her fired without a second thought, but now, she quits pretty much every day, smiling each time she gives me her notice.

But her not paying my tickets was a low blow. My car—my baby—was impounded, and I have an important meeting with Denis on site at the restaurant so we can finalize a couple of things.

Now, I'm walking out of the office with the keys to her bus in my hands. Okay, so it isn't an actual bus, but it's damn close to one.

I click 'unlock' on the key fob and get in. My knees are pressed against the dash, and the steering wheel is so close it's practically cutting off the air to my fucking throat. I fumble around on the side for the buttons to change the seat's position and give me some leg room.

Once I'm situated and circulation returns to my legs, I touch the keyless starter button, and the car starts right up.

I buckle in and am on my way. Soft music plays in the background when all of a sudden, a girl's voice starts filling the car.

Soft at first, and a bit annoying, so I push the button on the touch screen to switch to the radio. After clicking it once, nothing happens, so I try it again. And again, nothing happens.

I'm too busy trying to weave my way through traffic in this huge behemoth of a vehicle, so I try to block it out. And I'm somewhat successful, that is, until the shouting starts and scares the shit out of me. Someone yelling about letting it go.

What the fuck is this? I press the button again, this time for the satellite radio, and still the fucking song about letting it go is playing. The voice gets higher and higher. The music gets louder and louder as I desperately try to turn it down.

Unable to silence this current Lauren-induced nightmare, I grab my phone, dialing her number, still trying to turn down the volume but having no luck.

She picks up after one ring.

"Yes," she answers, obviously annoyed that I'm bothering her if the tone of her voice is any indication. Well, good, I'm annoyed, too.

"Something is wrong with the car," I yell into the phone that I'm holding in my hand as I tap the screen, putting her on speaker.

"Well, whatever you did, undo it," she advises then continues, "I told you before you took it that if you break it, you pay for it."

I breathe out an aggravated sigh. "I didn't break anything. I can't get the radio to shut off." Meanwhile, the song has started—*again*—the voice breaking in with the fucking letting it go.

"Oh that, yeah, I know. I have to get it checked. It's like it's frozen," she says and immediate starts laughing at herself. "Get it? Frozen?"

I look at the phone, wondering if this is really happening, if I'm really having this conversation. "I don't get it," I huff while the lady sings about the cold never bothering her anyway. "How the fuck do I get her to shut up?" I shout over the music.

"Oh, yeah, I don't know. I tried to Google it, but nothing came up." I hear her typing like this conversation isn't even bothering her.

"You 'Googled' it," I deadpan and then repeat because surely, I heard wrong. "You Googled it?"

I can practically hear her eyes rolling. "Yes, I Googled it. What else would I do? Google knows everything."

"Lauren, I'm about to puncture my eardrums if I have to keep listening to this girl go on and on AND ON about letting it go and the fucking cold never bothering her. How do I turn this shit off?" I touch every single button on the screen.

"You aren't the only one. I just don't know what to do. I guess I have to call the dealer." Her voice is flat.

"You should call them the minute you call impound and find out how the fuck to get my car back," I snap, right before the radio yells 'let it go' again.

"Yeah, yeah. I'm on it. Is that all you called for?" She is brushing me off. Just when the piano drift starts again.

"That's all," I grumble. "Thank god, I just got to my meeting. This fucking song is the soundtrack from hell, I'm sure of it," I state before disconnecting and turning off the car. Of course, I'm shocked and dismayed that I can still hear it playing. It isn't until I open the door that the radio finally shuts off. I'm hoping—praying, really—that it resets itself. Grabbing the keys and my phone, I shut the door and don't even bother to lock it, thinking Lauren would be lucky if someone stole it.

When I open the door to the restaurant, the smell of wood and paint hits me. This is my favorite part of my job. Creating something. I may not be good with my hands, but I have the gift of vision and conceptualization, which is what I get paid for.

Denis walks up to me, wearing his regular cargo pants and construction boots. "Hey, you look much better than you did last time." He holds out his hand to shake mine. No kidding, I almost died the last time he saw me. I just nod to him and head over to the bar area where the plans are spread out.

I look up seeing the staircase coming along nicely. I notice that the glass blocks are installed exactly as I intended them to be, so that when patrons head up the stairs, they can see through them to the downstairs area. The rounded booths will be great for a group of friends who want some privacy; each booth can be seen from downstairs as well. I can't wait until the draping comes and is installed, completing the look that I was going for—like a cozy fort. A sexy high class but still cozy fort, obviously.

I look around to see the tables that will be scattered throughout the middle of the vast space are all stacked up in the corner. "You also got some high-top tables, right?" I ask as I look around for them.

"I did, yes. Those are coming in next week along with the stool version of those chairs." He motions toward the chairs stacked next to the tables. I run my hand along the bar top, a heavy mahogany wood that is smooth and shiny, sexy. It's the only rustic touch in the space; the base of the bar is a frosted glass with lights that appear to be embedded in its panes. The barstools look like they're made of thin metal rods, giving them a sleek, modern appearance. The whole back wall of the bar area is mirrored, causing the space to look bigger. The shelves, which will be made from the same frosted glass as the base of the bar, have yet to be installed.

I see Serena heading toward me. Oh, Serena, with the glossy brown hair that flows down to her waist and those long, lean, toned legs that she's flashed at me enough times in her efforts to entice me. Her eyes never wavering from mine, she saunters over to me like a huntress tracking her kill.

I smile as I take in the red suit that pours over her curves like it was made just for her. With the money she has, it probably was.

Serena is one of the backers of this venture. It's one of her 'side jobs' as she calls them. She made the bulk of her money from the style app she created.

"Austin," she sings in her Southern accent. "I didn't know when I got here that my day was about to get a million times better with a visit from you." She walks right up to me, hugging me close as she tilts her head and kisses the underside of my jaw.

I move away from her and her blood red-stained lips. "Serena, I didn't know you would be here," I say over her head and mostly to Denis.

As hot and gorgeous as Serena is, my dick knows that if I go there with her, she'd do whatever she could to sink those bright-red talons into me. Plus, she sucked off Noah and swallowed. So, yeah, I know it's crazy, but my mouth is never getting near hers. Ever. For those reasons, I haven't taken even a little sip of what she's constantly offering.

I disentangle myself from her clutches and look around. "This is going to be a huge success, I can feel it," Serena states as she continues to eye me up and down with blatant carnal interest.

"I think so, too. Denis, you said you had something to discuss with me, something in the kitchen?" I look at him pointedly, seeing a look of surprise before he finally gets it.

"Right, right." He nods. "I think the plumber said something about…" He stops talking once we get inside the kitchen and the door slides closed behind me.

"Fuck me, she's like a vulture." I try to shake her touch off of me.

"Opening night will be interesting." Denis knows she'll probably plaster herself to my side and never let go.

I shake my head, not wanting to even think about it. "What else do we need before the final touches come together?" I ask him as my phone beeps in my pocket. I take it out, looking at the screen and seeing a text from Lauren.

Car will be out of impound as soon as you head down there and fill out a form. Sorry, I can't do it, because the car is in your name.

I shake my head.

You have to drive me there. This is your fault after all.

She answers in a matter of seconds.

Great, I can't wait. Good news, I can sing along to the song!

Fuck me, that goddamn song starts up in my head again.

Forget it. I'll ask Noah.

I text Noah next, asking him to pick me up at my office in an hour. Looking at my watch, I notice that I have to get back or I'll have to drive the car to Lauren's house.

"Okay, so when are we doing the photos?" I ask Denis as we walk back out of the kitchen. I scan the area and see that Serena has either left the building or is hiding somewhere, probably ready to pounce.

"I have to talk to Jake at the PR firm, but I'm thinking the night of the opening before everyone comes in would be best." Denis replies while taking his own phone out to take some notes.

"Perfect." I say good-bye and head back out into the hot sun. My good mood is short-lived when I see what is sitting there, awaiting me, in front of the restaurant. What I begin thinking of as the vessel to hell, aka Lauren's minivan, waits to transport me back to the office on a ride filled with the song that will surely haunt my nightmares for a long time to come. Fuck my life.

CHAPTER FIFTEEN

Lauren

I'm typing up the notes for tomorrow's meeting when my keys drop on my desk with a big clank.

"Never a-fucking-gain." I look up at him with a smile on my face, which is wiped away the minute I see red lipstick on his shirt collar.

"You better not have had sex in my car," I snap at him, getting up from my chair. "You are having my whole car shampooed." I wag my finger at him and hope that he can't see how fast my heart is beating. The pit of my stomach burns at the mere thought of him having sex in my car.

He looks at me as if I have two heads, his brows furrowed in confusion. "Seriously, don't you ever have sex at night?" I ask him. "It's what normal people do."

"I don't even know what the fuck you're talking about right now." He puts his hands on his hips.

"You have skank all over your collar." I point to the lipstick.

"Oh, that." He reaches to exactly that spot before smirking at me.

"I thought you were at a meeting. Or does a booty call qualify as your meeting these days?" I ask, glaring at him. "Good times."

"You wouldn't know a good time if it hit you in the face."

I roll my eyes and scoff at him as I cross my arms over my chest. "Ok, whatever you say." I look past him to see that our fighting has drawn a bit of a crowd. Peeking around the corner is Carmen, along with Steven and Barbara, who is standing there watching us over the glasses perched on the tip of her nose. "You had sex in your office and now my car. Jesus. Can't you control yourself?" I grab my keys off my desk while I lean down to grab my purse.

"Are you always this uptight?" My body stills while he continues, "Maybe if you loosened up a little, you would still be married."

The minute the words leave his mouth, I hear a gasp from Barbara, but that isn't what gets me. What gets me is the fact that he is right. Maybe if I weren't so uptight, I would still be married. Maybe if I lived a little, Jake wouldn't have cheated. I don't know what hurts me more, the fact that I'm questioning myself or that he thinks these things of me. All I know is that my heart just hurts.

I place my purse on my desk as I gather my things. I do not make eye contact with him or acknowledge him in any way.

My coffee cup, my Post-it notes, the picture of my kids that I put next to the computer all get tossed into my purse, overfilling it.

I grab my keys off the desk and walk away from him, never once looking at him. Not once giving him the satisfaction of knowing that he hit his mark and hurt me. All the pranks in the world couldn't have come close to hurting me as much as the words he just spoke did.

"Lauren," he says softly, right when I'm about to turn the corner. "I didn't—"

I turn around, the hurt now mixed with anger. "You didn't what, Austin? You didn't mean to insinuate that I'm uptight and that's the reason my husband had an affair and left me? Well, good job, Austin, you guessed it in one," I hiss at him, trying to keep my voice from cracking.

"Lauren, I didn't mean—" He walks up to me and reaches out with one hand to touch me.

"No, no, it's fine. And you're right, that's what happened." I side-step him and use my hands to block him from touching me. I hear the elevator ping and turn to hurry around the corner to slip inside the open door right before it slides shut.

The last thing I see before the elevator door closes is Austin turning the corner quickly, racing up to the door. He's too late, though; it closes in his face, right before I hear what I assume is his hand slapping the closed door.

I press the button for the lobby repeatedly, ridiculously hoping it will make the elevator go faster than it is. I know it won't work, I know this, everyone knows this, but I keep pressing the button anyway.

The door opens to the lobby, and I'm thankful that it is empty. I run toward my car and don't look back. Austin parked it exactly where I left it this morning. Thank god for small favors.

Opening the door, I throw everything inside as I rush to get in the car, get going, and get the hell out of there before I can allow the first tear to fall. Because it will. It's just a matter of time.

My eyes fill with tears, blurring my vision. Starting the car and making my way out of the parking lot, I pull up Penelope's number on my phone.

If I'm on Bluetooth and on my phone, thankfully that overrides the music.

"Hey," she answers cheerily.

"Hey." I angrily wipe away the tear that has made its way over my lashes and onto my cheek. "I'm not going back. I'm sorry. I really tried to tough it out. I hate to put you in this position, but I…I just can't go back," I finish as my voice cracks.

"Hey, now," she whispers, her voice softening. "I don't give a fuck about the job. Are you okay?" I shake my head no while more tears fall freely.

"I'm going to hang up now. I'll grab a couple of bottles of wine and head to your place. Is this a case for Alanis Morissette?" she asks, because everyone knows Alanis Morissette is the wronged, hurt woman's anthem, no matter how old they are.

"I already have the CD in my player at home," I sniffle.

The phone beeps and I see it's Austin calling me on the other line. I quickly decline his ass.

"Okay, I'm going to go call Barbara and let her know that you aren't coming back," she assures me. "See you in an hour."

"I think she probably knows. There was a scene." I'm not sure how much of a scene it actually was, but to me, it felt like all of my co-workers were there to witness my humiliation.

"Oh, fuck. No worries, hon, I'll take care of it." And she clicks off just in time for the fucking "Let it Go" chorus to ring, loud and clear, through my car.

I make it home in record time, climbing out and thanking the powers that be that the kids are staying with Jake tonight. Every second week, he gets a mid-week sleepover, and tonight is that night.

I open the door, letting myself in, dumping everything down by the door. I walk straight to the kitchen, open the fridge, and grab the open bottle of wine from the door.

Ripping the cork out of the bottle and not bothering with a glass, I bring the bottle to my lips, gulping down enough wine to begin the process of soothing my jagged little edges. Somewhat.

I'm about to go for a second big swig when the back door opens and Kaleigh walks in. She looks at me and drops her yoga mat.

"What happened?" She rushes over to me.

I take that swig before answering her. "I'm uptight, apparently." I allow those hurt feelings along with the tears I've tried to keep at bay to consume me. "According to Austin, it's why my husband left me," I whimper before bringing the bottle back to my lips and finishing it off in one long pull.

"What are you talking about? Explain, please." She goes to the wine fridge in the living room and comes back with another bottle. She looks for the corkscrew, slamming drawers in an effort to find it quickly.

I pull off the jacket that I was wearing today and climb up onto a stool, while she pours two glasses of wine. Handing one to me, she offers a toast. "To assholes, and to the women who think they're fucking the prize."

I nod in agreement and finish the glass off. I don't think I even stop to breathe.

My phone rings from over by the front door. I don't even move to get it, but Kaleigh does. "It's Austin. I'm assuming this"—she points to the bottles of wine—"has to do with him?"

I don't answer verbally; instead, I just offer her a jerky nod yes. She presses decline, and I see her fingers move over the screen. "Don't bother," I tell her. "I already quit."

Her eyes snap up. "What did he do?"

"Well, he borrowed my car, possibly had sex in it, and when I called him out on it, he called me uptight. Me. ME, MEEE!" I shriek while pulling the bottle of wine closer to me. "We need to play Alanis." I start pouring myself another glass.

"Fuck, I'm going to hide the sharp knives," she murmurs as she heads into the living room and plugs in my phone. Her fingers move across the screen, and in no time, Alanis's angry, raspy, knowing voice is serenading us in commiseration.

"After he said I'm uptight, which I totally am not. Remember that time I gave Jake car head in the driveway?" I ask her.

"Yes, I was very proud of you." She comes around the counter to sit on another stool and listen to the rest of my story.

"Well, after that, he said that maybe if I loosened up a little, I'd still be married." I look at her, letting the pain I feel at that moment show. "I'll admit, maybe he's onto something, but it's not the whole reason. It's because that skanky whore waved her non-saggy tits in my husband's face, and he made the decision to sample what she was offering." I look up at her with tear-filled eyes. "Right, Kay? I mean, you don't think Austin is right, do you?"

"Abso-fucking-lutely not," she says vehemently. "There is no fucking excuse whatso-fucking-ever for a married man to cheat on his wife. None. Not even if Gisele Fucking Bündchen comes in and sits on his dick while wearing goddamn angel wings."

"I'm totally in agreement," I mumble to myself as I get up and try to walk away, but my spinning head stops me before I can even take a step. I reach out to steady my woozy self with a hand on the counter. "We need pizza," I tell Kaleigh as I let go of the counter, mentally crossing my fingers that I don't fall.

Once the spinning stops, I make my way up the stairs, taking my tight skirt off when I reach my bedroom, and face-planting on my bed. "He's such an asshole. Right, Kay?" My voice comes out a bit muffled seeing as I'm facedown on the bed.

"I took my Post-it notes. Haha, take that." I turn my head to the side, away from her. "I think I really liked him," I admit quietly, while Kaleigh gets on the bed next to me. "I should have known better, right? No happy for me." My eyes get heavier and heavier as I continue blinking. "I need a little nap," I whisper right before I drift off to sleep.

CHAPTER SIXTEEN

Austin

"Maybe if you loosened up a little, you would still be married."

As soon as the words left my mouth, I wished I could call them back. I didn't even have to see her face to know I hurt her. Her body went rigid, and for a moment, I thought she was going to let me have it. Hell, I wish now that she had, because what she gave me instead of the dressing down I deserved was a million times worse. Despite her best efforts to mask it, I don't think I will ever forget the wounded look on her face. I immediately wanted to pull her into my arms.

I wanted to tell her that I really was an asshat. But instead, I just stood there, watching her pack up all her things, even the fucking Post-its.

When I realized what she was doing, I tried to reach out to her, but she just dodged me and blocked my hands like she was protecting herself—from me—before she turned and practically ran away. And I fucking let her.

As if that were not bad enough, of course, Carmen, Steven, and—even worse—Barbara were all watching and heard the whole thing. Carmen and Steven refused to look at me and quickly dispersed, while Barbara just stood there shaking her head at me in disappointment. "That is going to cost you more than you realize, Austin." Leaving me with that bit of wisdom, she walked around me and went back to her office.

"Fuck, don't I know it," I mutter under my breath as I head into my office, pick up my phone, and try calling Lauren.

No surprise, she must have declined the call, because it goes right to voice mail after two rings. "Motherfucker."

I try calling her again right away, and as expected, it goes straight to voice mail. "Lauren, please call me back. I want to apologize. I was way out of line," I say before I finish with a plea. "Please, Lauren, just call me back."

I end the call and decide to text her.

Call me, please!

I sit at my desk, watching the phone for the gray bubble with those three blinking dots, but they don't appear. Nothing at all happens. The message isn't even marked as read. I don't know how long I stare at my phone willing her to call back or reply, but the next thing I know, Noah comes waltzing in. "Whoa, dude, who killed your dog?" He throws himself into the chair in front of my desk.

"I fucked up," I confess, looking back down at my phone.

"Nothing new there. What happened now?"

"I may have told Lauren that if she weren't so uptight and she loosened up a little, that maybe her husband wouldn't have left her and she would still be married." I don't even finish getting the words out before he's pulling out his phone. "What the fuck are you doing?"

"I'm making sure I clear my schedule for your funeral," he says, earning himself a glare from me.

"Fuck off, asshole." It's the only thing I can say right now. "Let's go get my car, and then I'll pass by her house. She has no choice but to answer the door, right?" I ask him as we walk out to the elevator.

I see Barbara come out of her office and head straight for me. Her mouth is pressed together in a tight line. I cut off whatever she's going to say by holding up my hand and stating, "Not now, Barbara." I press the elevator button.

"I think my balls just crawled back into my body, and that look wasn't even directed at me," Noah murmurs from beside me as we watch Barbara turn and storm away. "If I were you, I wouldn't drink or eat anything that anyone else, especially someone who is a female or an employee here, offers you," he advises as he follows me into the elevator.

We make it down to the impound lot, where I fill out all the forms and show all my documents in order to get my car out. It takes about forty-five minutes, and the whole time we're there, I've got my phone in my hand. I've tried to call Lauren about fifteen times now, and each time, the call goes straight to voice mail.

Once I get my car out, I make my way over to Lauren's, parking my car at the curb. I take a deep breath, but my door is whipped open. I look up and see Noah.

"As your friend, I'm going to try to talk you out of this." I shake my head, ignoring him. I get out of the car and walk to her door. "This is a really, really bad idea. Women who are pissed can do evil things. I mean, she wasn't even that pissed at you when she almost made your balls explode."

"I have to see her," I say and then knock on the door. When I hear the locks click open, my heart literally skips a beat and a smile starts to creep across my face. It's quickly replaced with a frown when I see that it's Kaleigh who opens the door—with what appears to be a machete in her hand. Okay, so maybe not a real machete, but it sure as hell is a knife that looks like it can easily debone a chicken and probably take off a man's—hopefully not this man's—hand. She comes outside, closing the door behind her as the sound of Alanis Morissette is playing in the background.

"You have some nerve showing your face here," she spits out at me.

"Is Lauren home?" I sound like a dork. Obviously, she's there, her car is here.

"She is," she confirms as she sways a little. I look a little closer and can tell that she is totally blitzed.

"Whoa, there, little lady." Noah wraps an arm around her shoulders to avoid the knife to the dick.

"I need to talk to her," I say.

"Not going to happen. Not now, not ever." she continues, "You fucked up bad." She is now pointing the knife at me, and her voice is rising. "Really, really bad."

"Babe, can we put the knife down?" Noah pleads with a smile, and she smiles at him while bashfully giggling.

"Can I please just talk to Lauren for two minutes? Then I'll leave, I promise," I practically beg.

"Nope," she replies and then turns around, grabbing the door handle and talking to us over her shoulder. "If you're not gone in two minutes, I'm calling the cops and telling them you're stalking me." I scoff at that, and she glares at me. "And show them the inappropriate dick pics you sent me."

I turn to look at Noah, who says, "I may have showed them to her and she might have forwarded a couple of them to herself."

"Can you please tell her that I was here and ask her to call me? Please, Kaleigh?" I beg as she slams the door in my face and flips the locks with loud clicking sounds.

I hang my head, while Noah pats me on the back. "She'll call." He assures me. "Or send someone to kill you. I mean, she did say Donkey Kong."

I shrug his hand off me and walk back to my car, wishing I could just start this day over or at least go back to the moment when I walked back into the office after my meeting.

Noah gets in his car and goes home, while I head to my condo. I go straight into my bedroom and throw myself onto my bed. I scrub a hand down my face as my mind runs back over my day. Fuck! This is a such mess.

I get up, tossing my jacket onto the chair in the corner and pulling my shirt out and unbuttoning it. I shrug it off and see the red lipstick on the collar. The same damn lipstick that started this whole fucking nightmare. I wad up the shirt and throw it straight into the fucking trash.

The next day, I get to work earlier than normal. I wait anxiously for eight o'clock to roll around, so I can see her the minute she comes in.

When it hits eight-ten, my hands start to get sweaty, and my shirt starts feeling a bit tight around my neck, so I undo the collar. An email ping comes from my computer, and I turn to look at it when I see Carmen sit down at Lauren's desk.

I get up and go over to ask her, "What are you doing?"

She smiles at me. "I'm your new PA. Isn't this exciting?"

I don't say a word to her. Instead, I march right over to Barbara's office. The door is open, so I just walk in. "What the fuck is Carmen doing?"

"She's your new PA. Not only did Lauren quit, but Penelope also cancelled her contract with us, leaving me without a reputable temp agency to rely on, so I did the only thing I could do under the circumstances." She takes off her glasses and leans back in her chair, steepling her hands together in front of her as she taps her pointer fingers on her lips. She looks at me with disappointment radiating off of her. "You fucked up so bad here, Austin. I'm not even sure if you actually realize the depth of what you've lost."

"I know. I know I did. I called her to apologize, but she didn't take any of my calls. I even went by her house, but her sister wouldn't let me see her," I tell her, hoping it will soften the blow I know she's about to deliver to me.

She sits up straight in her chair, looks me dead in the eyes, and starts to speak to me in that soft but angry, firm, and concise tone she used on me when I seriously messed up as a kid. "You told that beautiful, vivacious young woman that she is undesirable and that's why her husband left her. And you have the audacity to think that because you say sorry she is going to forgive you? I must have dropped you on your head when you were younger." She shakes her head.

"Austin, you have to know that she had feelings for you, just as you have them for her. It sure as hell was obvious to all of us who were thoroughly enjoying that dance the two of you were doing. Hell, we were getting ready to start a pool for when you two would finally get it together and *get* together. What you're not getting is that it was going to take a lot of bravery and trust and faith on her part to take that step. The last man she had feelings for wounded her, Austin. And the next man she thought she might possibly open up to just wounded her, too. Men wonder why women turn into raging bitches? Think about what SHE has been through at the hands of men she's cared about, and there's your answer." She waits a beat for that to sink in before continuing.

"You needed an assistant, I did the best I could. Carmen was available, and even after that display yesterday, was still willing. You need to understand that Lauren will never come back here, Austin, and it is highly unlikely that she will ever give you the time of day to deliver that apology," she finishes as if she didn't just gut me with that speech. Fuck, what have I done?

I'm so mad at myself, I can't help the glare I aim at her as I ask,

"Aren't you the one who says never say never?"

"I also taught you how to be sensitive and kind-hearted. What happened there?" She raises an eyebrow at me.

I turn and practically storm out of her office, coming face-to-face with John. "Hey there, buddy. You're looking a bit uptight today," he remarks as he puts his hands in his pockets.

"Fuck you." I walk away from him, hoping he doesn't follow me, but hearing his breathing beside me, I know that I'm not that lucky.

"Did you really call her out in front of everyone?" I look over at him when he finishes asking the question.

"I didn't do it in front of anybody. They were just there," I say as I walk back into my office. "Close the door."

"Oh, now you want privacy?" he asks, chuckling. "All kidding aside, I heard that it was brutal. You're lucky no one caught that on video. That shit can go viral, and the next thing you know, you're all over the Internet as the World's Worst Boss."

I tolerate him until he walks out and then start my day. My emails come in all fucked up. Nothing is entered in my calendar. My meetings aren't even entered. I have no idea where I'm going. I pick up my phone and call Carmen.

"Hiyeah," she greets. And, really, is that even a word?

"Have you sent me the emails that came in today? Did put all the meetings that I have next week in my calendar?" I look at my computer screen.

"No, I assumed you would do it," she replies.

"No, I don't do it. You do it," I bark and then hang up. It just gets worse from there. The notes she enters make no sense. She is confusing projects and entering things in the wrong places. She can't even get my coffee order right.

For the next two days, I text Lauren, begging her to call me. I've even driven by her house a couple of times to try and catch her or the kids outside, but so far nothing.

Finally, it's Friday night. I shut down my computer and text Barbara.

Go see Lauren. Double her salary. I promise, I won't even talk to her. We can do everything by email. Do whatever it takes, but just get her back.

Her reply comes right away. It's a picture of Lauren sitting on her couch, laughing. There's not a stitch of makeup on her face. She's wearing a pair of black yoga pants and a tight tank top, and she's holding a glass of wine. Her hair is piled on top of her head. I've only ever seen her dressed professionally, and she always looked hot, but she looks comfortable and effortlessly pretty now. That isn't what really gets my attention, though. No, it's Barbara, who is sitting right there next to Lauren, a glass of wine in her hand, and they are both laughing.

I reply with one word.

Traitor.

I send Noah a text.

Tomorrow night. You, me, drinks, women, good times.

He answers right away.

It's on like Donkey Kong.

Fuck me. She's left her mark all over my life and on everyone in it.

CHAPTER SEVENTEEN

Lauren

It's been four days since I've spoken to Austin. Four very long, very boring days. I called Penelope and begged her to find me something, anything. So far, she has nothing.

I've rearranged furniture and reorganized closets and cabinets. I've done a big deep cleaning of all the bathrooms. I've gone through the kids' toys, closets, and drawers. I've stripped the beds and washed all the bedding. I forced myself to stop when I found myself eyeing the windows.

Tonight, the kids left to go to Jake's until Monday night. Leaving Kaleigh and me to entertain ourselves. I had great plans to Netflix and chill, but she came in with Barbara, of all people, following right behind her after the kids left. Barbara came bearing gifts, and by gifts I mean wine, so I wasn't about to tell her to leave. That would be rude, plus, I like Barbara and I missed her.

We laughed over wine about everything and nothing at all. Neither of us bringing up Austin, which made me happy and sad all at the same time.

It was when she was getting up to leave that Kaleigh left us alone to talk.

"You have to know that we all miss you," she says, emphasizing the 'all' as she reaches for the empty pizza box in the center of the table.

I shake my head a bit sadly, hoping I don't start tearing up again.

"We do. He does especially." The way she refers to him makes my heart beat just a tad faster. Makes it hurt, too.

"He humiliated me," I tell her, taking the box out of her hands so she can see me. "And he didn't even know it. My husband had an affair with our son's teacher." I drop the box back on the table.

"He would never—" she starts, but I hold up my hand.

"I know he wouldn't, and I understand that he didn't know, but what he said hit close to home. Very, very close to home."

"He's miserable. I replaced you with Carmen." She laughs a bit evilly. "She barely knows how to email at all, so forget it if there's an attachment. And let's just say that she and Excel are a big, fat no-go."

"Good. He deserves it. Asshat," I grumble as I sit down. "I know you have your loyalties, I understand that." I grab a Kleenex from the side table and dab at my eyes. "I will never, ever put you in the middle. I like you, and I'd like to continue our friendship."

"Please come back," she pleads. "I'm begging. I'll give you whatever you want, just name it."

"I don't know," I say, but I'm thinking about it. Who am I kidding, I'm so, so, so, close to saying yes.

"Just think about it. Go out tomorrow night with your sister. Get dressed up. Drink, flirt with hot guys, have fun. Then call me on Sunday, and we'll talk," she says as I walk her to the door. "Flirt a little for me, too." She winks at me, gives me a quick squeeze, and walks out the door.

"So, are you going to go back?" Kaleigh asks from the stairs where she is sitting.

"I don't know."

"I think you should. Don't let him chase you away from a job you genuinely liked." She gets up and makes her way down the rest of the stairs. "Now, let's discuss outfits. Are we doing slutty maids or slutty school girls?"

I look at her like the crazy person she is and ask, "Why do we have to do slutty anything?"

"Because sluts have more fun." She shrugs. "Or so I've been told."

I stare at her and wonder, not for the first time, how the hell I'm related to this woman.

The next day, we spend the afternoon lounging in the backyard. At three, I go up to my room to take a nap, because let's be honest here, I'm a single mom of two who thinks that eleven p.m. is a late night.

My nap lasts a solid two hours, and when I wake up, I'm almost tempted to cancel this debacle that Kaleigh is planning. I'm about to tell her that we should just stay home when the door flies open and she comes through it, telling me, "Don't even fucking think about it. Get your dusty vagina in that shower. You will exfoliate and shave— *everywhere.*"

"Jesus, Kal, it's not dusty." I storm into my bathroom and slam the door. I lean back against it, thinking to myself that she might be right. It's probably a little bit dusty.

I walk over to the sink and look at myself in the mirror. I'm hot, I'm young, and I'm single. Tonight, I'm going to go out, drink some cocktails, flirt with men, and maybe, just maybe, have sex. Hot, no-name sex. Okay, well, maybe not sex, sex. Maybe just some kissing and I'll give him my number. And if he's really hot, maybe my real number. Definitely not my real name, because you know, he could be a stalker. Oh, for Christ's sakes, I'll most likely just have some drinks and come home drunk.

I wash and dry my hair, setting it in big curlers so it will be wavy. I do my makeup darker than usual, with a smoky eye in dark brown and gold tones.

I walk out of the bathroom and stare at the outfit I picked out this morning. A tight peach high-waisted dress that goes to mid-thigh. In case that isn't short enough, there is a V-notch in the center that shows off my inner thighs spectacularly, especially when I walk. I've paired it with a black strapless bustier. It's tight, too, holding the girls in place and making them appear firmer than they really are. I put on a chunky black necklace. The whole outfit is put together with black strappy heels. My feet will be screaming in about an hour, but the shoes are sexy as fuck. Well, at least that is what Kaleigh says.

I grab my Michael Kors black wristlet and put the essentials in it. "Are you ready?" I yell down the hall.

Kaleigh walks out of her room, and I'm left speechless. Her outfit consists of a pair of white lace looser-fitting short shorts with a small, shiny black belt. Her top is a black tube top. I know for a fact that she isn't wearing a bra, mainly because her breasts don't need it. She finishes this look with a seriously sexy pair of black open-toe, lace-up stiletto boots. "Let's go get us some dick!" She raises her hands in the air, and I can't help but laugh.

Before I can answer her, I hear a honk outside. "CAB'S HERE!" she yells in her best Jersey shore accent.

I shake my head and say a prayer to whomever is listening at this point that I come home tonight, safe and sound, and with both shoes.

Two hours later, I'm finally sitting down after dancing my ass off. When we got to the club, Kaleigh, of course, knew the bouncer, so we walked right in and were given a booth. The booths sit in a section that is a bit higher than the dance floor. You can get to this area by using the set of six stairs leading up here around the dance floor.

Bottle service is a whole different ball game. The club that we're at is called Light Night, which is weird, because it's almost pitch black with soft light moving around the room.

I'm finally drinking my vodka and cranberry when the Drake song "One Dance" comes on.

I stand up, throwing my hair back, putting my hands in the air as I yell how much I love this song. I grab Kaleigh, and we run back out onto the packed dance floor.

I sway my hips to the beat of the song, singing out loud with Drake.

I feel a pair of hands land on my hips, and I slowly turn around to smile at the guy who put his hands on me. He's cute. Tall with shaggy hair. He smiles at me and pulls me to him. I go with it and live in the moment. Singing the song and moving my hips, I'm having fun taking in the scene all around me.

As I scan the room, my eyes land on a familiar pair of green eyes that I haven't seen in almost a week. I don't have time to think, let alone escape, before I see him making a beeline right to me. My hands fall from my dance partner when I feel his heat against my back.

"Get lost," he demands, using a tone of voice that unmistakably conveys the message not to test him on this.

I whirl around to face him, pissed off that he thinks he can come here, interrupt my dance, and try to ruin my night. I'm about to tell him to go fuck off when he grabs my hand and drags me across the dance floor and out the side door into the cool night.

I try to yank my hand out of his once we get outside, but I'm suddenly pushed up against the wall. I'm about to say something when I see the look he is giving me and snap my mouth shut.

"Don't push me, Lauren, not now," he warns me, and I look at him.

He is dressed in low-slung, tight blue jeans that mold to him. A baby blue button-down, tight-fit, tailored shirt has two buttons open at his neck. His sleeves are rolled halfway up to his elbows, and his silver Rolex is on his wrist.

"Don't push you?" I question, pushing off the wall and squaring my shoulders. "Don't push you? You have some nerve, Austin." The alcohol is giving me a little bit more courage. "You called me uptight, and I was in there enjoying my night when you charged over there like…like…I don't even know what the hell that was all about, except for the fact that I wasn't the uptight one in that scenario. Hmm, who needs to loosen up now, Austin?" I taunt.

"You drive me nuts! I can't sleep! I can't think! I can't even fucking get anything done at work without thinking about you!" He roughly runs his hand through his hair, his shirt tightening across his chest with the movement.

"So, I come out tonight. I'm going to kick back, have a few drinks, and not think about you. But of all the places, you're here, looking like this." He gestures to my outfit, his eyes running up my body from my shoes to my face.

"What's wrong with how I look? I look good!" I cross my arms under my breasts and cock my hip to the side.

"No, Lauren. No, you don't look good. You look fucking amazing. As usual. I tried to ignore you. I turned my back. I wasn't going to pay you any attention at all. But when I turn around, there you are on the dance floor, swinging your ass with that douche all over you," he grates out angrily.

"So? I'm here to have fun, too, Austin. And I was! Until you marched over there like some crazy man and dragged me out here. What the hell was that, huh?" My voice rises as my anger ratchets up a few notches.

He steps further into my space, and I'm now sandwiched between the wall and Austin. He tips his face down so we are nose-to-nose. I can't see the rest of his expression, but his eyes are blazing.

"I didn't like it, Lauren," he rumbles in a quietly angry voice.

"Why, Austin? Why did it bother you?" I whisper, completely

114

mesmerized by that look in his eyes. I should have paid attention, though, because instead of answering me, his lips come crashing down on mine.

CHAPTER EIGHTEEN

Austin

I spend the whole day Saturday running a 5K through the park and rearranging my emails in alphabetical order. Fucking Carmen.

Noah picks me up at seven, when we hit up a pub and watch the Yankees kill it again. At the end of the ninth inning, he suggests going to Light Night Club.

Shaking the doorman's hand, I make my way over to the corner bar. We have spent many nights closing this place down. This is one of the first clubs to hold our names. I look around, taking in the beauty of it.

The minute I scan the booths, I see her. The woman who has been a thorn in my side. Tonight, she looks like she just walked off the red carpet. Her hands rise to the sky, taking her skirt up to dangerous levels.

I stand up straight, draining the bourbon in my glass in one gulp. I make eye contact with the bartender and raise my glass to get another shot.

He pours my shot and passes it to me, and I shoot it down in one gulp, signaling for another. When I look back over to the dance floor, I see some douche with his hands all over Lauren, while she shakes her ass.

She turns around to put her back to his front, and her eyes scan the area around her. The minute they land on me, it's like I've been lit up from the inside.

I take the last shot and make my way over to her. I know exactly when she feels me, because her body goes stiff.

I look at the idiot she's dancing with and motion with my head for him to move on.

"Get lost." My voice is tight, my mouth doesn't even move, since I'm talking through my clenched teeth.

The douche doesn't even try to fight for her. He just puts his hands up in defeat and walks away.

She turns around, all pissed off, but before she can say a word, I grab her hand and drag her across the dance floor, through the throngs of sweaty bodies dancing, and out the side door into the cool night.

I don't stop till I'm in the middle of the alley. She tries to yank her hand out of mine, but I push her against the side of the wall.

"Don't push me, Lauren, not now," I warn her.

She looks me up and down before she squares her shoulders and opens her mouth to let me have it. "Don't push you? Don't push you? You have some nerve, Austin. You called me uptight, and I was in there enjoying my night when you charged over there like...like...I don't even know what the hell that was all about, except for the fact that I wasn't the uptight one in that scenario. Hmm, who needs to loosen up now, Austin?" She finishes her rant with her hands on her hips and her breasts heaving with her anger.

"You drive me nuts! I can't sleep! I can't think! I can't even fucking get anything done at work without thinking about you!" I snarl at her as I rake my fingers through my hair, half tempted to pull it out of my head. That's how crazy she makes me.

"So, I come out tonight. I'm going to kick back, have a few drinks and not think about you. But of all the places, you're here, looking like this." I don't even attempt to hide the fact that I let my eyes run up the length of her body.

"What's wrong with how I look? I look good!" she huffs in outrage as she crosses her arms under those luscious tits and throws her hip out to the side.

"No, Lauren. No, you don't look good. You look fucking amazing. As usual. I tried to ignore you. I turned my back. I wasn't going to pay you any attention at all. But when I turn around, there you are on the dance floor, swinging your ass with that douche all over you," I grit out as I lean even further into her space.

"So? I'm here to have fun, too, Austin. And I was! Until you marched over there like some crazy man and dragged me out here. What the hell was that, huh?" Her voice rises as her anger climbs. Well, so what? I'm getting angrier, too.

I step even further into her space, backing her right up against the wall. My chest is heaving against hers, and she tips her angry face up to mine so we are nose-to-nose. "I didn't like it, Lauren," I hiss out.

That seems to take the wind out of her sails a bit. "Why, Austin? Why did it bother you?" she whispers.

I'm still feeling anger, but now it's mixed with lust and confusion. I don't know why I didn't like it. So instead of answering her, I do the only thing I can in the moment.

My mouth crashes down on hers, and I run my tongue along her plump lips. She whimpers, and I use that opening to slip my tongue into her mouth, sliding it against hers. She kisses me right back, meeting my ferocity with a hunger of her own. The taste of her invades my mouth. A small moan escapes her, and the lust I'm feeling kicks up. I move my hand up and into her hair, where I pull it, tilting her head back to look into her eyes.

She watches me with a stunned but way-turned-on expression. Her breathing is erratic, her lips are swollen from kissing me, and her eyes are hooded with desire. I don't move. She does. She pushes up onto her toes and fastens her lips to mine, nipping on my bottom lip and then soothing the sting away with her tongue before slipping it into my mouth. She twirls it in a circle, dancing with mine in the hottest kiss I've ever had.

Her hands slide from my chest around to my back and down to my ass, where she presses me into her.

I let go of her mouth, trailing my lips across her cheek to her chin and down her neck, licking, nipping, and sucking as I go. She is panting, and the hand on my ass squeezes it, while the other one claws at my back.

I go back to her mouth to get another taste of her. She's the drug and I'm the addict. I've never wanted someone so much in my life.

Not just her body, though her body is meant to be worshipped, but her head, her heart. I want it all.

My tongue moves with hers, deeper into her mouth. She wraps her arms around my shoulders and gives a little hop, telling me what she wants. I lift her legs and wrap them around my waist, lining her pussy right up to my cock. I groan from the sheer pleasure of feeling her against me.

I was trying to hold myself back, not sure how fast or far she wants to go, but that last move pushes me to the brink of my control.

I let go of her lips, and she whimpers and attempts to chase my mouth with hers in an effort to get them back together.

I look to the right and left and see that there is a gate locked on the side so no one can come in that way. The dumpster a couple of feet from us shields us on the other side.

"I can only be a gentleman for so long, baby," I whisper roughly in her ear and then roll the lobe between my lips. Her head falls back, hitting the wall.

Her legs are locked around my hips, and I pin her in place against them with my body as I grab her hands, moving them above her head and holding them there with one hand wrapped around her wrists. "I've dreamt about this moment since I watched you get out of your car." I grind my cock into her. She replies with a moan that echoes through the alley.

She tries to push off the wall, but my body holds her in place. "Hold on tight, baby. Lock your legs around me." I order as I feel her ankles shift against the small of my back, securing her to me. I run the hand that was holding her at her ass over her hip and up her side.

My hand is open on her side, and I use my thumb to lightly stroke the swell of her full breast as I tell her, "I used to sit at my desk, watching you bend over yours, hoping to get a look at this." I glide my hand between us to cup her tit and give it a light squeeze as my thumb moves over her hardened nipple. Her lips part as her head drops back against the wall and her eyes drift closed.

"Don't close your eyes now, Lauren," I whisper as I push her top and the cup of her bra to the side. I look down to see creamy flesh and her hard, pink nipple springing free. I don't even wait or take a breath before I lean down and run my tongue over it. I suck the whole thing into my mouth and then give it a light bite before I roll my tongue around it and go back to sucking. "Fuck me," she hisses.

I look up at her, while she looks down at me. "Don't mind if I do," I reply, planning to do just that.

CHAPTER NINETEEN

Lauren

The minute his lips touched mine, my knees buckled. Totally turned to Jell-O. I've never experienced anything like that in my life.

You always hear about that kind of kiss, the one that will totally rock your world. You wait for it to happen, hoping with each kiss that it will be the one, that it's *that kiss*.

Well, if the fluttering stomach, sweaty palms, and panting are anything to go by, it appears that I just had the best kiss of my life. Right here in the middle of an alley with the Asshat I hate. Okay, maybe I don't hate him, but I thought I did. So, while my brain may not have liked him, I can admit that my heart and vagina lusted after him.

Not only am I now dry humping him, I'm pretty sure I'm going to fuck his brains out. Or he is going to fuck my brains out. Doesn't matter, because either way, I'm getting laid.

As soon as my legs let go of his hips, I pull my bustier back into place and smooth my skirt down. He grabs my hand and pulls me back inside the club. We don't stop; we just head straight to the front door and back outside, where he flags down a cab.

"My place or yours?" he asks as I look up at him.

"Mine." I wasn't going to do this in a place I wasn't comfortable.

"Oh, shit. Kaleigh?" I look back to the club door that is still letting in the people who are waiting in line.

"She's with Noah. She's good." He pushes me gently into the back of the cab. My knees are still weak and not totally functional, so of course, my heel gets stuck in the pavement and I dive into the cab, sprawling across the seat on my stomach. I lie there giggling at the display of my sexiness. I sit up and move my legs so Austin can get in.

He gets in, closes the door, and gives the driver my address. "Come here." He pulls me into his lap to straddle him, my knees coming to rest on the seat by his hips.

His hands go straight to my ass, squeezing it, before they roam up my back to the base of my neck, where one makes its way into my hair, the other locked around the small of my back holding me in place.

He closes his fist around my hair, giving it a little tug as he thrusts his cock up against my center.

My head drops back as a groan leaves me.

"No sex in the cab," the driver admonishes from the front.

"No worries," Austin assures him.

His fisted hand in my hair guides my mouth to his, where I open for him immediately as his tongue darts in and out of my mouth. Our kiss is frantic, leaving us both breathless.

He pulls my hair, my head rolling back and to the side as his mouth starts working my neck. "I can't wait to be inside you," he whispers. "Can't wait to fuck you." His words shoot straight through me, and my clit throbs in response. "If I slid your panties to the side, would your pussy be wet for me, Lauren?"

I look at him innocently, a small smirk playing on my lips. "Why don't you find out for yourself?" I will hold nothing back with this. I've held back for too long. His hand releases my hair, skating down my neck, then my arm, until they finally land on my hips. He stops for a second, and I grind down on him. "Don't stop." I lean forward and nip at his neck and then suck on it.

"Oh, I'm not stopping, baby, not at all," he promises right before his hands rub down my thighs and then back up. Once, twice, making me shiver with anticipation each time. On the third pass, he brings the front of my skirt up with his hands.

The tips of his thumbs rest against the soaked black lace of the panties I'm wearing under my skirt. "Next time, don't wear panties. I'll finger fuck you in the restaurant. Got it?" I can barely focus on what he's saying, my body is so keyed up waiting for him to touch me.

Using his left thumb, he hooks the lace to the side, grazing through my wetness as he drags the material over.

"Next time? Next time, I'll suck your dick in the car before we even get to the restaurant," I whisper in his ear before I rise up on my knees a bit, giving him space to enter me. He groans out his reply just as the car breaks suddenly.

"Okay, Romeo and Juliet, it's twenty-eight fifty. Is that cash or credit?"

I get off his hips, while he grabs his wallet from his back pocket and swipes his card. "Keep the receipt." He grabs my hand and exits the cab. He waits for me to get out before slamming the door closed.

"Let's go, Mr. Mackenzie. I have plans for you," I tease him as I walk ahead of him, adding a bit more swing to my strut. "You made some promises back there. You're planning on keeping them, right?" I ask coyly.

"Oh, I'll be fucking keeping those promises, alright. Tonight, tomorrow morning, tomorrow afternoon, and then again tomorrow night. The question is, do you think you can handle me?" He comes at me, picking me up, my legs wrapping around his waist, my hands around his neck as I lean down and kiss him hard. I lightly lick across his lower lip before I drag it back across and push it inside his mouth. Our tongues tangle as my back hits the door. My stomach flip-flops, and my heart jack-hammers in my chest. "Open the door, Lauren. Now," he roughly demands, and my core quivers in response to the tone of his voice.

"I don't have my purse," I tell him but snap my fingers. "Wait! I have a spare!" I tell him as I rush over to the potted plant on my front porch, pushing it over and bending to pick up the key. Okay, fine, I may wiggle my hips a bit in the hopes that he is watching. And from the groan that comes out of him, it seems he is.

I head back to the door and feel his chest at my back as I push the key into the lock. His arm snakes around my waist and he slides his hand down from my belly to cup my pussy. "Not so fast," he says right at my ear. I whimper as I wait to see what he'll do next. "I didn't check if you're wet yet."

My head falls back on his chest, and the hand not holding the key still in the lock latches on to the forearm banded around my waist. I tilt my face up so he can kiss me. He presses his lips to mine and against them, he whispers, "I'm going to finger fuck you right here, and you're going to come for me, and come hard, right now, Lauren." I moan my agreement, to which he replies, "But you can't make a noise. Can you be quiet, Lauren?" I shake my head no.

"Fuck, no. I've been quiet for ten years, Austin. This time, I'm yelling. Shouting. Groaning." I widen my stance to give him more access. "Touch me, Austin. Please," I beg.

It's his turn to groan as the hand that was cupping me moves quickly to join the other in hiking my skirt up to my hips. The cool night air skates across my now exposed skin, but with him pressing what feels like a very sizeable erection into my ass, my overheated body barely notices the temperature.

"You know what I'm going to like more than finger fucking you?" He moves my panties to the side, gliding two fingers over my sensitive clit and right into me. "Eating your pussy."

"Yes," I hiss, the small of my back curving into an arch that forces my ass to press into his hard cock. My nipples tighten, almost to the point of discomfort. My hips move with his hand as he fucks me, hard and fast, with his fingers. I'm soaked and hot and throbbing, which is clearly evidenced by the ease with which he's able to enter me. I grind my ass on his hardness as my hips continue rocking with his hand. "I'm going to come," I tell him, knowing it's coming.

"I know. Your pussy is squeezing my fingers. God, so fucking tight," he groans as he moves them faster, rougher. My hand moves from where it was clutching onto his forearm, snaking around me and then between us to palm his cock. I rub him through his jeans, up and down. His cock is huge, and I can't wait to have him inside of me. It's been so long, so, so very long. "Come on, Lauren, come on my fingers so we can go inside and I can eat this pussy." He pumps them in and out of me. My wetness is now leaking down his hand and my inner thighs. "So fucking wet. So fucking tight. So fucking hot. You're going to come on my fingers, then you're going to come on my tongue. And then you're going to come on my cock. *Over and over and over again.*"

And that's it, that's when I come, and come hard. I moan out my orgasm with a barely coherent "Oh my god, so good." My hips move with his fingers to draw out the orgasm that has been lingering since the moment I set eyes on him tonight.

I'm not completely sure my legs can hold me up right now. Thankfully, he still has one arm around my waist, while the other hand is still in me. He slowly removes his fingers, and I turn around, grabbing the hand that was just inside of me.

"That was so good," I purr, looking him right in the eye as I bring it to my mouth. "Got me all excited." I suck one of his fingers into my mouth. One of his fingers that's coated in my cum. I suck it deep into my mouth, twirling my tongue around it. "You know what gets me even wetter, hotter, hornier?" I ask, drawing another finger in my mouth. "Sucking cock," I tell him, and before he can reply, I'm on my knees in front of him, wrestling with his belt. The need to get him out is intense for both of us.

I get his belt undone, open the button with both hands, and slowly pull the zipper down. I open the front of his pants, slide my hands along his abs into the waist band of his jeans, and carefully push them down his hips. When I move the material over his impressive cock, my eyes take in their first unhindered glimpse of him—long, hard, and thick, and all mine.

CHAPTER TWENTY

Austin

When she sank to her knees after sucking herself off my fingers, my cock jerked painfully against my zipper. Jesus fuck.

Her hands fumble with my belt and then the button. She starts sliding the zipper down slowly. I put both hands against the door over her head and look down to watch, more than ready to enjoy the show.

My dick pops right out, since I didn't bother with boxers tonight. I see her eye my dick, and from her expression, it seems that she likes what she sees. Good. She licks her lips before her tongue darts over the head of my cock in a slow, wet swipe, licking up all of the pre-cum that coats the tip. She pulls her tongue back in, almost like she's savoring it. Then she runs it back over it, a little "hmmm" sounding in her throat.

I use one of my hands to push her hair off her face and hold it to the side, so I can watch her take me in her mouth. She looks up at me, our eyes connecting as she takes the tip in her mouth. Sucking in a little more each time she bobs her head. My pants move further down my hips when I start thrusting shallowly into her warm mouth.

She curls her tongue around the head again and then takes in more of my length into her mouth. Her hot, slick tongue slides along my shaft, while her mouth covers me as she takes me deeper into her mouth.

The need to grab her head and fuck her face is strong. I grab her hair with both my hands and thrust my hips forward. When she groans, I pull her hair a little harder, and she sucks me harder in response. It seems that my girl likes to have her hair pulled. No problem there. I make a mental note to grab her by the hair when I take her from behind.

That mental image has me thrusting into her more forcefully. I take stock of her face, scared I'm going too deep, but she's lost in what she's doing and uses her hands to pull my hips into her.

"Can you take me in all the way to my balls?" I ask her, watching as she starts to do just that. Taking her time as she takes me in deeper each time. She moves one of her hands and wraps it around my shaft, taking her mouth off me to run it over my balls. Her tongue moves from one ball to the other, while her hand continues to work my dick.

She lifts her eyes to mine and warns, "Get ready, Austin. I'm going to take in your whole cock, right down to your balls. It's big, bigger than I've ever had"—she gives me a sexy little smirk—"but I like a challenge." She runs her flattened tongue up my shaft from root to tip right before she slips her mouth over the crown and takes me all the way to the back of her throat.

Swear to god, my knees go weak and my head falls back in ecstasy. "Fuck," I hiss out. I pull one hand from her hair to brace myself against the door as I tip my head down to watch her.

I hear—and feel—her humming while she moves up and down my cock with her mouth, hollowing out her cheeks as she goes. I see her hand on my shaft, while the other is buried in between her legs. "Where is your other hand?" I pull her hair, so she takes her mouth off my cock. My cock cries in protest.

"Buried in my pussy," she says with a smile as she closes her eyes to enjoy the pleasure she's giving herself. I stand here watching, still gripping her hair in one fist, as she continues to stroke my cock with her other hand.

"Okay. Play time is over, Lauren. Open the door." I pull up my pants before I bend down to lift her to her feet. She looks a little stunned at the sudden change in plans and surprised when I pull the hand that was playing with her pussy to my mouth, sucking her fingers clean. I groan as her taste explodes on my tongue. Sweet and tangy, like a ripe peach on a hot summer fucking day.

One taste isn't even close to being enough. I let her open the door, but once we're through it, I slam it behind me and yank her back into my front. Her ass is still bared, and my cock is still wet from her mouth. I know if lift her up right now, I'll slide right into her to the hilt in one smooth stroke.

She must be thinking the same thing, because she pushes back, grinding her ass against my crotch. My hand wraps around her front, going straight to her pussy, her panties still moved aside, as my fingers move on her clit.

"Wet," I tell her as I apply a bit of pressure and make tight circles. "Fucking wet, and hot," I groan, easing up to a gentle tease as I switch to bigger circles. "Know what's going to make this pussy wetter?" I whisper into her ear while I remove my hand from her pussy with one last flick to her clit.

I turn her around, almost roughly, pushing her back against the door. No lights are on in the house, but the lights from the street glow outside, streaming through the windows and softly illuminating the foyer.

She is panting, her eyes are hooded, and she looks at me in question. I smirk at her as I move to my knees in front of her. It's my turn to devour her now. I press my face against her pussy, inhaling deeply. She smells as good as she tastes, and I can't help the groan that escapes as my tongue darts out to lick her wet, slick slit from bottom to top. I use my hand to part her lips, revealing her swollen clit just waiting to be sucked.

Her pussy isn't bald; it's got a neatly trimmed landing strip that runs all the way down. My tongue flutters against her clit, teasing her. Her back arches, causing her hips to jerk forward. "Now, now. Patience," I admonish her while I lick her again, slower this time, my tongue buried between her parted lips as it travels up and back down the length of her, purposely avoiding her clit.

She whimpers and squirms as her pants become almost jagged. My tongue dips into her opening, in and out, mimicking what my cock will be doing shortly. I'm the one looking up now, watching her. Her head rolls against the door. One hand is at her side, resting flush against the door, while the other has found its way into my hair.

"Do you want to come on my tongue or my fingers?" I watch her go crazy with need.

"Cock," she breathes, pushing my face into her pussy. I close my mouth over her clit, sucking it into my mouth while tormenting it with my tongue at the same time. Her head thrashes, the hand not in my hair is now fisted at her side, and her moans are interrupted by words as she says, "Fuck, I'm going to come." She never once lets go of my head as she works her hips against my face. "So good." I continue to focus on her clit as I use my finger to fuck her, moving it in and out as I nibble and suck her clit until she begs me to make her come. "Make me come, Austin, please. I need to come."

I suck harder and then bite down on her clit once before I start sucking again. My finger is moving inside her, and I hook it to find her G-spot. When I do, I make sure to pass over it with a little tap each time my finger enters her. I feel her walls tightening around my fingers and then fluttering. I let go of her clit while still massaging her G-spot, and tell her roughly, "Come, Lauren. Come all over my finger. Come for me now, baby." I go back to sucking her clit, and I feel her legs start to shake as her orgasm starts to rush through her. She comes on my hand with a scream, and I continue to lick her slowly as I bring her down. My hand is now planted against her belly, holding her up as I feel her start to slump.

I stand and pick her up, her body pliant, loose, and sated. Her limbs wrap around my neck and my hips. She starts kissing up my neck to my ear, where she whispers, "Please tell me we aren't finished."

"Not even fucking close," I promise as I head up the stairs to her room. Tossing her on the bed, I palm my aching cock and tell her, "We're just getting started."

I look down at her, legs spread, arms raised over her head. She looks at me looking at her and then lets her eyes drift closed for a brief second as she gives her body a little stretch before she gets up on her elbows.

"What are you waiting for?" she asks me. "You said we were just getting started." Sitting up now, she reaches behind her to take off her chunky necklace and throws it on her nightstand, where it lands with a clump. "Do you want me to undress myself or would you like the honors?" She tilts her head to the side, her hair rumpled. She looks fucking perfect.

Her bedroom has a huge picture window, and the light from the street lamps flows into the space, illuminating her with a backlit glow. "You're taking too long." She rises up onto her knees. Her skirt is still shoved up around her waist, and she reaches to her side to lower the zipper of her top. A quick shuffle of the garment, and it falls to the bed silently. The only sounds in the room are my breathing and my gasp when I finally see her tits in all their glory. Perfect round globes that are plump and topped with tight pink nipples that call out to be sucked, to be played with, to be teased.

"Jesus." She pulls the skirt from around her waist and brings it up and over her head, her tits bouncing with her movements. I'm staring to the point of gawking when I notice that she is about to take her panties off. "No, not yet. That's for me to do."

She nods her head, watching me from her bed, on her knees, wearing her fuck-me shoes and a black lace thong.

I kick off my shoes, pull off my socks, and unbutton my shirt all the way down, shrugging it off my shoulders. Now, it's her turn to gasp and gawk. My body is lean, with no fat. The time at the gym and running keeps everything off. My six-pack abs are key to everything. "Jesus right back at you," she whispers, moving forward on her knees, getting closer to me at the end of the bed.

Her hand fists me, slowly working my cock up and down, as she asks, "Condom?" I reach into my back pocket for my wallet and pull out three. "Only three? We'll have to make them count, then." She leans down and bites my nipple then sucks the sting away.

I move my hands to her tits, cupping them in both hands as I squeeze both nipples between my thumbs and forefingers, lightly at first to gauge her reaction. When she moans, I roll them between my fingers more firmly, and she moans louder. When I pinch them hard, she throws her head back and moans out a curse. I let one nipple go as I lean down, taking the peak into my mouth as I continue pinching the other. Her hands work almost frantically on my cock at this point, and if she continues at that pace, I'm going to come like some teenage boy in her hand.

I move her hand off me and continue palming both breasts with my hands, squeezing, kneading, massaging. "Cover me," I demand of her, motioning to the condoms lying next to her on the bed. "Cover me now."

She puts the corner of the wrapper in her mouth, tearing the top off and pulling the condom out of the package. "I haven't done this in a really, really long time," she confesses as she rolls it all the way down my cock, squeezing the tip to get the air out. "Just like riding a bike,"

She chuckles while she starts to stroke me again.

"How much do you love your panties?" I ask her, fully prepared to replace them, several times over if she wants me to.

"Not as much as I love the thought that you're going to rip them off me," she groans, nipping at my jaw as my hand grips one side of her panties, ripping them clean off her.

"On your back, middle of the bed, legs spread wide for me." I don't have to ask her twice, because she turns right around and crawls to the middle of the bed, showing me her perfect, heart-shaped ass as she goes. She looks over her shoulder at me as she eggs me on. "This is a position I look forward to—*later*." Then she moves to her back and lies down with her head on a pillow.

She cocks her knees, placing her shoes flat on the bed as she slowly spreads her legs, wide enough that they fall to the side. She's quite the sight, there in the middle of the bed, open and ready and wet for me, just for me.

I put my knee on the bed and move to her, my cock harder than it's ever been, knowing without a doubt that it's about to sink into pure heaven.

I pull her knees up, pushing them back and causing her pussy to tilt. Holding her legs in place, I tell her, "Guide me in, Lauren." She takes my condom-covered cock in her hand and rubs me through her slick slit to the opening of her pussy. Slowly, she pushes the head in and removes her hand for me to take over. I watch as I sink all the way into her.

Her pussy grips my cock so tight, it's being strangled in the best possible way. I hiss out a breath at the pleasure at the same time she moans, "So good." Tightening my hold on her knees, I pull out and then slam back in with a little snap of my hips. Her pussy is getting impossibly tighter with each stroke. "Oh, god," she moans as one of her hands land on her nipple, while the other slowly trails down her body to her clit. She runs her fingers through her slit and around me as I tunnel in and out of her, getting them wet then bringing them back to her clit to circle. I plant myself all the way in her, balls deep, afraid to move for fear that I'm going to come before her. I just need a second to gain some control, but she's got other ideas. "Move, Austin, please!" she begs as she squirms beneath me, tilting her hips and taking my cock deeper into her heat.

I start to move in earnest, pulling out and then slamming back into her so hard the headboard bounces off the wall a few times. "Yes, yes, yes!" she chants, the finger on her clit rubbing faster and faster as her pussy pulses and tightens around me.

I don't stop. I just keep pounding into her, the sounds of our heavy breathing and skin slapping together filling the air.

The harder I pound, the tighter she becomes. "I'm going to come," she breathes. Her hand is now rubbing back and forth, almost violently, over her engorged clit. "Harder," she begs, pulling her legs back further as she tilts her hips up to meet my thrusts as she moans out her orgasm. Her pussy clamps down on my cock, pulsing and rippling around it as I move. The hand between her legs never stops, and the sensation of her climax coupled with watching her let go is the last straw for me. I continue to pound into her, bottoming out with each stroke, as lightning shoots down my spine into my balls, and I follow her over the edge. I come harder than I ever have in my life, so hard that I vaguely wonder if it might break the condom. Her orgasm hasn't stopped yet, either, and her pussy is milking me, squeezing every single drop out of me.

With my cock still buried inside her to the root, I let go of her legs, wrapping them around my waist as I fall onto my elbows by her head. "That was..." I pant out, trying to catch my breath and gather my scattered wits about me, while she wraps her arms around my neck, bringing my weight down on top of her.

"It was," she agrees, kissing my chin and then my lips between her own heavy breaths. "Definitely something we need to do again." I don't get a chance to agree with her, because her mouth has covered mine and all thoughts are gone as I lose myself in Lauren.

CHAPTER TWENTY-ONE

Lauren

The light streams into my room, landing right on my face like the beam of a flashlight. I groan, trying to grab something to block it out. I reach for the covers, trying to bring them up to shield my face, but they won't budge.

Soft butterfly kisses landing on my shoulder make me smile. *Austin.* Best. Fucking. Night. Of. My. Life. Well, besides having my children. Okay, best fucking *sex* of my life.

I don't respond to the kisses. His finger plucks at my nipple, rolling it between them, waking my body up and making it ache for him. "I know you're awake," he says between kisses.

"I need food," I reply. "No sex until we have food." I move deeper into his embrace. His hard cock pushes against my ass.

After the first time, we took a nap, and he woke me for round two with his mouth between my legs before I wound up riding him like a rodeo queen. I think I shocked his ass when I suddenly swung off him, mid-ride, and remounted him, reverse-cowgirl style. I wasn't surprised that when presented with my ass, Austin spanked it. No, what surprised me was how much I liked it. With his back to the headboard, me facing forward and looking at us in the mirror over my dresser was like watching my own personal porn. It was one of the hottest moments of my life.

Jake and I had what I always thought was an exciting and active sex life, but one night with Austin had me thinking that maybe it wasn't quite adventurous as I'd thought. Despite the years we'd had together and the level of comfort I'd felt with him, I've never let go like that during sex before. But after my divorce, I knew the next time I brought a man into my bed, I would be asking for and taking what I wanted. That wasn't something I did with Jake; with him, I followed his lead and took what he gave. It wasn't bad per se, but I think I knew deep down that something had been missing in it for me.

"Food," I repeat when his hand moves down my stomach to cup me. I ignore his hand and stretch my body. Muscles hurt in places that I didn't know could hurt from having sex.

"Okay, I'll go start the coffee." He's still trying to play with me. I slide out of bed and head into the en-suite bathroom in my bedroom. "I'm going to have fun playing with that ass later," I hear him say right before I close the door.

After using the bathroom, I look in the mirror. My makeup is still half on; the mascara isn't that bad, though a bit smeared. I take the time to remove it and wash my face. Tying my hair high up on my head in a messy bun, I brush my teeth. Once I make my way out, I immediately smell coffee.

Grabbing the shirt he wore last night, I put it on. It's huge on me, but I leave the top three buttons undone and button the rest, leaving him plenty of room to reach in if he wants to. I head downstairs and into the kitchen.

He's there, jeans on and buttoned, leaning against my counter, his feet crossed in front of him, drinking a cup of coffee.

His hair is tousled from sex and sleep, and a five-o'clock shadow has crept over his handsome face. I go straight to the coffee machine and reach up to grab a cup but see that he has made me a cup already. "I didn't poison it," he says, the mug shielding his smirk but not the smile in his eyes.

Before I can reply, I hear the front door open. He looks at me with a surprised look. "It's probably Kaleigh." I shrug and see his face start to relax. "Or my parents," I add, giggling into my coffee mug when he looks close to panicking.

Kaleigh comes into the kitchen dressed in a man's dress shirt and boxers, her purse hanging off her arm while her other hand holds her shoes.

"Look what the slut dragged in," I say, leaning against the counter next to Austin.

"Funny, funny, ha ha. I take it the cobwebs have been cleared out?" she fires back.

"Oh, there are definitely no cobwebs in there," Austin murmurs with a little smirk as he throws one arm over my shoulder. "Isn't that Noah's shirt?" he asks.

"I hope you told him you were leaving, Kaleigh." I look at Austin. "She isn't exactly known for sticking around the morning after. She, um, likes to leave before it can get awkward," I explain as I take a sip of my coffee.

"He's going to lose his shit," Austin states.

"Did you use my almond milk?" Kaleigh asks while he continues to drink his coffee and shakes his head no. "Oh. So, you used the breast milk, then?" Austin spits his coffee out of his mouth all over the counter.

"What?" he questions, looking into his cup and then looking at me.

"She's just messing with you." I laugh. "You are going to clean up that mess." I point to the counter that now has his coffee splattered all over it.

"I'm not messing with him. I ordered frozen breast milk this week and switched it out." Kaleigh looks at me, while I look inside my coffee cup. "You put butter in my potatoes, remember?"

"You let me drink someone's breast milk?" I throw the coffee down the drain along with the rest of the milk. "That's sick, Kal."

"Where the fuck do you even order breast milk from?" Austin is looking under the sink for cleaning products. "Do we need to get, like, a hepatitis shot or something?" he asks, coming up with some Windex in his hand.

"I ordered it online." She shrugs her shoulder. "I switched it yesterday morning after the kids left." She nonchalantly studies her nails, while Austin and I start to freak out.

"What if the woman has a disease? Jesus! Could we catch it?" Austin turns to me. "I feel a little funny." He puts his hand to his stomach, making me roll my eyes.

"Relax, it was from a reputable website for mothers who can't produce enough milk," she assures us right before someone starts banging on the front door.

"Kaleigh! Are you in there?" Noah yells from outside.

Austin smirks at her and walks to the door to open it. "Hey, man." He steps aside for him to walk in. "Come in. Can I get you some coffee? With or without breast milk?" Noah just looks at him like he's crazy.

"What are you doing here?" He walks into the kitchen and eyes me in Austin's now buttoned-up shirt before shifting his gaze to Kaleigh.

"You took my shirt? And then you just fucking left?"

"She's not good with the whole morning-after thing," I add helpfully, while Kaleigh shoots me a glare and the middle finger.

He turns her around on the stool as he cages her in between his arms with his hands braced against the counter. "I thought we said we were doing yoga this morning?" He leans into her.

Austin laughs from beside me, where he stands after closing the front door. "You couldn't do yoga if you tried." He continues laughing while Noah glares at him.

"Plus, you said we could do the down-dog thing," he whispers to her.

"What's the down dog?" Austin asks me in a whisper that is not at all quiet. I shrug my shoulders as I shush him and continue to watch the scene in front of me.

"Don't you two have to be somewhere?" Kaleigh looks back at us.

"Nope," Austin and I answer at the same time and then look at each other and smile. His smile melts me, so I wrap my arms around his waist as he throws his over my shoulders, bringing me closer to him.

"Come back home with me," Noah asks her, leaning in and tracing her jaw with the tip of his nose. "Please."

"Okay," she replies, and I gasp at her in surprise. She never lets her guard down with men, *ever.* "Besides, I think Austin is going to kill me for making him drink breast milk." She tries to make it seem like this isn't a big deal, but I know better.

Noah looks at Austin as he stands back, making room for Kaleigh to get up and gather her stuff. "You drank breast milk, dude? Can you die from that?" He slips his hands in his pockets.

Austin stills next to me. "No, you can't. Now, go away before he goes nuts," I order before turning to Austin. "You can't die from drinking breast milk," I reassure him. "Well, unless the mother had like HIV or something."

Noah bursts out laughing, grabbing Kaleigh's hand, and dragging her back out the door.

"We need to get tested," he states.

"I was just kidding. She wouldn't really try to kill me. Anyway, I was thinking maybe we could shower. I'm feeling very, very dirty," I whisper to him.

He grabs me around the waist, my body molding to his like it was made for him. We walk upstairs, where we make good use of our hands and mouths—and that third condom.

When nighttime comes, he gets dressed to go home. I'm a little down. We haven't talked about where this is going, but I'm not stupid enough to think that it's going anywhere. So, I tuck it down, bury it, and try to just live in the moment.

Later that night, he texts me.

Missing you.

I'm not sure what to say to him, so I send a casual reply.

Me, too ☺

I don't hear from him the rest of the evening, and then the next day, I make my way to work. I messaged Barbara last night, telling her I would give it another chance. She was very excited. I dressed in a tight black pencil skirt that I paired with a white fitted, button-down shirt with three-quarter length sleeves that has a faux rolled cuff, making it appear as if the sleeves are rolled up to my elbows. I finished the outfit off with a smoking hot pair of Ferragamo patent-leather, pointy-toe stiletto pumps.

I walk in and see Carmen at the reception desk. Her reaction to seeing me is less than friendly. I don't bother questioning her on it, I just walk back to my desk.

I put my purse on the desk as I look into Austin's office and notice he isn't in yet. I walk to Barbara's office to tell her I'm here, but she isn't in yet, either. Looking at my watch, I see it's almost eight, so they both should be in soon.

Walking back to my desk, I come face-to-face with a furious Austin, who is just walking out of his office.

"What are you doing here?" he asks with his hands on his hips, and my heart sinks a bit at his reaction.

"I work here. Barbara asked me to come back, and I agreed." I put my hands on my hips now, too.

He grabs my arm, bringing me into his office and slamming the door.

"You can't work here. I don't sleep with women I work with." I look at him in confusion.

"What?" I ask, not sure I understand.

"I don't sleep with women I work with. I think it's pretty straightforward," he barks.

"So, you're saying that you won't be with me if I work for you?" I ask him, now folding my arms over my chest.

"I'm telling you that you aren't working here, so we can continue sleeping with each other."

"Well, then that settles it. We won't sleep with each other," I bait him. He drove me out once, he won't do it again. "When we slept together, I hadn't agreed to start working for you again, so that doesn't count," I tell him right before there is a knock at the door.

"Go away!" Austin yells, but the door opens anyway with Barbara peeking in.

"Oh, good, you're here. I see you've found out that Lauren decided to come back. You're welcome." She takes in the tension in the room and looks at her watch. "It's been two minutes. How can you guys be fighting already?"

"It's nothing," Austin says as I stare him down.

"He's trying to fire me, because, apparently, he doesn't work with women he has slept with." I look over at Barbara, who closes the door behind her.

Then I look at Austin, who throws his hands in the air. "Why did you tell her?" he asks.

"Oh, please, she changed your diapers." I look at Barbara and then back to him. "Besides, if she hasn't already, Kaleigh would have told her."

He looks at the ceiling in his office, pinching his nose. "How did this happen?"

"Well, you had sex with Lauren, that's how," Barbara cuts in. "Which isn't that bad, Austin. I might have to change the employee handbook back now that it appears that fraternizing with a co-worker is okay," she teases.

"No, it's not okay," Austin snaps. "I don't shit where I eat." He looks at me. "Not now, not ever."

"Fine, no big deal. We forget it happened and move forward since it won't be happening again." I shrug my shoulders in an attempt to make light of it, while, in truth, my heart is breaking. "It wasn't that great anyway."

"Liar," he snaps as I turn to walk out.

"Now, if you guys will excuse me, I have work to catch up on." I turn and walk out before I break down.

I close the door behind me as Austin calls my name. I ignore the desire to go to him, ignore my aching heart and hurt feelings, and ignore the thoughts that we could have been starting something amazing.

CHAPTER TWENTY-TWO

Austin

I had the best sex of my life. I was walking on cloud nine. I was smiling at nothing. Then I walked in, saw her in the office, and I snapped.

I promised myself that I would never let my dick get involved with my work. Then there she was, in a tight skirt and a white shirt, and all I thought about was making those buttons scatter as I ripped that shirt off and fucked her tits.

My cock saw her and immediately stood up to salute her. Then she said the words I dreaded. "I work here."

Now, here I am, three days later, sulking in my office. While she comes in smiling every day like nothing happened. I see her bend down and have to stifle a groan. I see her chewing on her pen and think about her sucking my cock. I can't think straight. I can't even walk next to her without fighting the urge to push her up against the wall and fuck her so hard she can't walk afterward.

I'm watching her while she talks to Steven, her arms crossed over her chest and leaning back. Today, she's wearing one of those tuxedo shirts for women, with rows of pleated material down the center. I wonder if she's wearing a lace bra underneath? All I know is, if I see her laugh one more time at something he says, I'm firing him. I pick up the phone to call her.

"Yes," she answers, and I swear my cock knows when she's close, because he twitches.

"I need the specs for my meeting with Dani." I look over at my screen, knowing she sent it twenty minutes ago.

"I sent it to you already," she huffs and then turns back to her screen. "Yep, it says 'sent.' Did you refresh your screen?"

"Obviously, Lauren," I grate out. "Can you just bring me in the hard copies so I can go over them?"

"Sure." She hangs up and prints out the pages, then gets up to bring them to me right as Steven steps in her way, causing the papers to drop to the floor. She bends over to pick them up, her ass pointing straight at my office window. Steven doesn't even notice that ass; he just helps her pick up the papers.

I groan and throw my pen down, trying to get my thoughts together so when she comes in, it doesn't show that I'm affected by her.

I adjust my cock and mentally tell him to knock it off.

The door opens and she walks in, handing me the papers. "Here you go. Do you need me to attend the meeting?" she asks, and I can't say anything. Today, she has her hair tied up in a ponytail, and I want nothing more than to untie it so I can run my fingers through it. I just nod, pretending to review the plans.

"Fine. I'll meet you in there. I'm going to get myself a coffee. Would you like one?" she asks me over her shoulder as she walks out of my office.

"Sure, no laxatives or breast milk, please." I watch as she rolls her eyes. I continue to watch her as she walks past my office, a little swing in her hips and a small smile playing across her beautiful face. Like me, I know she's thinking of that morning, that incredible morning. It feels like it was ages ago, but it's been only four days.

Every night on my way home, I go out of my way to pass by her house just to see if she is there, hoping to catch another glimpse of her. Each and every night, I wish I could text her, call her, go to see her. But I can't.

The knock at the door jolts me out of my thoughts, and I look up to see Carmen standing there, leaning against the door jamb. "Hiyeah. I called, but you didn't answer. Dani is here," she informs me, and I nod as I get up, grabbing my jacket, and making my way to the conference room.

Dani and Lauren are in there gabbing away about new recipes. I can't help but notice how everyone has taken to Lauren. She gets along with everyone.

She looks over at me, feeling me staring at her. She smiles at me, her smile different than the smile she gives anyone else. It takes over her whole face, her eyes, her cheeks, and her body relaxes.

"Hey." She points to the table. "Your coffee is there."

Dani sees me and walks over to me, hugging me, and kisses my cheek. "Hey there, we missed you on Sunday." My eyes fly right to Lauren's.

"Yeah, sorry, I was…" I don't finish. I just look down at the pictures on the table. The restaurant is almost done. "Oh, wow, these are beautiful. I love the booths." I look and see that the booths are exactly like I wanted them to be, but now each also has a chandelier that hangs over the center of the table that gives it the appearance of falling rain.

"Yes, that was Lauren's idea. When she described it, I thought right away about the booths, so I told Chris. We are having a soft opening this weekend to make sure everything goes as planned, and then next weekend, it's go-time. I have a couple of celebrities coming. I even hit up your friend, Cooper Stone, and he's bringing his wife, Parker, with him."

I sit in the chair, looking at the pictures, while she talks, only half listening. "So, do you have a date for this or not? I can set you up with this girl I go to Pilates with. She is very detail oriented, and she just wants a good time."

My head snaps up, shooting straight to Lauren. "Um, no." I see her looking down at the pad in front of her. "I'm not bringing a date."

Dani laughs at me. "Serena will be there anyway." My eyes leave Lauren and shoot to Dani.

"Excuse me." Lauren pushes off from the table and walks out.

I look at Dani. "Is that all? Did we need to go over anything else?"

"No." She looks at me then at the door that Lauren just went through. "Jesus, are you and Lauren…" She motions with her fingers.

"She works for me, so that answers your question."

"Right." She gathers all her papers. "I'm going to hit up John before I leave. I'll see you Sunday?" Every Sunday, we all get together for dinner.

"I'm not sure," I reply, because I'm hoping that Lauren quits tonight.

I walk back to my office, expecting Lauren to be there, but her computer is shut off. I check my watch and see it's only two-thirty.

I pick up my phone and call her on her cell. She picks up after the first ring. "Sorry, I'm so sorry I had to leave," she says, almost frantically, without even greeting me.

"Is everything okay?" I'm ready to run out if she needs me.

"Yes," she sighs. "Well, not really. I might have to call in sick tomorrow. Kaleigh has strep throat. She has a fever, and she's at my parents' house now, because the last thing I need is for anyone else to get sick."

"What?" I'm trying to follow her, but she is rambling.

"Kaleigh had a fever, so she went to the doctor. She has a throat infection. She is the one who watches my kids after school while I'm at work. Except, tomorrow is a staff development day, and she's sick, so I have no other backup."

"Okay, don't worry about it." I go to my computer to check my calendar, seeing that there's nothing on my schedule till Monday. "What are you going to do with the kids tomorrow?" I ask her, not exactly sure why, but I do it anyway.

"I have no clue. Hopefully, keep them from killing each other. Listen, I'm just getting home, so I need to go. Sorry about just taking off like that," she apologizes softly.

"It's fine. I'll call you later to check in," I tell her and then hang up.

I block out my day tomorrow, sending a message to Barbara that I'm going to be working from home.

I have no idea what the fuck I'm doing. But the next morning at nine a.m., I'm standing on Lauren's porch, hoping she doesn't turn me away.

I hear the door locks turning and hold my breath. Rachel opens the door, still in her pajamas. I squat down to talk to her, asking, "Hey there, is Mommy home?"

She smiles at me, showing me a missing tooth, her lips shiny with what I'm assuming is syrup. "Mommy!" she yells loudly. "Asshat is at the door."

I put my head down, laughing at the nickname. "What?" I hear her voice from somewhere inside the house as she makes her way to the door. She is wearing a short pink cotton robe, loosely tied at the waist, the front a bit open on top so you can see her camisole. Her hair piled up on her head, she places her hands on Rachel's shoulders. "What are you doing here?" She looks down at me.

I rise up from the squat position. "I came to see if you and the kids would like to go ice skating?" I ask her, and not waiting for her to invite me, I walk past her, kissing her on the head.

I shrug off my jacket, throwing it on the pile next to the door with the other jackets. Then I turn and look at her. "Is that bacon I smell?"

"Real bacon," Rachel says, turning to run back into the kitchen.

I look at Lauren questioningly. "Kaleigh makes them eat vegan bacon, but I picked up the real deal yesterday, so it's like Christmas morning." She laughs as she pulls her robe together at the top of her neck. "Austin, what are you doing here?" she asks me again, and before I have a chance to answer her, Gabe runs into the room.

"Are we really going skating?" His eyes are wide with anticipation. "Mom, can I bring my stick so we can shoot some pucks?" He then turns to me. "Is it okay if I bring my stick?"

"You play hockey?" I ask him.

"Yeah, I want to, but Mom says I have to choose one sport, so I chose soccer." Gabe looks at his mom.

"I used to play college hockey with Cooper Stone. Have you heard of him? He's retired now, but he was a big deal when he was playing."

"You used to play with Cooper Stone? Matthew Grant is my favorite player of all time! He's still a rookie, but he's awesome."

I smile at him. This kid obviously wants to play hockey. "How about next Sunday, if it's okay with your mom, I ask Cooper to join us on the ice?"

"Mom, please? I'll do all my chores." Gabe turns to his mom and begs.

"First off, you're at your dad's next weekend. And second, you don't have any equipment, and this isn't the right time for me to be buying stuff," she answers him.

"I have extra gear," I pipe in. I totally don't, but I'll buy whatever he needs me to buy.

She looks at me. "How about we go do the skating thing and see how you like it? You've never really been on skates, Gabe," she proposes gently, and he must see it as a win in his favor, because he jumps up and hugs her, repeating 'thank you' over and over again.

"Rachel, we're going skating!" Gabe yells, running out of the room.

"You look cute," I tell her because she does look cute, but it's more than that.

"We aren't dating, Austin. You can't talk to me like that." She shakes her head. "Please, don't make this harder for me." She keeps her voice low, and I advance on her, but she quickly brushes past me and heads into the kitchen, picking up the kids' breakfast plates on her way to the sink.

"What do we call you if we can't call you Asshat?" Rachel turns to me on her way up the stairs.

"His name is Austin, so no more of that language, young lady. Now, go get dressed," her mother instructs from the kitchen. Gabe grabs her hand to hurry her upstairs to get dressed.

I head into the kitchen, finding Lauren bent over, loading the breakfast dishes in the dishwasher. Her ass taunts me, and my cock is hard and ready to slide into her.

Looking over my shoulder to make sure we're alone, I walk over to her, placing my hands on her hips.

Her body stills and then stiffens once my hands land on her. I press my hips forward so she feels me. The warmth of her body penetrates right through me. She snaps up straight, keeping her back to me. "I can't seem to forget you," I whisper in her ear as I sweep her hair to the side and kiss her neck. "I can't think." I run small kisses up the side of her neck as she tilts her head to the side to give me better access. I'm about to slip my hand inside her robe when I hear someone barreling down the stairs.

My hands leave her hips and I back away from her, while Lauren slams the dishwasher closed. "I'm not quitting my job just so you can have your way," she hisses as she walks past me. "Get ready, because there are more games to play, Austin."

She walks upstairs as I watch her, and I swear there's a distinct swing to her hips.

CHAPTER TWENTY-THREE

Lauren

He showed up like he just walked off a fucking catwalk modeling casual men's fashion. His faded blue jeans fit him perfectly, hugging him in all the right places and making his package look huge. Okay, fine. He's very well endowed, but fuck, those jeans just emphasize that fact. His blue Henley molds to his chest, shoulders, and arms, highlighting all his muscles right down to his trim waist, where the hem is tucked in at the sides in a way that's obviously just his style. Topped off with his black leather jacket, the whole outfit looks like he should be riding a bike instead of driving a Porsche.

Then he sweet-talked my kids, mostly Gabe, with the hockey bullshit. And then, the crème de la crème was him grinding his fucking cock into me while I was bending over. I swear I almost raised myself up on my tippy toes to get him to slide in.

Since Sunday, I've masturbated every single night with him starring in all my dreams. He wants me to quit. Well, fuck that! I'm going to make him regret he made this stupid rule, even if I give myself blue balls, or a blue vagina, or whatever.

I grab my yoga pants, because nothing molds to a woman's body quite like yoga pants. I pair them with my blue off-the-shoulder sweater that stops just above my waist and gives a little peek of my stomach, but not too much. I wear a blue lace bra underneath it, which is the same color as the sweater. It's a mom outfit, but a sexy mom outfit, or at least I hope it is.

I text Kaleigh right before I go downstairs.

Hope you're feeling better and that Mom isn't making you want to commit suicide.

She responds right away.

It's Noah, she's with me. I'll take good care of her.

I look down at my phone, confused.

I thought she was staying with my parents?
She was until she walked in on them playing Tarzan and Jane. Your mom looks hot in a loincloth, BTW.
Ewwww! You're a sick man. Off to the arena with Austin. Tell her to text me later.
*He finally got over that 'don't shit where you eat' bullshit? No.*I answer him right away and then throw out, *Know anyone hiring?*
You can come work for me. I definitely won't want to have sex with you.
Funny guy. Okay, well, if you have a real suggestion, let me know.
I'm serious. I need a PA to keep my shit in order, and I heard you're the best. Think about it. Let me know. That way, Austin's balls won't get swollen again. BTW I will never ask you to get me coffee or food.

"Mom! Come on, let's go!" Gabe yells from the bottom of the stairs. I take in my appearance. Yup, sexy yet still conservative.

"Coming," I shout as I start walking down the stairs. I see Austin taking me in from my feet to my shoulders, his eyes lingering on the lace bra strap. "Okay, are we all ready to go?" I smile big at him, while he tries to adjust himself discreetly. Score one for me.

We all pile into the minivan, and I throw the keys to Austin, since I have no idea where I'm going.

We pull into an otherwise empty parking lot. "Maybe it's closed," I contemplate, looking around.

"No, I have the key. I've practiced here since I was three, so the owner just gave me a key when I turned sixteen. I called Craig to let him know I was going to be here so he knew. He only uses it on Saturdays and Sundays at this point."

We walk in, and Austin turns on the light. The cement walls are lined with pictures of kids. I walk along the wall, while Austin walks behind the counter, getting a key out of the drawer.

Walking to another door, he opens it up. "Okay, let's see what we got. Rachel, what size do you wear?" he asks her.

"Twenty-eight," she replies, having no idea and just throwing any number out. He comes out of the room and looks down at her with a grin and his hands on his hips.

"She's a three, Gabe is a five, and I'm a six and a half," I tell him.

He comes back with three pairs of skates. Handing Gabe his first, then me mine, and then Rachel hers. "There are no girl skates, sorry, kiddo," he apologizes to Rachel as she sits down and he starts to tie her skates. I'm surprised when I see that Gabe has already tied his skates. "I'm ready," he informs us.

Austin looks at him. "Go into that room. There are some helmets and gloves." He motions over his shoulder to the room he just came out of.

Gabe goes in and comes back out with helmets for him and Rachel. "Can I get on the ice?" Gabe asks, and Austin nods his head while he finishes tying Rachel's skates and then calls me over.

"I think I can tie my own skates, Austin." I sit in front of him, while he is on his knees, readying the skate for my foot as I lean forward a bit, shifting my shoulder so my shirt slips a little, giving him a glimpse of the sheer lace bra under my shirt. I know right away that he's seen it when he groans loudly. I smile innocently at him. "Oops! Sorry about that." I hold my shirt up.

When my skates are tied, he takes his out of his bag and puts them on. It takes him a couple of minutes until he's done.

We make our way to the ice. Rachel, who ran to join Gabe as soon as she was ready, isn't skating. She is attempting to make snow angels on the ice.

Gabe, on the other hand, is skating like he was born to do it.

"I thought you said he hasn't skated," Austin says.

"He hasn't, really, just maybe once or twice." I watch him zig-zag from one end of the rink to the other.

"Kid's a natural," he comments, getting onto the ice, holding out his hand for me. "Let's play," he invites.

I grab his hand, put one foot on the ice, and slip right away. I grab onto Austin with my other hand so I don't fall. He doesn't even budge, while I flail around a bit.

"So, you hold onto the wall with one hand and my hand with the other, okay?" he instructs, skating to the side of the rink.

I'm holding onto the wall for dear life while I've got my other hand around Austin's in a death grip "This isn't fun," I deadpan, concentrating on not falling on the slippery ice. "Nothing about this is fun."

I look over at Gabe, watching him shoot a puck into the empty net. "Where did he get the stick?" I ask, attempting to skate.

"From the back room. Focus on your feet. Glide from left to right." I just glare at him. "Go away," I tell him, letting his hand go and clinging to the wall with both hands. I watch him skate away backward, smiling at me before he turns around and skates to Gabe. The two of them are shooting pucks while Austin gives him tips.

The rest of the day is spent at the rink. Rachel gave up on skating but figured out how the intercom worked, so she gave us a play-by-play of nothing. By the time we walk out of there, Gabe looks at me and asks if he can join hockey next season instead of soccer. I look over his head at Austin and see him smirk.

"Um, we'll see, Gabe. I need to speak to your father first. Okay?" I say as I get in the car, watching Austin open the door for Rachel and picking her up so she can get in her booster seat.

He gets in on the driver's side, and I'm momentarily shocked by how it looks, as if we've been doing this forever.

"What do you guys think about grabbing burgers for dinner?" He adjusts the mirror so he can look to the backseat at the kids.

We all agree to get burgers at Five Guys before we head home. By the time we finally do get home, it's past seven and Rachel is dragging her feet.

"Okay, Rachel, bath and bed," I urge her when we get inside. Gabe asks if he can call his father, and I nod yes. He runs upstairs with my phone in his hand, leaving me and Austin alone.

"I think I'm going to head home," he says to me.

I look at him standing at the front door, "Thank you for today. You didn't have to do that." I walk toward him. When I'm finally in front of him, I lean up on my toes, wrapping my arms around his shoulders. "You looked pretty hot out there." I whisper, pressing my chest to his, watching his Adam's apple bob up and down as he swallows. "Really hot, so hot." I kiss his jaw.

"Are you quitting?" His voice is almost cracking.

"Nope." I smile. "I love my job, I'm good at my job." I press deeper into him, his cock resting on my stomach.

"Okay. I should go." He's seemingly unsure of what to do. I let him go, watching as he turns the handle of the door. "I really, really wish you would quit," he says before stepping outside.

"I really, really wish you would get over it." I hold the door in my hand, leaning against the jamb. "So I could show you that I'm not wearing panties," I tease him, watching his mouth drop, right before I close the door on him and collapse against it.

Gabe comes back downstairs with my phone. "I had so much fun today. Thanks, Mom." He hugs me and then runs back upstairs.

I look at my phone and see that Austin has already texted me.

Were you serious?
I don't joke about panties. Ever.
What if I fire you?
You wouldn't dare.

After that, he doesn't text me back. I bring up my recent texts and text Kaleigh.

Tell Noah to call me after nine to discuss his proposition.
I really hope your proposition isn't about sex.
Are you still high?
No. Maybe. Yes. I'm so sick. I hope you catch it.
Gee, thanks.
He said the job is yours and to tell him when you want to start.
How does next Monday sound?
It sounds like I need to have sex with him. He's so hot taking care of me. I should give him a blowjob.

149

With a throat infection? He might catch it!!!
In his dick?
No, dumbass, in his throat. Gotta go.

I start to make the plans in my head. Taking a huge leap of faith by switching jobs, just so I can have sex. Really, really good sex, awesome sex, the-best-sex-I've-ever-had sex. Yep, decision made. Now, I just have to get through the week and that stupid club opening, and we are in the home stretch.

The week went by faster than I thought. I've already spoken with Barbara about leaving. She is sad to see me go but excited that Austin will finally be in a better mood.

It seems blue balls don't suit him.

I also didn't help matters by coming in all week wearing tight clothing. One day at lunch, I left my panties in his drawer. I watched him open the drawer and take them out while looking at me. I smiled at him and waved. He got up and slammed the door and then closed his blinds. I can only imagine what he did, but I don't think I'll ever get the panties back.

Then there was the day my shirt accidentally unbuttoned when I went to bring him files. It gapped opened so much, he could clearly see the sheer, cream-colored bra I was wearing, along with my nipples that were standing up to greet him. Oops, my bad. He actually snapped a pencil in half that time.

But nothing—nothing—beats my last day. I'm wearing a tight black skirt that clings to my body from my waist to right below my ass, where it then flares out with a ruffle. I wear lace-topped, thigh-high stockings.

Before I leave for the day, I walk into his office to ask him a few questions about the party we are attending tomorrow.

"So, what time should I get there?' I ask him, propping myself on the arm of the chair.

"I told everyone to get there at six. We have to be out front to do the red-carpet thing by eight, so I want to make sure everyone is on time." He tilts back in his chair.

"Perfect. I guess I'll see you there, then." I turn to leave and then stop. "Oh no, I think I have a tear in my stocking!" I say, looking over my shoulder at him watching me. "Right on the knee." I bend over, knowing full well that my skirt will rise just enough for him to see the border of lace stretched across the center of my thigh. He lets out a tortured groan and then a string of curses as I walk out the door. "See you tomorrow, Austin."

CHAPTER TWENTY-FOUR

Austin

I'm about to consult Google to find out if a man can die from blue balls when Lauren struts into my office asking questions about tomorrow. I'm almost tempted to close the door and fuck her on my desk.

All week, she has been torturing me. One day, she left her panties in my drawer. I slammed my door, drew the shades, and sat at my desk picturing her sitting on it, legs spread, in front of me, as I jerked off with them. I came all over them. Hard, too.

The next day, her shirt popped open, accidentally, giving me a perfect view of her tits in that sexy-as-fuck bra, her nipples hard and ready for me to bite and suck. That just reminded me of how incredibly responsive she is when I play with them. *Fuck me.*

Then the straw that broke the camel's back was right after she finished asking me the questions about the party. As she was walking out of my office, she bent over, and that fucking hot-as-hell skirt she had on rode up. She was wearing a fucking pair of thigh-highs and the tiniest pair of sheer panties. So tiny and sheer, I could see her pussy lips. *Motherfucker.*

I'm about to throw something across the room when John comes in, heading over to sit on the couch. "Hey there, man. I heard that someone got their period this week." He jokes with me just as Noah walks in.

"Jesus, did this week go slow or what? I didn't think it would ever end." He slaps John on the back and sits next to him on the couch. He looks over at me, then tilts his head and asks, "Are you sick?"

"He isn't sick. Lauren is holding her vagina hostage till he lets go of this whole 'I don't shit where I eat' bullshit," John explains.

"It's not bullshit," I snap at them both. "What if we have a good run and then she gets mad at me, we break up, and she sues me for sexual harassment?" I look at them both.

"What if you spend the rest of your life banging the best pussy of your life?" Noah fires back. "Listen, if you want, she can come work for me."

I sit up in my chair right away. "Not a fucking chance in hell. You've fucked every PA you've ever had."

"That was before. I'm a changed man. I went to the strip club yesterday to meet a client, and my dick didn't even twitch. In fact, he was bored. I think he might have even yawned." Noah looks down at his crotch.

John studies him. "No shit, you got the bug?"

Noah just shakes his head. "I did. By the way, I'm bringing her tomorrow." He leans back "She's so fucking hot. She can put her legs behind her head, man."

"I don't want to know that shit!" I yell. "That's Lauren's sister."

"She's not your sister." Noah turns to look back at John. "And she can hold them there." He raises his hand for a high five. Both of them have shit-eating grins stretched across their faces.

"Is Lauren bringing a date tomorrow?" John asks me.

"No," I snap, then think to myself that she fucking better not be bringing a date. But if she is, I have to know.

I pick up my phone and text her.

Are you coming alone tomorrow?
I'm hoping I'll be coming with you, but I'm not sure.

I throw my phone down. "Jesus, she's making my life impossible."

"Poor baby. Just fucking get over it. Have sex with her, work with her, and then I'll have a lot fewer complaints in my email." John gets up. "Now, if you bozos will excuse me, I'm going home to have sex with my wife. On the couch, because we can."

"You liar," Noah says. "Married people only fuck in a bed. Google it." He winks at John as he walks out.

"Let's go to the gym. You can work out your frustration there." Noah gets up. I do the same and follow him out. I spend the next three hours beating the shit out of a punching bag and working my body to near exhaustion.

Now, I'm in the car on the way to the party. I get there right before six, leaving my car at the valet. Walking the red carpet, I see the media setting up and wave at a couple of reporters I know. Opening the door, I walk in, and I'm speechless.

I see Scarlett, the event planner, walking up to me.

"So, what do you think?" she asks as I take in the room. There are dimly-lit chandeliers everywhere, casting the room in a sexy glow. White roses are placed around the entire space in mirrored vases. All the tables have a little lamp that looks like a martini glass is filled with little fake diamonds that are the lights. Once the overhead lights are turned off, they'll give an almost intimate lighting effect.

"It's really sexy." I watch the wait staff getting into their position.

Chris walks over to me, wearing a suit without a tie. "Didn't Scarlett do good?" he asks.

"She did." I look at the door and see John coming in. He's wearing a custom-made black suit with a black tie. Dani walks in wearing a black dress, followed by Barbara and Steven, who are both dressed to the nines.

"It's so beautiful," Barbara says. "This is my favorite one yet."

I look around taking in the booths. There are buckets set up at each one for bottle service. "You guys go reserve a booth now so we don't go crazy later."

When I turn back around, my heart skips a beat as I see Lauren walking in. She looks breathtaking.

She is wearing a coral-colored jumpsuit. It dips down dangerously low in the front and comes up to wrap around her neck, leaving her shoulders exposed. I'm watching her look around when I see the valet guy running back in, calling her name, and she turns around to greet him. With her hair tied up on top of her head, I can see that her back is bare all the way down to her waist. As if that isn't sexy enough, there is a slit on the side of each leg running up from her ankles to the tops of her thighs, giving a good view of her toned legs. She's got on a sexy-as-fuck pair of gold stilettos with fake diamonds on them that I would kill to have digging into my back later. A simple pair of diamond earrings finish her look.

When she walks over to us, I can see her pant legs swish around her with each step, giving me a peek of her legs. "Sorry I'm late, I took an Uber," she explains, and I rake my eyes over all of that exposed, silky skin.

I just stand here, taking her in. The need to grab her hand and claim her as mine is a war I'm internally waging with myself.

"Holy shit, Lauren, you look amazing," Dani exclaims when she comes back over to us after reserving a booth. "I love this color on you."

"Thank you so much. Oh, look, there's Barbara. I'm going to go say hello." She walks away, and we all watch her go. And we aren't the only ones, either. The wait staff has all taken notice of her. The bartender spots her saying hello to Barbara, and he makes a beeline over there, giving her a fake smile and talking to her. She tosses her head back and laughs at whatever he said, and my blood boils.

I make my way over to her side just in time to hear her order herself a lemon drop martini. "I'll have whiskey on ice," I tell him right before he walks away.

"Can I have a word please, Lauren?" I ask her.

"Sure, but I didn't get my drink yet. How about later?" she says while she talks to Barbara and ignores me. She stands next to Barbara, talking, so I lean on the bar next to her, hoping that me being this close is throwing her off her game.

The bartender puts the drinks on the bar in front of us.

"Shall we toast?" Lauren asks. "To new beginnings and to letting go." She smiles at Barbara, who winks at her and clinks her glass. Both of them sipping and smiling as I take my whiskey and down it in one shot.

"Picture time," Scarlett announces.

"Picture time?" Lauren asks next to me.

"We always take a group picture before the opening of the club for the wall," Barbara explains.

I grab her hand in mine, our fingers intertwining as I walk us over to the red carpet where the photographer is waiting.

She tries to shake her hand free, but I don't let her. I take my place in the middle, next to John. I let go of her hand, bending down to whisper in her ear, "Don't fucking move," I tell her through clenched teeth. "Not one fucking inch. Don't test me." She rolls her eyes at me.

We spend the next forty minutes snapping pictures. Finally done, we walk back inside and each grab a champagne glass, with which we toast our hard work.

I drink my glass watching Lauren watching me. I smile at her, watching her eyes dilate, knowing she wants me just as bad as I want her.

I walk over to her. "You look beautiful." I rub her cheek with my thumb. "Come home with me."

Her eyes on me are smiling. She steps closer to me, then her eyes go over my shoulder and she stills. Her face changes, her smile is gone, her spine is straight. "Jake?"

CHAPTER TWENTY-FIVE

Lauren

I knew showing up tonight dressed like this was going to cut him at his knees. I've never felt as sexy as I do in this outfit.

But I'm not the only one dressed to kill. Austin is in a custom-tailored navy blue suit and a crisp, stark white dress shirt with the top two buttons undone and no tie. Silver cufflinks rest at his wrists next to where his name is monogrammed and his silver Patek Philippe watch peeks out. Polished brown Ferragamos—what can I say, I'm a shoe girl—complete the whole package, and what a package he is.

I tried not to watch him from my spot at the bar, but I saw him heading my way out of the corner of my eye. When he grabbed my hand, intertwining our fingers, I knew I would be going home with him. Well, that and when he told me not to fucking move. I was almost tempted to move just to see what he would do.

Looking at him while we toasted, I was so proud of everything he did. I watch as he walks over to me. "You look beautiful," he tells me while he rubs my cheek with his thumb. "Come home with me." I step closer to him, ready to tell him I'd go anywhere with him. Smiling at him, I glance over his shoulder for one second, and that one second changes my night.

My smile fades, and my spine stiffens as anger rushes through me. "Jake?"

Jake walking in with Camilla on his arm brings me back a bit. I didn't attend many of his functions when we were married, because there was always something going on at home.

Austin turns to see what I'm staring at, watching Jake and Camilla walk toward us, his hand holding hers. "What the fuck?" he says under his breath.

I don't have a chance to tell him everything I need to.

"Hey, Lauren, what are you doing here?" Jake asks when they stop in front of me.

"Um…" The words stay lodged in my throat.

"She helped make tonight happen," Austin answers for me, putting his hand on the exposed skin at my lower back. "Austin Mackenzie." He offers his hand to shake Jake's.

"Jake Watson, Lauren's husband." He shakes Austin's hand.

"Ex," I say, gulping down the rest of my champagne. "Ex-husband." I look to Jake and then to Camilla. "Gabe's former teacher. Lots of exes in the room." I laugh nervously.

"Oh, wait." Jake snaps his fingers. "Are you the Austin who took the kids skating?"

Austin grabs champagne from a passing waiter and hands it to me before he places my empty glass back on the tray. "That would be me. We took the kids out last Friday. They had no school."

"Are you two dating?" Jake asks, surprised, his eyebrows going up.

I don't know how to answer this. We've never really discussed the status of our relationship. Having sex, yes, driving each other insane, yes. Dating, um… it's complicated. "We are," Austin states. "If you'll excuse us, I see someone we need to say hello to." When he grabs my hand, I nod at them and follow him wherever he takes me.

He walks over to a couple who just walked in the door. From the shouting that wafts in and the flashing cameras, I know it's someone important. "Cooper," Austin greets, raising his hand to him.

The couple walks over to us, and I can't help but stare at them. The man is huge and gorgeous, obviously not as gorgeous as Austin, but still mouth-droppingly handsome. Austin lets go of my hand to shake his friend's and bringing him in to hug him. "Asshole," Austin says. "Good to see you," Cooper replies with an easy smile at him.

"Thanks for coming."

"Wouldn't miss it for the world. Plus, we get to spend the night in the hotel, where I plan to take full advantage of Parker." I look to the woman at his side who just rolls her eyes.

"Please, he's all talk. Lately, he falls asleep before the twins." She laughs at her husband.

"I'll show you falling asleep," he tells her, then turns to look at me. "This man has no manners. Cooper Stone." He reaches out for my hand. "This is my wife, Parker Stone."

Austin laughs at him. "This is the guy I used to play with in college. He's now retired and playing Mr. Mom."

"And loving every fucking second of it." He leans down to kiss Parker's lips.

"So, how did you two meet?" Parker looks at me.

"I'm his PA." I take another sip from the champagne.

"Are you the one who turned his testicles the size of boulders?" she asks me, laughing. "I saw the picture."

I grab the glass with both my hands, laughing as well. "How is it everyone saw this picture but me?"

"Oh, I can send it to you. I think it's Cooper's screen saver." She laughs at Austin, who is groaning next to me.

"I'm going to fucking kill Noah." He puts his hands in his pockets. I don't get a chance to say anything else, because there is more yelling coming in from outside, and the camera flashes are going crazy again.

"I guess Matthew has arrived," Parker says to the group, and we don't have to wait long before the door opens and in comes Matthew.

He's got black hair that is parted on the side, a bit longer on top and shorter on the sides. His slim-cut black suit is cut perfectly for his frame. His dark gray shirt is paired with a shiny black tie. With the way his jacket hangs open, showing off his muscular chest, it's plain to see that he spends a fair amount of time in the gym. "Matthew!" Parker shouts, waving him over. He looks over his shoulder and sees Parker waving. He gives her a big smile and turns to guide himself and the woman who is by his side over to us.

They start to head this way, zig-zagging through the crowd, which has grown, and occasionally stopping to say hello to people on the way.

"Hey, Mom, Coop," he greets them both with a hug and kiss for Parker. "Where is Karrie?" He looks around for whom I assume is the woman he walked in with.

The blond woman is talking to a man who is kissing her hand and laughing with her. She looks amazing in her figure-skimming white dress. The top is off-the-shoulders with sexy little sleeves that cling to her biceps, and the dress hugs her in all the right places as it tapers down her thighs to stop just above her knees. Her thick hair hangs loose around her bare shoulders. Matthew spots her and walks right up to her, grabbing her hand, completely unfazed that the other guy is still holding her other hand.

Right before they get to us, she pulls him to a stop and says something to him. He leans down and kisses her on the mouth, and it's not just a peck either. No, that's a kiss one gives their lover, the kind of kiss that you feel all the way down to your soul. When he finally lets her go, he takes her hand and closes the distance to us.

"Well, that settles that," Cooper murmurs as he sips the beer that the waiter just delivered to him.

When they make it to us, Parker smiles at the girl and greets her. "Karrie, you look beautiful."

Cooper looks her up and down and smiles at Matthew. "Good luck, son." Matthew glares at him.

"Austin, this is my girlfriend, Karrie." Matthew pulls her into his side with a hand around her waist.

"I'm not his girlfriend. I'm his chaperone." She holds out a hand to Austin and then to me. Austin and Cooper both bust out laughing at Matthew's glare at her.

"I'll show you a chaperone." Matthew stares at her, and she glares back at him.

"Good luck finding me," she quips. "I don't have to be with you until next week." She tries to pry his fingers off her hip.

With that, he laughs and grabs a beer off the tray from the waiter who is walking past us. "Try to run. I dare you," he challenges her. "Remember the last time you tried that." He takes a pull of his beer. The memory must be something, because her cheeks turn pink.

"Lauren, do you dance?" Parker asks when Rihanna's "This is What You Came For" comes on. I nod my head and then down the rest of my champagne, handing the empty glass to Austin.

"I love to dance," I say, while the guys all groan.

"Let's go get a booth," Matthew says. "The dance floor looks cramped."

"I'm going to dance. Who is coming with?" Karrie heads for the dance floor, not even acknowledging Matthew's comment. Parker follows her, and I follow Parker.

The three of us find a spot on the dance floor, where we are joined by Dani. The four of us are moving to the beat of the music, hands in the air, hips shaking. Singing along with the music as it changes from one song to another.

I don't know how long we are out here, but I can't help but notice that a group of guys has circled us and are trying to cut into our group. The lights dim, with the glow of the chandeliers softly lighting the room.

I look around to see where Austin is, and I don't have to look far. He's standing at the railing, looking down at us with Cooper on his left and a woman hanging on his right side. She is wearing a red one-sleeved lace dress that is very tight and very short. Her hands are wrapped around his arm, while she whispers in his ear.

"I'm going to get something to drink," I inform the girls and then head over to the bar. I stand at the side of the bar, trying to get the bartender's attention, but there are so many people.

"What do you think you're doing?" I hear from my side. I turn to see Jake there, alone. I look left to right and try to find Camilla.

"I'm getting myself a drink." I lean one arm on the bar to take the weight off my shoes.

"I meant, what do you think you're doing with that guy?" His hands go to his pockets, and it's then I see that he's gained weight around his stomach.

"I really don't understand your question, which is none of your business for that matter." The bartender finally comes over.

"What can I get you?" he asks.

"Two shots of tequila." I look to Jake. "What are you having?" He shakes his head no to the bartender.

"You can't possibly be serious about this guy. He has player written all over him," Jake chides, while the bartender puts the shots down in front of me.

I down a shot, pressing my lips together as the liquid burns all the way down. I look back at Jake. "You can't judge a book by its cover,

Jake. After all, you didn't look like a cheater, yet that is what you are." His mouth tightens into an angry, grim line. I take the next shot and tell him, "You don't get a say about who I date. Not now, not ever." I look back at the railing and see that Austin isn't there anymore, and neither is the woman who was hanging all over him. My heart sinks, and my stomach is burning with devastation.

Camilla chooses that moment to find him. "I couldn't find you anywhere." She leans into him and kisses him, putting her hand on his face. The big round diamond can't be missed.

I look at them both, while the bartender places another shot in front of me. I quickly down that one before looking back at them. "Congratulations on the engagement." I point to her hand. "Excuse me," I say, trying to walk past them, but Jake stops me by grabbing my arm. I raise a brow in question as my eyes look from his hand on my arm to his face.

I don't get a chance to say anything further before we hear a roar from behind me. "Get your fucking hand off her before I break every single bone in it." I look over my shoulder to see Austin's angry face glaring at Jake.

Jake loosens his grip on my arm, and I snatch it back. "Good luck, Camilla. You know what they say, once a cheater, always a cheater."

And with that parting shot, I walk away from the three of them to make my way to the bathroom.

CHAPTER TWENTY-SIX

Austin

We stand upstairs above our booth, looking down at the four women dancing, the four of us watching closely.

What the women don't realize is that they are attracting attention—a lot of attention. Cooper is next to me, his arms crossed over his chest and his eyes narrowed practically to slits. Matthew stands next to him, growling every ten seconds, and I wouldn't be surprised if steam started pouring out of his ears. The only one calm about all this is John, who is leaning against the railing, looking at us. "Suckers." We all turn to glare at him.

Cooper leans forward. "Um, you mind explaining what you're doing with Karrie?" he asks, turning his head to Matthew.

"Nope. She's mine." He sips his water. "She's just fighting the inevitable."

"She left you once. What makes you think she won't try it again?" Cooper asks.

"I handcuffed her to my bed for four days." He smiles at the memory. "I dare her to try it again."

"You know that's kidnapping, right?" Cooper grins.

"Would you let Mom leave?" he asks him, knowing full well that he wouldn't even let Parker leave for four hours. "Just get on a plane and take off for God knows where?"

"I hope you used comfortable cuffs." Cooper laughs as he looks back down at his woman.

"Exactly," Matthew states. "Now, I'm going back down there, because I've given her enough space." He walks down the stairs and onto the dance floor, going straight to her. He moves in right behind her, his hands landing on her hips as he brings her closer to him. She doesn't move until he whispers something in her ear, then her arms move up his chest and around his neck.

"Austin." I look to the right and see Serena coming up the stairs. "I've been looking everywhere for you." She kisses me on the cheek and holds onto my arm.

"I've been here all night." I look down at the dance floor. The girls are still going at it, but Matthew has taken off with Karrie.

"Isn't it fabulous? We did it, we've got another hit." She digs her claws into my arm, while I try to shake them loose. "We could rule the world, in and out of bed," she purrs. "Don't you think?"

I shake my head at her audacity and huff out an annoyed laugh as I firmly peel her hand from my arm. "Serena, that's never going to happen. Ever." I look down and see that Lauren is heading to the bar.

I walk away from Serena and down the stairs. I head in the direction of the bar, talking to different people on the way down, thanking those who have showed up. I see Noah and Kaleigh walking in.

"This place is insane." Noah looks around. "Congrats, man." He shakes my hand.

"Your shirt isn't even buttoned properly," I point out to him.

Kaleigh shrugs her shoulders. "I can't help it if he dresses like a guy on GQ. Where is Lauren?" She looks over my head.

"Oh, shit. Is that Jake and the home wrecker?" She looks toward the bar.

I don't even wait to hear what she says next. I turn to make my way over to Jake and Lauren when I see her try to walk away as he stops her by grabbing her arm. My blood boils, my hands clench into fists at my sides. "Get your fucking hand off her before I break every single bone in it," I growl at him, my voice loud and angry, causing the people around us to turn and look.

Lauren jerks her arm away from him. She looks at Camilla and says, "Good luck, Camilla. You know what they say, once a cheater, always a cheater." Then she turns and moves through the crowd toward the bathroom.

"I know you're just playing around with her," Jake states as he steps in front of me.

"I knew you were stupid. I just didn't think you were a fucking idiot, too." I look from him to his girlfriend, who holds his one hand in both of hers. "You not only downgraded, but you got the cheapest knock-off on the shelf." I turn to Camilla. "I was waiting to see if you remembered me, Camilla. I wasn't sure if you would. But I'm sure you remember Max?" Her face pales the minute I mention my good friend's name. "He's doing well. You know, after you fucked him out of house and home. Made him lose everything, and for what?" I snarl at her and then look back to Jake. "If you think you're the first student's father she's fucked, think again. You're just this year's model." I glance at her in disgust. "I bet she's already fucking someone else right now. After all, the game is over for her. You gave up everything. The thrill is gone."

I scan the room, my eyes going to the last place I saw Lauren. "She hides a second cell phone. Max found it in her tampon box." I leave the fool with that tidbit and head to the bathroom.

I wait outside the bathroom for two minutes, or maybe it is two seconds, before I knock on the door. "Coming in," I shout, walking in and nodding hello at the girl handing out paper towels. Lauren is at the sink washing her hands. "We need to talk," I tell her while she looks at me in the mirror, her mouth hanging open.

She shakes the water off her hands and then grabs the towels from the attendant. "I'm not really in the mood to talk right now." She wipes her hands, throws the towels away, and then walks out.

She gets out the door, and I snap into action. I grab her hand and drag her the other way toward the office. "Austin, really," she says as I hear her heels clicking against the floor behind me.

I open the door to the office I have used in the past to discuss the floor plans, then close the door behind us and lock it.

She walks into the room and to the window that overlooks the whole club. "I'm really not in the mood right now, Austin." I stare at her. "I honestly just want to go home." I walk over to the window, standing next to her while she looks out.

I spot Jake and Camilla fighting right where I left them. "She is called

'Camilla the Cunt' in my circle of friends. One of my best friends, Max, married to a great woman, a father of three. She taught their oldest son." I see her look at me, so I turn to look at her. "He's an idiot."

"It doesn't matter." She shrugs her shoulders. "It really doesn't matter. If it wasn't Camilla, it could have been someone else. Who knows? And with you"—she laughs out—"I am so out of my league with you. I have kids, I'm a mom. I'm not cut out for this." She points to the dance floor. "This is your world. That blonde is your world." She laughs humorlessly and turns to walk away. "I guess that policy was the right call after all." She starts to walk away as my hand snaps out to hold hers, my fingers folding into hers. We both look down at our hands, but she slowly pulls hers away. "I can't do this."

"Are you about done now?" I ask her. "I'm a lot of things, Lauren, but I'm not a liar or a fucking cheat. I want you." I close the distance between us, running the back of my fingers from her shoulder to her elbow. "Only you. You drive me absolutely fucking crazy, and you keep me on my fucking toes. You make me want everything, and I've never wanted everything. I've only wanted me. Now, I want you and everything that comes with you. I want the dinners at the table. I want laughter. I want the kids' banter. Fuck, I even want Rachel calling me Asshat, but not all the time." I chuckle as I see her smile. "I want more Sundays like the one we had when we woke up together."

I pull her to me as I wrap my arms around her, placing a kiss where her shoulder meets her neck. I feel the shiver that runs through her in response. "Austin," she whispers, her chest rising and falling with her nerves. "I would really hate to cut off your dick," she says quietly, "but I will. If that doesn't work, Kaleigh will finish the job."

I push her against the door, taking her mouth before she says anything else. The need to taste her more powerful than my next breath. My mouth devours hers, while her mouth matches my need with her own.

Our tongues are tangling together when her hands go straight to my belt, my hands going for her ass.

I leave her mouth, running my lips down her neck to the plunging V at her chest. Pushing the material off her breast, I bend to take her nipple into my mouth. I suck on it deeply, and her head falls back against the door, her hands stopping their assault of my belt.

"Austin," she moans, lifting a leg to my hip, my hand holding her leg then roaming up it and dipping into the slit to slide along the back of her thigh. I glide my hand all the way up to cup her bare ass.

"You better be wearing panties," I warn her before giving her nipple a soft bite. Releasing her leg, I squat down in front of her, both hands roaming up the backs of her legs until they get to her ass.

"Oops, my bad. I guess I forgot to put panties on." Her breathing turns a little deeper as my hands squeeze her ass.

"Fuck," I hiss, realizing that this whole time, she has had nothing on under this hot-as-hell outfit. I stand up just as she reaches behind her neck, unclips the top, and in one swoosh, the material glides down her body until she's standing in front of me, gloriously naked, except for her gold shoes.

She cups her breasts in her hands and asks, "You ready to drop the whole 'don't shit where you eat' bullshit?" Her eyes close as she rolls her nipples between her fingers. I would give away my soul right now to touch her. Her tongue darts out to lick her lips, and one hand moves down her body as she buries it in herself.

My hands are in my hair, pulling at the strands, as my cock jerks against my pants as if to question why he's not already buried in her. "Fuck. Fine," I give in as I start undoing my pants.

"You would do that for me? For us?" she asks.

"Anything," I tell her then place my forehead on hers. "Anything for you," I whisper, knowing I would give her the fucking moon if I could.

"Good, I quit." She smiles. "Now, how about you show me how much you've missed me?" I pull my pants down to my thighs, reaching into my pocket to grab my wallet and a condom. I cover myself quickly, but it still takes longer than I want it to.

I pick her up. "Really sorry, but this is going to be fast. I promise you I'll make it up to you," I tell her as I plunge my cock into her and fuck her, hard and fast, against the door. No talking is necessary as our bodies, heaving with our need for each other, do the talking for us.

I pound into her over and over again until her pussy finally clamps down on me and she yells out my name. I stroke into her roughly before I plant myself all the way in her and follow her over the edge into orgasm. She's wrapped around me with her arms around my neck and her legs around my waist. My head is resting on her shoulder as I catch my breath. "Tell me you'll come home with me."

She giggles. "Can I say no?"

"Try it, I dare you," I challenge her right before there is knocking at the door.

"Austin, are you in there?" The whiny voice calls from the other side.

"Fucking Serena," I mumble. I place Lauren down on her feet, where she picks up her outfit, sliding herself into it, and fastens it at the neck. I take care of the condom and buckle up. I drop a kiss on her lips right before the door swings open and Serena stands there. "Hey, the door must have been stuck. Serena, this is my girlfriend, Lauren." I grab her and bring her close to me. "Lauren, this is the owner of this place, Serena."

CHAPTER TWENTY-SEVEN

Lauren

The door swings open, and the brunette from earlier comes in. "Hey, the door must have been stuck. Serena, this is my girlfriend, Lauren," Austin introduces, curling an arm around me and bringing me in closer to him. "Lauren, this is the owner of this place, Serena."

I smile at her. "It's a pleasure to meet you."

She looks me up and down, the disdain obvious in her expression. "Hmmm, likewise." She turns her attention to Austin. "We haven't chatted or taken pictures yet."

"Sorry, Serena, but we have to go. We took pictures earlier, and I'll make sure that Scarlett sends them to you," Austin says as he takes my hand and leads us out.

We make our way back to the booth that was reserved for us. Cooper is sitting there with Parker on his lap, John and Dani are sitting next to each other on one side, and Noah and Kaleigh are seated opposite them on the other side of the booth.

"Hey," Kaleigh greets when she sees me. "Where have you been?" she asks, leaning over Noah to look at me. They slide over in the booth, giving us space to sit down. Austin sits first and then pulls me down on his lap. Kaleigh leans in and whispers conspiratorially in my ear, "You totally just had sex!"

I gasp loudly and look at her, denying it by shaking my head no. "Oh, yes, you did. You are glowing and have the 'I've just been fucked' face. Trust me, I know that look."

Everyone is talking amongst themselves and the music is loud so no one is really paying attention to our conversation. "You're crazy," I tell her.

"I'm starving," I say loudly, and everyone agrees.

"Pizza?" Dani suggests, standing up. "Let's go." We all get up to make our way outside.

I hold Austin's hand as we leave the club. Some fans have spotted Cooper, and hc goes over to them to take some pictures. While he's doing that, the rest of us climb into a huge black party bus that Scarlett has ordered for guests who drink and don't want to drive home.

"I can't wait to take off these shoes," Parker whines, propping her feet up in Cooper's lap.

"You can wear flip-flops tomorrow when we go skating with Austin," he tells her.

"Skating?" I ask.

"Oh, yeah. I was telling them about Gabe, and since Matthew is in town and wants to run drills with Cooper, we are all meeting at the rink at noon."

"Oh, that sounds like fun. Can I come?" John asks from his side of the bus.

"Can you skate?" Austin asks.

"Well, not like you guys, but I can keep up," he states as Dani laughs out loud.

"Honey, I love you dearly, but you can't skate." Dani leans over and kisses his cheek.

"I'm coming," Noah announces from his seat.

They talk and make plans for the next day, while I take it all in. We spend two hours at the pizza place, laughing over their stories from the 'old days.'

Austin asks me, "Your place or mine?"

"I'm going to Noah's. So you can go home and have loud monkey sex without me hearing it." Kaleigh runs up behind Noah, who has already flagged down a cab.

"Let's swing by my house and grab some clothes for tomorrow," Austin suggests, yelling at Noah to wait for us.

We wave good-bye to everyone as we cram into the cab. "You live near each other?" I ask.

"I couldn't leave my boo," Noah jokes.

We pull up on their street, a chic, modern neighborhood, where all the houses are three stories high.

We get out of the cab. I look at Austin's house. It's white with a brown, wooden door. There is a huge window above the door, trimmed in black, and narrow, long rectangular windows are on either side of it.

When he pushes the door open and the lights come on, I take in the modern, masculine space that looks like it could be in a magazine. "You live here?" I ask him, walking into the all-white sunken living room. The back wall is the showpiece of the room with its floor-to-ceiling windows.

"I live here." He laughs. "Want to come see the upstairs?" He holds his hand out for me to take it.

We head up the stairs, which are black and look like they are held together with wire. "Should I take off my shoes?" I ask him when we make it to his room and I see the plush white carpet. His bed sits in the middle of the room, overlooking a wall of windows. He walks in, touching something on the wall so that the lights turn on. Walking further into the room, he opens the door to his walk-in closet, except it's the size of a bedroom. "Jesus, how many suits can one person own?"

"Should I ask about your shoe collection now?" He turns to me while grabbing his bag from the shelf, throwing in a couple of pairs of pants, then going to the wall that has drawers, where he opens a couple and pulls out socks and shirts. "Should I pack boxers?" he asks with a smirk.

"I don't know. Should I go to work on Monday without panties?" I smile back at him and yawn.

"You know, we could stay here and then go back to your place tomorrow." He shrugs off his jacket and kicks off his shoes, pulling his shirt out of his pants and unbuttoning it from top to bottom before shrugging the shirt off and throwing it in the basket in the corner. His pants are next to go. "Sleep with me in my bed?" I look back at the huge bed with its thick, white covers and think that it looks like a cloud. "I want you in my bed. I want to roll over when you're not here and still smell you on the pillow." I take the pins out of my hair, letting it fall down to my shoulders.

"Are you going to do dirty, dirty things to me?" I ask him, unclipping my outfit so it falls to the floor. I kick it over to join his pants. "I just need to take off my shoes." I walk out of the closet to the bed, bending down at the waist to unclip my shoes when I hear him groan behind me. "Like the view?"

"Change of plans." He picks me up and throws me on the bed. "I want to feel those heels digging into my back when I fuck you hard."

"Well, since you asked so nicely"—I spread my legs wide—"let's put those marks on you."

By the time we finish, I think I see the sun coming up, my body is well used, aching in places that I will feel all day. My shoes are gone, long ago thrown somewhere in the room.

I turn to look out the window, Austin curling around me, where we both fall into a deep sleep.

The alarm next to his bed wakes us up, both of us snuggled under his blankets that really do feel like a cloud.

"We need to get to your house." Austin kisses my neck while he cups my breast.

"I need to call Jake and ask him to bring Gabe early." I yawn, blinking my eyes to stay awake.

I get up from the bed to call Jake, who sounds as tired as I am, and he doesn't argue with me about dropping the kids off early.

I borrow a pair of his basketball shorts that are so big they go down to the middle of my calf, even rolled at the waist, and a blue Hugo Boss t-shirt. My shoes dangle in my hands as I make my way from his car to my front door.

Thinking that this is what they call the walk of shame, I look over my shoulder at Austin. He is dressed in blue jeans, a tight t-shirt, and his aviator glasses. He didn't shave this morning, so his face is covered in light stubble. The thought that there is nothing shameful about spending the night with him crosses my mind.

"Remember the last time we were at this door?" Austin asks while gripping my hips. I, of course, move fast before my neighbors get the chance to experience a replay.

I unlock the door, walking straight up the stairs to my room. "I need a shower so bad." I dump the clothes in my hands on the bed. Austin is already without his shirt by the time I turn around. "What are you doing?"

"Conserving energy," he answers while he picks me up and tosses me over his shoulder.

The shower lasts until the water coming out feels like ice pellets hitting our skin, my legs are limp, and I need a nap. Having awesome sex is freaking exhausting.

We are both now dressed and downstairs having coffee together. He sits at my table, reading the Sunday paper, while I flip through the living section. Every now and again, he takes my hand and kisses it.

It's almost as if we have been doing this forever. The doorbell rings, and I get up to answer it. "I think the kids are home," I tell him, getting up to answer the door.

Opening the door, I'm tackled by Gabe and Rachel, who run to me.

"Mom, is it true we are skating with *the* Cooper Stone and his son, Matthew?" Gabe rushes out without taking a breath.

"It is. Austin is friends with him." I ruffle his hair and kiss him. "He's in the kitchen. You can go say thank you."

"Sweet!" He runs into the kitchen, yelling.

Rachel has her head on my stomach and her hand around my hips. "I need a nap," she says.

I look up at Jake, who looks like death. He's wearing a baseball hat, and his face is a greenish pale and unshaven. He looks ragged. "Why are you so tired?" I ask her.

"The babysitter put her to bed at one a.m." Jake takes off his hat to scratch his head then puts it back on.

"Okay." I look over at him standing there. "Go put your things away while I talk to Dad."

I watch as she heads into the kitchen and then hear her greet Austin in her special way. "Hey, Asshat, you're here." I laugh quietly when I hear giggling coming from Rachel and then Austin telling her he's going to tickle her till she gets his name right.

I look back at Jake, who I'm assuming has heard that Austin is here. "You okay?" I ask him, my hand on the doorknob as I lean on it.

"Camilla and I have ended our engagement." He looks at me and then to the side.

I don't say anything, because what can I say at this point?

"I'm so sorry, Lauren, for everything. I ruined it." He looks back at me. "I ruined everything, and for what? For a woman who collects fathers."

"I don't know what you want me to tell you, Jake." I cross my arms over my chest.

"I was a fool. She played me." He takes his hat off again to scratch his head.

"You wouldn't be the first," Austin says from behind me. "Sorry to interrupt." He puts his hand around the back of my neck and kisses my temple. "The kids are getting ready."

"I should go," Jake says. "Tell the kids to call me later." He walks away from us with his head hanging down.

I wrap my hands around Austin's waist, while he uses his foot to close the door. "Do I have anything to worry about?" he asks while hugging me. My face rests against his chest, listening to his heart beating faster than normal.

"Not in this lifetime," I tell him honestly. "No matter what happens between us, Jake and I are over."

"Okay." He squeezes me.

"Asshat, can I do snow angels again?" Rachel yells from upstairs, her voice coming closer.

I hide my face so she doesn't see me laughing, then I turn around. "Rachel, it's Austin."

"I know dat, Mom." She's coming down the stairs, chanting, "Asstin, Asstin Asstin."

I continue laughing and so does Austin. "Well, it's better than Asshat."

Half an hour later, we walk into the arena and see Cooper standing in workout clothes and chatting with a bald man, laughing at whatever they are talking about.

"Look what the cat dragged in," Austin says to Craig as he moves in to hug the old man.

"I couldn't miss my two best boys on the ice again." He looks at both Cooper and Austin.

"Hey," Cooper greets Gabe, who is standing next to me, gawking shamelessly. "You must be Gabe. I heard you're really good." He ruffles his hair. Gabe continues to stare and has still not said anything.

I nudge him with my hip. "Um. You're Cooper Stone," he whispers, and everyone laughs.

Cooper laughs, too, and is about to reply when he looks over at Rachel. "Do you skate, too, or are you just a princess?"

"I'm a princess, and I only skate if I can make snow angels." Rachel smiles.

Parker walks in with Matthew and Karrie following her.

"Hey, guys," she greets us as she goes to Cooper's side. "Who are these guys?" she asks me.

"These are my children," I say, smiling at her. "This is Gabe, who, believe or not, never stops talking." I hug him sideways. "And this is my girl, Rachel."

"She's a beauty." Parker smiles at me in return. Rachel leaves my side to go tap Matthew's leg. He stops talking to Karrie and smiles at her before squatting down in front of her. "Hey there, Princess."

"Will you be my boyfriend?" Rachel asks, while I gasp out loud and Austin groans beside me.

"Um," Matthew mumbles.

"Rachel, what are you doing?" I question, going to her.

"Well, Auntie Kay has Noah as her boyfriend, and you have Asshat." Cooper bursts out laughing. She looks at Austin and smiles. "Sorry, Asstin. So, I want one, too, and I want him." Rachel points her thumb at Matthew, who is in stitches.

"I would really, really like to be your boyfriend, but Karrie is my girlfriend, and it wouldn't be fair to her."

"Oh, that's totally okay. I give him to you," Karrie says to Rachel. "No take backs, either." Cooper and Parker are now laughing even harder.

Matthew stands up and glares at Karrie. "I'll show you no take backs later." His tone is fierce, but Karrie looks at him and then down at her nails. "Can't. I'm busy."

"You're busy, huh?" he mocks. "Really? With no phone, no car, no purse, no wallet?" He smiles at her.

"Matthew," Parker whispers. "You didn't."

"He must have lost the handcuffs," Cooper chimes in. "Okay, why don't we go get ready to skate?"

"How about the girls go out for cupcakes and coffee?" I ask them.

"Is Noah coming?" Cooper asks while walking to the rooms in the back.

"I would love to go for coffee," Karrie says. "You guys can be my getaway."

"You can run, but know that I'll always catch your ass and drag you back," Matthew warns with a wink, then turns and jogs into the back.

"That man is a..." Karrie stutters. "He's a...he's a..."

"He's an asshat," Rachel helps her out, smiling at me and then Parker and Karrie, making everyone laugh.

"Okay, babe." Austin kisses my lips. "Come back, and for the love of god, whatever you do, make sure you bring Karrie back with you."

I look at Karrie, who looks like she is about to blow steam out of her ears, just like in the cartoons. Before she can explode, Parker goes up to her, seemingly averting that crisis. "Honey, I'm so, so sorry." With that, we all head out to go have chocolate cupcakes and coffee.

CHAPTER TWENTY-EIGHT

Austin

We spend three hours doing drills and practicing stick handling. We play a two-on-two game, since Noah never showed up.

Matthew shows Gabe little tricks, and I have to give it to him; he soaks in every word, following up Matthew's instructions to a T and getting into it right away, hungry for more. When we call it a day, he actually groans and moans.

Craig is there when we skate off the ice. "That boy, with a little bit of coaching, could be out of this world. He's a natural." He looks at Gabe. "I got one more left in me." He looks from Gabe to me.

"What does that mean?" Gabe asks, taking off his helmet and spitting out his mouth guard.

"He coached Cooper and me. Now he wants to get his hands on you." I watch his face turn from confusion to awe.

"Can I?" he asks me. "You think you can talk to Mom?"

"I think we could talk to her about it," I say to him while I whip my jersey off, throwing it into the bag that holds all my equipment.

Gabe finishes before us and goes back to help Craig clean the ice on the Zamboni.

"Kid has the itch," Cooper says, unwrapping the tape from his legs. "Where is the father in all this?" Cooper knows all about being a stepfather.

"He's around." I shrug. "He cheated on her with the kid's teacher. Found out she's Camilla the Cunt." I unwrap my legs also.

"Holy shit, no way!" Cooper shouts. "You think you're ready for this?" He knows I don't have any experience with kids.

"I know that with her come them; they're a package deal. The kids are easy. It's the ex I'm not sure I can deal with," I finally voice my fear. "He broke up with Camilla, so now he's free. What's to say he won't try to get her back? They don't just have a past, they have kids. Can I even compete with that?"

Cooper throws his ball of tape in the garbage. "Oh, I know what you mean. When I met Parker, her ex was always away. The minute he spotted us together, all of a sudden he had second thoughts." He looks at Matthew to see if he is listening. Matthew is listening, and he just nods his head and agrees with him. "But I knew that the minute I found out she had kids, I didn't give a shit. I wanted her, all of her."

"How do you compete, though?"

"You don't, you be you," Matthew adds from his side. "As long as Gabe sees that you treat his mom well, you make her laugh, and she isn't sad anymore, well, that's all you really need to do." He smiles at Cooper.

I nod my head and think about everything while I get undressed and check my phone, seeing Noah texted me.

Sorry I missed today! Two words, my mother and Kaleigh.
Oh, Jesus! Is everyone okay?
Let's just say no more naked yoga in the living room.
I don't even know what to say to that.
There's nothing to say.

We get dressed, each of us grabbing our bags to head out. "Okay, buddy, let's go," I tell Gabe as he walks out in front of me.

"Shit," Matthew says. "They took the car."

"It's okay. I have Lauren's, and I can drive you guys back to the hotel." I open the trunk. "It really is a bus." I wink at Gabe, and he just smiles and drinks the chocolate milk he got from Craig.

The minute I turn on the ignition, the sounds of "Let it Go" fill the car, and Cooper and Matthew both groan. "I take it you guys know this song?"

"Why is it playing?" Matthew yells from the back, putting his hands over his ears.

"Because it's jammed inside the player and Mom didn't have it checked out yet," Gabe explains, his head moving to the beat of the music. "Dad used to do all that."

I look at Cooper, who raises his eyebrows at me. My eyes go from him to the road, letting everything sink in.

We drop Matthew and Cooper off at their hotel, and a couple of fans notice them and come up to ask them to take pictures. We say good-bye with a promise to see each other soon.

Once I turn onto the street and pull into the driveway, I jump out, grabbing my bag, while Gabe grabs his. I dump my bag into my truck, and then inside the house.

Music and the smells of something delicious cooking flow through the house, greeting us as we walk in. Pink's song "So What" is playing, and whatever is cooking smells amazing. I walk into the kitchen and see that Rachel is at the table doing some sort of homework, while Lauren is at the stove cooking.

"Hey," I greet, coming up behind her and wrapping my arms around her waist.

"Hey there. How was hockey?" she asks, stirring the tomato sauce she is making.

"Good. Great, actually. Craig wants to coach him," I tell her while she tastes it and lowers the temperature to let it simmer.

"Really?" She turns to drape her arms around my neck. "That's exciting," she says as she kisses my chin.

"Mooommm, I need help with math," Rachel groans.

"Coming," she answers. "I have to do homework. Are you going to stay for dinner?" She smiles. I think back to the bag I packed this morning and left on my bed.

"No." I smile. "I'm pretty beat."

Her smile slowly falls, but she replaces it right away with a forced one. "Oh, yeah, of course."

She lets go of me and moves to the table, my body missing her touch instantly. I watch her at the table, sitting down, explaining the math to Rachel. I watch her and think to myself, *Can I do this?*

"Okay, I'm going to head out," I say to her. She nods her head, getting up to walk me to the door.

"Are you okay?" I sense that her demeanor has changed.

"Yeah, I'm good. Just busy. It's Sunday, so we have to finish homework and stuff. Nothing you would know." Her last comment hits me straight in the gut. I lean down, kissing her on the lips, a soft kiss, a fast one. Totally different than I wanted.

"Mom, I got it!" Rachel yells again.

"I have to get back to her." She opens the door, and I walk out. I get in the car and pull out, looking back at the door, hoping to see her there, but instead finding it closed. I don't know why that pisses me off so much.

I take the long way home, trying to clear my mind.

I see that Noah's car isn't there, so I go straight to my door, opening it and letting myself in. There is nothing there to greet me. No noise, no music, nothing but silence.

It was something I used to crave. Now, I don't know what the fuck it is.

I throw my keys on the table by the door, taking off my shoes and walking to the fridge. It's empty. I slam it shut and grab the take-out menus from the drawer. I go through them, wondering what I want to eat. I know what I want to eat. I want to eat pasta at the table with Lauren and her kids.

Throwing the menus back into the drawer, I open the freezer and take out a frozen pizza, throwing it into the oven.

I walk over to the couch, grabbing the remote and turning the television on for some background noise. This is my life, the empty, the quiet. This is what I wanted, right? I never had ties, because I didn't want them. But two days with her and her kids, and it's something I'm rethinking.

The oven beeps, letting me know my pizza is ready. Getting up, I walk into the kitchen, my breathing and the low noise of the television the only sounds in the house. I eat the pizza alone, in the kitchen, leaning against the counter by myself.

I throw half the pizza away, thoughts of Lauren and how her dinner was so totally different than mine crowding my mind.

Turning off all the lights downstairs, I walk upstairs straight for my bedroom, where the unmade bed greets me. The pillow she slept on still has her indent. I throw my shirt in the basket next to the bathroom door and head to the shower.

By the time I've showered and shaved, it's almost eight-thirty. Grabbing my phone, I send her a text.

Hey

I sit in bed waiting for her to answer. Laying my head on the pillow next to hers, I hold it close to me. Her smell surrounds me, the memories of last night playing in my head.

After ten minutes of waiting, I text her again.

I miss you!

I'm giving her ten minutes, and then I'm just going to call her. I close my eyes waiting for her, resting my eyes, but I fall asleep. The next thing I know, my alarm is ringing for me to get up.

I look at my phone and see that Lauren texted me back.

Hey, sorry, I was giving Rachel a bath.
I miss you, too!
Okay, I guess you fell asleep. I'll call you tomorrow from work.
Eek! I'm working with Noah.

I blink my eyes a couple of times and then text her back.

Good morning. Fell asleep waiting for your text. Are you really going to work for Noah?

I toss my phone aside while I go into the bathroom and splash my face with water. Grabbing the phone again, I go downstairs, where I start my morning routine. It's still as silent as it was last night, so I turn on the television. The voices of the CNN anchors fill the silence while the coffee brews.

The phone rings in my hand, and I look down to see Lauren's number. "Hey," I answer, smiling.

"Hey. I thought it would be faster if I called you," she says, and I hear her moving around in the background.

"Did you sleep well?" I ask her, thinking about how much I would have loved to wake her up with my face between her legs.

"Yeah, I was exhausted." I hear her call out a five-minutes warning to the kids. "Sorry, it's hectic in the morning."

"I can imagine. Are you really going to work with Noah?"

"Um, well, seeing as I'm due there in an hour, the answer to that would be yes." She chuckles.

"You don't need to do this," I tell her while I pour myself a cup of coffee and take a sip. I can hear Gabe in the background asking where his lunch is.

"I'm doing this, so we don't kill each other." She moves the phone from her mouth to tell Gabe she already packed his lunch in his bag. "Sorry. I have to go. Rachel is not dressed yet. The bus is due in seven minutes, and Kaleigh didn't come home again."

I smile thinking of Rachel running around naked, calling me Asshat. "Okay, call me later."

She doesn't say good-bye, I just hear her yelling as the phone disconnects. The rest of the morning routine is uneventful.

Walking into the office, I groan thinking about training a new temp. God, I hope it's not Carmen.

I see a man sitting at Lauren's desk. "Good Morning, Mr. Mackenzie." He gets up to greet me.

His hair is perfect, his suit is perfect, and he follows me into my office with a small pad and pen in hand. "I've taken the liberty of going through all the emails to familiarize myself with the routine you have. I also see you like your meetings alphabetically arranged, which is perfect, since it's also how I like to file things," he continues as I shrug off my jacket and put it on the back of my chair.

"What is your name?" I ask him.

"Bruce." He folds his hands in front of himself. "I can't wait to get started."

"Can you tell Barbara I'm in, and that I would like to see her? Also, if a woman named Lauren calls, she always gets put through right away. No matter when she calls."

"Right away." He heads back to his desk and calls Barbara. She walks into my office five minutes later with a cup of coffee for me.

"Okay, what has your panties in a twist this morning?" She sets my coffee down and takes a seat in front of me.

I glare at her. "Nothing has me in a twist. I'm just wondering how long this has been in the works?"

"Since the second day, maybe, when she knew that you wouldn't cave and she couldn't fight her feelings for you anymore."

I smile, thinking over the last month and all the shit we went through. "Is he the best they got?" I motion to Bruce.

"The best they've got is Lauren. He's the second best," she replies, getting up to leave. "Now, I have lots to do. You let me know if you need anything," she says as she walks out.

Looking over my emails and schedule, I get lost in my work. There is a new space I've had my eye on that I'm itching to get into. Denis just sent me the plans. It looks like a lot of work, but it will be amazing if we can get everything done. My phone buzzes on my desk with a text from Noah and a picture.

I swipe across it, opening up his text.

My PA is better than yours!

Under the message is a picture of Lauren, with four guys around her desk as she smiles at the screen.

Fuck off! Is my only reply, but I go back and zoom in on the picture. She's wearing a peach-colored sweater today.

Dude, she is the shit, these chumps are eating her up.

I squeeze my cell phone in my hands and call out to Bruce.

"Yes, sir?" He sticks his head in.

"I need you to send two dozen roses to Lauren at Noah's law firm. The address is in my box." I turn down to see another text came in.

All jokes aside, she just cleared my schedule in ten minutes.

I pick up my desk phone, calling Noah's office, knowing she'll answer, and when she does, I smile. "Hey there, beautiful. How's your day?"

"Hey," I hear her say, hoping she's smiling, too. "It's going well. I haven't had to poison him yet. So, I call that a success." She laughs.

"What time is lunch?" I ask her.

"I have to meet with HR at lunch today and tomorrow."

"Really, what about dinner?"

"It's Monday, which means gymnastics for Rachel and a soccer game for Gabe. Rain check?" she asks. "The kids are with Jake on Wednesday. How about I make dinner and we can eat in bed?" she whispers, and my cock springs to attention.

"That sounds like a plan. I'll bring dessert."

"Is that what you're calling it now?" She giggles. "Okay, I've got to go. I just got called into the conference room."

"Talk to you later," I say and hang up. Why didn't she ask if I wanted to go with her? For that matter, why didn't I offer to meet her?

The rest of the day flies by, and by the time I finish my meeting with Denis, it's almost six-thirty.

There is a text from Lauren and one from Noah.

I read Lauren's first.

Thank you for the flowers, they are beautiful ;)

She also sent a picture of her smelling the roses with a sly smile.

I smile at her face, missing her like crazy.

The next is from Noah.

Way to piss on her leg. We get it, she's taken. Thank God, you didn't send a barber shop quartet to serenade her.

I laugh at him and answer with the middle finger emoji.

Closing up my computer, I head down to my car, wondering what field they're at and thinking about going to join them.

I call her cell phone, but there is no answer, so I go home, where I grab my stuff and go for a run.

I run for six miles, getting home soaking wet. Looking over at Noah's house, I see the lights are all off, so I go straight home, where I shower.

I pick up my phone and see that Lauren hasn't called me yet, so I call her back.

"Hey," she answers out of breath, "sorry I missed your call before. We were at the park."

I hear moving around on her end.

"Yeah, I know, I was going to meet you." I slam the door of the fridge that is still fucking empty.

"Oh, really?" She sounds sad. "I didn't know. I forgot about Rachel's play date with Emma. So they met us at the park."

I smile drinking my water. "Hot moms at the park," I kid with her.

"It was actually Emma's dad with us. Mom left them last year," she explains, while I hear things slamming from her end.

"Is this father hot?" I ask, anger shooting out of me.

"Um, I don't really look at him like that." I hear a door close. "Why would you ask that?"

"No reason, just wanted to know who you were spending time with, since it wasn't with me." Holy fuck, am I sulking? Is this me sulking?

"I wasn't with anyone. I was with Rachel, who was playing with a friend. I didn't go there on a date with him. What is this really about?"

"Nothing," I breathe out my frustration. "I just missed you today."

"I missed you, too. A lot," she whispers. "Like to the moon and back." I hear a smile in her voice.

We continue talking till we drift off to sleep. I haven't done this since high school, but smile when she sends me a text before I wake up.

Have a great day! Kisses in special areas!

I laugh to myself while I get ready and start another day that flies by. I won't say that Bruce is better than Lauren, but he is filling her shoes better than anyone else.

I try calling Lauren during the day, but the conversations are all short. Then after she gets home to the kids, it's almost impossible to get through to her.

I sit in my living room that night, holding my phone, wondering what she's doing. Wondering if Rachel brought home more math homework.

Wondering if Gabe is thinking hockey or soccer. I even wonder if Kaleigh is driving them crazy with tofu.

By the time she gets back to me, she's yawning and on her way to bed.

I toss and turn all night as sleep evades me. My mind plays through different scenarios in my head. What if I'm not good enough? What if she doesn't want me in her life with her kids? What if I fuck up and we fight about it?

The questions are endless, the answers never coming. I'm about to throw my phone out the window when Noah comes waltzing into my office.

"Hey there, stranger." He goes to my couch, unbuttoning his jacket and sitting down. I look at him looking at Bruce. "Well, at least you won't try to bang your new PA, right?" He laughs, brushing his hands into his hair. I notice that he has pink nail polish on.

"That really isn't your color." I point to his hand.

"Rachel painted my nails yesterday." He inspects his nails. "You should see what she did to my feet."

I throw my pen down and sit up straighter. "You saw Rachel yesterday?"

"Well, we had to babysit Rachel and Gabe so Lauren could bring her car in to get the radio fixed." he says it as if it's no big deal, and I'm suddenly pissed off.

"What?" I yell.

"A CD of *Frozen* was jammed in her player and was stuck on repeat, so it played it all the time. You know this," he reminds me as if I'm dumb.

"I know what you mean. What I don't understand is why you were babysitting."

"She needed help," he says with a pointed look at me.

"Why didn't she ask me?"

"I don't know, maybe because you hightailed it right out of there the minute family shit started happening on Sunday night?" He stands up.

"Fuck off!" I yell back at him. Bruce sits up in his chair a little straighter. "She was busy, so I left."

He glares at me. "You left or you took off, it's the same thing."

"Is that what she said?" I look at him, waiting for the answers. Did she think I didn't want to be around her kids?

"She didn't say anything. I just found it weird that she would ask us and not you. Kaleigh said to drop it, so I figured you didn't want to."

"I wasn't asked." I hold out my hands to the side. "I didn't even know."

I grab my jacket, ready to run out of the office, when Noah grabs my arm. "Where the fuck do you think you're going?"

"I'm going to tell her that I'm not scared of her kids."

"Think about what you're doing. You are planning to go barge into her workplace to profess this to her. Dude." He shakes his head. He grabs his phone and dials someone. "Babycakes, are you home?" He smiles and nods his head. "Okay. Austin needs to come over and do something. Can you go to my place? Pack a bag, or better yet, just bring everything with you." He smiles and then hangs up. "Okay, Kaleigh is leaving the door open for you. Go woo your girl."

"Woo?" I ask him.

"A meal, rose petals, champagne, lingerie, vibrators, cuffs. You know, romance."

"This, I can do." I make a list of everything I need to get. "I'm going to woo the fuck out of her."

I rush out of the office, the sound of Noah's laughter trailing behind me as the elevator doors close.

CHAPTER TWENTY-NINE

Lauren

It's been a long two days, made even more hectic because I was on edge. Ever since Austin hightailed it out of my house like his pants were on fire, I've been a mess.

Does he want to be with me? Does he just want a casual relationship, to be with me when I don't have the kids? Can I even be in that type of relationship? I'm not sure. I have my kids all the time. To top it all off, I can't seem to get in touch with him about tonight.

I huff out a breath as I get out of my car and walk up to my front door. Opening the door, I'm hit with thick white smoke and the fire alarm going off.

"What the fuck, Kaleigh?" I storm into the kitchen and come to a complete stop.

Austin is in my kitchen, wearing white Calvin Klein boxers and an apron. My mouth waters right away, but then I see the fire coming from the pot on the stove and notice that he is using the sprayer from the sink to douse the flame with water. "What in the world?" I run to the back of the house, opening the door so the smoke will clear out of the kitchen. I grab what I think is a kitchen towel that is sitting on the table. I pick it up and see what is underneath.

I gasp out in shock, because under the cloth is a mini sex store. I'm talking cuffs, a whip, butt plugs, balls, nipple clamps, bullets, cock rings, four different vibrators. He looks over at me. "Oh, that is for dessert."

I run to the smoke detector and start waving the cloth under it, trying to get it to turn off. "What is going on here?" I look at him and ask. "Why are you burning down my house?"

He looks at me, the water spraying across my whole kitchen when he turns around. "I'm trying to woo you." He turns back around and finally puts out the fire. "I'm cooking for you—flambéed steak—but I guess I put too much alcohol in the pan. It pouffed up too fast and got a little bit out of control." He reaches for a small rag to wipe up the water.

The alarm finally stops ringing and I run up the stairs to get towels. Throwing one at him, I put mine on the floor and start to walk on it across the floor in an attempt to soak up the water before throwing another one down.

"You went to work like that?" I look down at my outfit. I'm wearing tailored trousers, a white fitted shirt, and a matching jacket.

"First, you try to burn down my house. Now you're insulting my wardrobe!" I throw my hands up.

He drops his towel by his feet and storms over to me. He grabs me by my ass and hoists me up as his mouth crashes down on mine. His tongue slides against mine, and I pull him closer. I've missed him so much. The feel of him, the sound of his voice, even the annoying pen-tapping thing he does on the desk when he's thinking.

I moan into his mouth while the kiss turns frantic, almost desperate. Neither of us interested in stopping, he puts me down on the counter, right in a puddle of water. *Cold* water. "Fuck," I squeak out.

"Oh, shit. We should get you out of those pants." He quickly whips off my shoes. "Lift up," he urges, and I try to lift myself up on my hands, but they slip off the counter because of the water. I fall backward, and Austin face-plants into my stomach.

"Ouch," I whine, while he just laughs against my stomach.

"I'm supposed to be wooing you," he mumbles into my stomach while placing little kisses on it. "Romancing you."

"Ahh, I see. Nothing says romance or wooing quite like anal beads do." I chuckle, running my hand through his hair and looking around at my house. It looks like a bomb went off in here, but looking down at him with his lopsided grin, I can't be upset.

"The anal beads were for after the wooing." He smiles at me. "I missed you." He gets up and pulls me to a sitting position.

He puts my hair behind my ears, cupping my face in his hands. "This was supposed to be romantic." He kisses my lips softly.

"It is." I smile as I stroke my thumb across his cheek. "No one has ever tried to romance me."

"I was a dick," he says, and my eyebrows shoot up in surprise.

"Which time?" I ask him.

"When I left on Sunday." I look down, not ready for him to see how much it bothered me.

"It's okay." I smile up at him after a minute.

"It isn't okay. This is your life, and it's now my life."

I take his hands from my face and push him off me as I jump off the counter. "No." I grab the towels off the floor. "It's not your life. It's mine."

He grabs the towels from my hand, throwing them back down. "I worded it wrong. I want this, Lauren. I want to be there for you. To be the one who helps you. I mean, I'm pretty sure you can run the world from your phone"—he smiles—"but when you have too many balls in the air, I want to be who you call. I want you to know that I'm here for you not because I have to be, but because I want to be." Then his smile disappears as he continues, "And when you need your car serviced, I want it to be me who you call to help you, not Noah, not Kaleigh—but me." He motions to himself with a thumb at his chest.

"Austin," I whisper, "I'm not going to force my kids and my responsibilities on you."

He places his finger on my lips, stopping me from talking. "You aren't forcing anything on me. If anything, I'm forcing myself on you." He takes a breath and continues. "I want to be there with you when you go to soccer games, if I can. I want to be here with you when Rachel is running around naked. I mean, not to see her naked, that's weird, but I want to be here to throw you her clothes." He reaches for me. "And I really want to drive Gabe to hockey; it's our thing." He shrugs and gives me a smile. "I want to cook for you guys." My eyebrows shoot up. "Okay, I want to be here to order out for you guys. Let me be that person for you." His arms wrap around me, bringing me flush against him.

"Austin, what if you resent this whole thing and then feel like you can't leave?" I question him. "What if you have a headache and the kids yelling just makes it worse? I'm okay with this thing between us not having a title."

"I'm not." His voice is firm. "The last two days, I realized that this is where I want to be. In the middle of the chaos. Ask me," he whispers.

"Will you come to Gabe's soccer game tomorrow night?"

"Yes," he answers, smiling. "Now, can we have dessert?"

"What type of dessert were you thinking about?" I look back at the table of titillation and torture.

"I was thinking bullet, anal beads, and whip."

"Really? I was thinking nipple clamps, cuffs, and vibrator," I counter.

"Who wears the cuffs?"

I wiggle my eyebrows at him, while he looks at me with hooded eyes. "Oh, you are definitely wearing the cuffs this time." His evil laugh comes out. "Let's go upstairs. I want you laid out."

He jogs up the stairs after he collects the whip, cuffs, bullet, vibrator, nipple clamps, and anal beads. "Just in case." He winks.

I follow him up, shrugging off my jacket and shirt as I go. "You're lucky your junk didn't burn off in the fire." I enjoy the view of his ass in those white Calvins.

"That would have been a bigger disaster than your house burning down." He throws his toys down on the bed.

I slip my wet pants off, leaving me in my matching white lace bra and panties that are both sexy and delicate.

"Leave those on," he demands, his erection tenting his Calvins as his hand rubs it. The sight makes my knees weak and my pussy wet.

I get on the bed, moving to the middle and crossing my legs. "Okay, what next, sir?" I laugh.

"On your stomach for now," he orders me. "But first," he states as he reaches for the cuffs, then cuffs my wrists together in front of me. "On second thought, on your hands and knees, head to the wall." I get in position, looking over my shoulder to see what he is doing.

He has the whip handle in his hand while he tests it on his other hand. "You trust me?"

"It's kind of difficult to answer now that I have the cuffs on," I tell him, "but I wouldn't have these cuffs on if I didn't."

"Good, now, eyes facing forward," he demands. "Should have gotten the blindfold, too," he murmurs to himself.

I'm facing the headboard. The anticipation of what's to come has all my senses on high alert. I feel the bed move and then his heat hitting the back of me.

He opens my knees wider with his hands, sliding them softly up my inner thighs ever so slowly until they get to my pussy, where he starts rubbing me through the lace with two fingers. "Wet," he groans, and I hang my head. "I bet we can make this pussy wetter. What do you think?" he challenges me. His fingers are now gone but are quickly replaced with the tip of the whip, the square leather tip grazing me. His hand goes to my ass, which is only partially covered since I'm wearing a thong.

"So soft," he says, caressing it gently. my back arches, making my ass stick out more. Moving from one cheek to the other, he strokes me in a circular pattern. "Creamy white," he breathes. "Let's see how it looks pink." And then his open-palm hand comes down on my ass with a smack. It stings at first, like a pinch, but he soothes the sting with his hand, and the pain dissipates, leaving a warm sensation in its place. I wait for the next smack, but it doesn't come, and my heartbeat picks up the longer I wait.

Instead, he takes the whip and smacks the other cheek, and I moan. It's a different kind of sting than the one from his palm, more isolated, less painful, but it leaves my skin feeling warmer.

The next thing I hear is the buzz of the vibrator as he turns it on. He runs the vibrator along my lower back, the vibrations pulsing through me. He moves to my side, continuing to slide the vibrator against my back. He then moves it to my nipple, which hardens in response as he circles it. He slides the vibrator under the lace of my bra, pressing it down on the hard peak. The sensation shoots straight through me to my belly before it slowly spreads to my core.

"Austin," I moan as my hips buck from side-to-side. I hear him chuckle as he moves back behind me. He reaches between my legs with the vibrator, landing it straight on my throbbing clit. "Please," I beg, for what I'm not even sure.

"Not yet," he says, and I pull at my hands, the need to take care of myself great.

He moves my panties to the side, slipping the vibrator in between my lips and coating it with my wetness. My hips move on their own, and he smacks my ass to make me stop. "Not yet, Lauren." He smoothes his hand over the spot he smacked. "If I stuck my cock into you now, would you be wet for me?"

"Yes," I groan, closing my eyes to focus on the way the vibrator is rubbing up and down through my slit, the tip hitting my clit with each pass.

"What do you want?" he asks me, teasing me further by pushing just the tip inside my waiting cunt.

"To come," I tell him, exhaling slowly. "So much." My arms begin to wobble in their efforts to hold me up. "Please, Austin."

He pushes the vibrator all the way in, filling me up. My ass pushes back against him, the whip coming down on my ass, delivering a sting that runs straight to my clit. He leaves the vibrator all the way inside of me but turns up the speed, and my eyes roll back, my lids fluttering closed.

I feel him moving around my body to position himself in front of my face. With his boxers riding low on his hips, he taps my cheek and says, "Open." I immediately comply and take him inside my mouth, twirling my tongue around his head as the salty taste of his pre-cum floods my tongue. I take his head fully inside and bob my head, taking him deeper each time until the base of his cock is in my mouth and the head hits the back of my throat.

He drops the whip and uses both hands to pinch my nipples hard enough for the pain to turn to pleasure as it shoots right to my clit. He fucks my face while the vibrator buzzes inside me. I rotate my hips to get something moving, but he stops me with a smack to my ass. He moves one hand to hold my head in place by my hair at the back of my head, while the other hand holds the whip he brings down on my ass twice with a smack to each cheek. My hands fight against the cuffs now, the need to come so overwhelming I can barely breathe. I attack his cock with a vengeance, as the need to make him come so he can make me come drives me.

"I could fuck your face all night long," he groans as he brings the whip down on my ass a little harder this time. "Come down your throat," he moans as his hips thrust forward. "Over and over again." The vibrator continues working its magic on me, making me wetter than I've ever been as my juices run down my thighs.

He pulls his cock out of my mouth, and my arms give out as I fall to my elbows, my ass still in the air. He moves behind me, removing the vibrator from my pussy as it clenches to keep it in place.

I hear crinkling coming from behind me right before the wet vibrator moves from my pussy to my clit, where he uses it to apply pressure to my aching clit. My hips jerk in response, and he smacks my ass again.

"Fuck," I whimper into my hands. "Please."

The vibrations stop as he strokes into me in one long, smooth thrust. We both moan loudly as his cock stretches me, my wetness easing the way for him to plant it in me all the way to the root.

"Harder!" I push back against him, and he gives me what I ask for and fucks me harder. The sounds of our skin slapping together echoes throughout the room. My orgasm hovers right there, sparking beneath the surface, on the cusp of breaking free. My hands ball into fists around my sheet as I try not to move forward every time he thrusts himself roughly into me.

"So fucking tight. So fucking wet. So, so fucking hot," he grits out as he pounds into me even harder and faster. Finally—*finally*—as I'm right about to come, he smacks my ass, the sting exploding across my skin as the burn lights me up and I come all over his cock. He pumps into me twice more before he follows me and comes with a roar.

CHAPTER THIRTY

Austin

Our bodies press together as our chests heave for a minute, while we both try to catch our breath. I lean over and grab the key from the side table to unlock the cuffs.

Once they are unlocked, I see little red marks where she must have pulled the cuffs. I rub the marks with my thumbs, looking up at her. "Fuck, I didn't think this would hurt."

"It didn't." She smiles and closes her eyes. "Relax, Austin, you didn't go all Christian Grey on me. I'm fine." She laughs while I continue to rub the marks. "Next time, though, it's my turn to torture you. Did you buy a ball gag by any chance?" Her body shakes with her laughter. She turns herself around and lies down in her bed.

I laugh as I get off the bed to go into the bathroom to dispose of the condom. Washing my hands, I return with a warm washcloth. Gently opening her legs, I am about to wipe her when she snatches it from my hand. "What the hell are you doing?"

"I was going to clean you up." I look at her in confusion. "What's the big deal?"

"I just…" she starts and then stops. "It's weird." she stutters, and I snatch the washcloth back from her and open her legs again.

"You know, I've already been intimately acquainted with it. My fingers have felt it, my mouth has tasted it, and my cock has fucked it,"

I say as I gently clean her.

"Ok then, when you put it that way, please proceed," she gives in a little shyly. "Um, is this going to be an everyday thing?" She points between me and her as her voice softens with her question.

"You mean us having hot sex? That would be a yes. I would do that daily." I throw myself down on the bed next to her.

"And, um, we won't be doing this with, um, anyone else?" she asks a little nervously.

"Fuck, no. I don't plan on fucking anyone else, and I sure as hell hope you don't plan on it, either," I answer firmly.

"Ok, then. Well, I'm on the shot," she informs me. "And I haven't been with anyone since Jake left. I'm clean. I don't know the protocol on this whole sex-without-a-condom thing or how it works." She tries to sound casual, but the slight tremor in her voice betrays her nerves. That, and she closes her eyes to avoid my stare.

"I've never gone without one," I say honestly. I'm never with anyone long enough for it to get that serious. "I'm clean, but I got tested recently. You remember, it was during that time you made my balls swell up to the size of an elephant's." I try to alleviate her nerves by lightening up the moment with a reminder of our not-so-distant past shenanigans. It works and she snorts at the memory.

"So, maybe"—she gets closer to me and throws her leg over my hip—"we should try it without one to see if it works?"

"If what works? My cock?" I grip her hip with my hand before I slide it up her back to find the hooks to her bra.

"It's in the front." She unclips the bra so her tits spring free. Her pink pebbled nipples are begging to be sucked, so I do just that and take one into my mouth.

Her head pushes back further into the pillow as her neck arches. My cock is hard and ready for round two. She lifts her hips, pushing me to my back with her thigh as she follows me over and climbs on top of me. On her knees, bent over my torso, hands planted in the bed at either side of my head, she positions herself on top of my cock, and slowly, so fucking slowly, she lowers herself onto me. I know, in that moment, that this woman was made for me.

Holy fuck, the way her pussy grips me, I feel everything so much more intensely being in her bare. She's hotter, wetter, tighter than ever, and so much softer than I imagined. I moan at how good it feels.

"We are doing this again. At least twice more before tomorrow." I thrust up hard as she meets me with a downward thrust of her own.

And that is exactly what we do. After we clean the mess in the kitchen, that is, and I put away all the toys I bought. They're now in a box in her linen closet, up high under a pile of sheets.

The next day, I walk into work with a lighter step. I woke up with her in my arms. I had her this morning when we woke up and then again in the shower. It's going to be a good day.

Bruce is there with my messages as soon as I walk in, and I greet him with a smile. I don't say much more to him.

I get a text from Noah.

So, how did the wooing go? Did she set your balls on fire?

I laugh, thinking of the fire I started cooking.

The wooing was fine, minus me setting fire to dinner. My balls were not involved. Next time, it's pizza.

I don't know what you did, but she is in a fine mood, she even brought me coffee. I won't drink it. Because there is the chance that she may have poisoned it after I told her she had that just-freshly-fucked face.

How have you not been sued for sexual harassment yet?

Your guess is as good as mine.

I laugh at that last text and by the time I look up again, it's almost six-thirty. I stand up and stretch as my phone rings and I see that it's Noah.

"What is it?" I say in place of a greeting.

"I'm not making this phone call right now," he whispers into the phone. "But I thought you should know that Jake the Snake has showed up to talk to Lauren, and she asked Kaleigh and me to take the kids to the park."

"What park?" I ask, grabbing my jacket and keys, rushing out.

"The park at the corner by her house."

"Why are you whispering?"

"I'm playing hide-and-seek. Fucking hurry." He disconnects the phone call.

I run out to my car, not knowing whether I should head straight to Lauren's or go to the park. My mind says go to the park, so that is where I head first.

I see Rachel running around with Noah chasing after her like a monkey. Parking the car, I head over toward them. Gabe sees me and starts running to me. "Austin, my mom says I can play hockey!" He holds his hand up for a high five. I high five him, then pull him in to hug him, happy that I was able to make this happen for him.

"Asstin, you came to play?" Rachel asks as she runs to me with Noah and Kaleigh following behind her, holding hands and looking at each other.

"I came to see if you guys wanted to go out for ice cream?" I suggest the first thing that comes to mind. "How about we go see if Mom wants to come with us?"

"Ice cream!" Rachel jumps into my arms and surprises me so much I almost drop her.

"Let's go get Mom." I walk to my truck, an upgrade from the Porsche I had last week.

I pull into her driveway and see that Jake the Snake's car is still there.

So, I make the kids walk in first and then follow them in. "Mommy, Asstin came to have ice cream!" Rachel shouts as soon as she gets into the house.

We find them in the kitchen sitting at the table. Lauren sees me, and her eyes light up with a smile to match. "Hey, you," she says as I walk to her and lean down to kiss her softly.

"Hey. I thought I would surprise you and the kids." I look at Jake and nod. "But if you're busy—" I stop talking, because she holds up her hands.

"No, that sounds like a great idea. Jake was just leaving anyway." She looks at him, giving him a smile that he has to recognize is fake.

Jake slaps the table and gets up. "Yeah, I was just leaving. Gabe, Rachel, come give Dad a hug and kiss!" he calls for them.

They come back into the room and give him hugs and kisses, and he asks if they want to come over that weekend. "I know it's not my weekend, but I can take them if you guys have plans," he addresses us both. Lauren has now stood up and is standing next to me, and I've got my arm around her shoulder.

"Gabe has hockey on Saturday afternoon," Lauren says to him, "so maybe after that."

"I have hockey!" Gabe shouts with glee.

"That's right, dude. I didn't get a chance to tell you, but I spoke with Craig and he can start you on Saturday."

"Yes!" he cheers. "Mom, I'm going to go and tell Jesse." He runs out of the house.

"Well," Jake says, "I guess I'll just be going."

Rachel runs over and jumps into his arms and kisses his cheek. "Bye, Daddy."

He says a quick good-bye to both of us and walks out the front door.

Rachel looks at Lauren. "Are we still going for ice cream?"

"Sure, go grab a sweater." She doesn't have to ask her twice. Rachel rushes out of the room looking for her sweater.

"Are we going to discuss what happened here?" I look at her, asking about the elephant in the room.

"There really is nothing to discuss. He came crawling back. Telling me how him leaving was a mistake." She shrugs her shoulders, while my heart stops, my stomach drops.

"What does that mean?" I try not to freak out.

"It means exactly what you think it means. He fucked up. I mean, did it hurt me? Yes. Did I want to go all Beyonce on his ass? Fuck yeah. But it's over. I've moved on." She comes over to me. "I'm hoping that you are on the same page as me?" She kisses me on my neck.

"We are exactly on the same page. I will say," I tell her while I look down on her, "he gets a pass for today, because he got fucked over. But"—I push her hair behind her ears—"this is the last pass he gets. Next time, I'm going to tell him exactly where to go fly his kite." I smile at her. "If you know what I mean." I kiss her nose, watching her smile.

"I know what you mean. Now, can I have some ice cream?" She puts her hands on her hips. "It's Thursday, it's spin class day."

"Really?" I'm surprised I didn't know this.

"Really. I take spin classes on Mondays, Tuesdays, Thursdays, and sometimes on Saturdays. Usually, I drop Gabe off at soccer practice and then hit up the gym where Rachel goes to the play area."

"Baby, if you want to work out, all you have to do is tell me. You can ride me all night long," I whisper to her while taking her in my arms.

Her hands curl around my arm while she picks off invisible lint. "Oh, I'm going to ride you all night long"—she moves her hands around my neck, pulling my ear to her lips—"as soon as you buy that ball gag." I feel the huff of her laughter across my cheek as I turn my face to kiss her lips.

"I found my sweater!" Rachel yells from somewhere in the house, her footsteps coming closer. I wait to see if Lauren will drop her hands, but she doesn't, so I bask in this second victory tonight. The first being her obviously negative reaction to Jake's presence there and whatever it was he wanted to talk to her about. "Asstin, can you carry me on your shoulders?" She comes into the kitchen as she tries to pull on her sweater. "Are you strong like Noah?" She pets her sweater.

Lauren puts her hand in front of her mouth to stop the laugh from escaping, while I glare at her. "I'm a thousand times stronger than Noah." I grab her and toss her in the air and then catch her and flip her upside down while she giggles.

I finally put her on my shoulders, and we start walking toward the ice cream parlor. Gabe sees us walking down the street and runs to catch up to us after saying good-bye to his friend Jesse.

The four of us walk down the street, me holding Lauren's hand, while Rachel sits on my shoulders, her feet tucked under my arms, and Gabe holds Lauren's other hand as he talks non-stop about hockey.

We eat the ice cream and then make our way back home, almost the same way we came, except now Rachel is telling us all about how she needs a cat, because everyone has a cat, *everyone*.

When we walk back into the house, Lauren starts issuing orders for bath and homework. They both go to their respective rooms, while Lauren looks over at me and says, "I have to do the dishes. Come sit and talk to me." She walks to the kitchen, rolling up her sleeves as she starts cleaning the dinner dishes and putting them in the dishwasher. I don't sit on that stool; instead, I get up and move to stand next to her. When I lean my hip against the counter, we start talking about our days. I undo the top button on my dress shirt. "I need to bring over clothes for when I come here after work."

Her hands stop moving in the water. "Um, is that what you want?" Her eyes avoid me, and I grab her chin with my fingers to bring them to mine.

"I want that very much," I tell her honestly before I lean forward, kissing her lips. I lick across her bottom lip, and she opens for me to slide my tongue in. I grab her waist to bring her closer to me while my tongue plays with hers. My hands roam to her ass, cupping her to bring her even closer. I almost forget where we are, until I hear Rachel's voice calling from upstairs. "Mom, the bubbles are finished." We both groan as our lips separate.

"Coming!" Lauren yells. "Why don't you sit on the couch and watch television?" She suggests before she walks upstairs. I'm about to go sit down when Gabe comes downstairs with his notebook.

"Austin, can you help me study for my spelling test?"

I toss the remote on the table. "Sure," I'm surprised at how excited I am that he asked me. "Where do you want to do this?" I look around.

"I'll just sit on the floor, and you can tell me the words." He lies down on his stomach, a piece of paper and a pencil in front of him.

I go through the list of words, while he gets all but two of them right. "You know what I used to do when I got my words wrong? I'd write it out ten times," I tell him, and he inwardly groans. "I know it sucks, trust me, but it worked. And you know what else? That's going to be something you'll be doing in hockey. Well, not the writing, but the repeating stuff over and over. It's how you'll train your muscles to memorize the movements of your plays. It's the same idea with your spelling words, except instead of training your muscles, you're helping your brain memorize the words through the repetition of writing them over and over."

The comparison to hockey does the trick, and he nods his head as he starts writing the words. When he finishes, he says, "Okay, let's try it again." He grabs another piece of paper, and by the time we're done, he has all the words memorized. He is so happy, he gives me a high five before running upstairs to tell his mom. Truth be told, I'm happy, too. It felt good that he asked for my help, and it felt even better when I saw how my efforts actually did help him.

I finally turn the television on and see that it's almost nine p.m. I stretch out on the couch, waiting for Lauren to come down. When I hear her footsteps, I look up and what I see has me sitting straight up.

She is walking to me wearing a short, pink satin robe, which falls to just over her ass. Tied loosely at the waist, the middle gapes open, showing me that she isn't wearing anything under it. She doesn't say a word, just comes right to me, pushes me back against the couch cushions, and straddles me before she crushes her lips on mine. She slides her tongue into my mouth, her taste filling it.

She slowly starts to rock herself on me. My cock sprung to attention the minute she sat down and is now starting to throb. She finally peels her lips from mine. "You know what really turns me on?" She starts to unbutton my shirt. I'm looking inside her robe, which has fallen open further, showing me her bare breasts. My hand reaches in to cup one of her plump breasts as my thumb grazes over the peaked nipple.

"No fucking clue, but whatever I did, I'm going to do it again," I say, leaning down, taking her other nipple in my mouth as she grinds down hard on my cock.

"You. Doing homework with Gabe, carrying Rachel on your shoulders. It was so hot, my pussy got wet just watching you." She leans down to bite my nipple as a hiss comes out of my mouth.

I don't have a chance to do anything else before she is off me, grabbing my hand and leading me upstairs to her room. I'm barely through the door when she closes and then locks it. She brings me to the bed, positioning me in front of it. Kneeling in front of me, she quickly undoes my belt and works my pants and boxers down as my rock-hard cock slaps up against my belly. She gives my hips a little push so that I sit down and spread my legs as she moves in between them. "The whole time, all I could think about was your cock in my mouth and taking it to the back of my throat. I'm not sure you know this about me, Austin, but I love giving head." I'm panting as her hand wraps around my cock, giving it a few quick strokes. Pre-cum pools in the slit, and she licks her lips. "Mmmm," she hums right before she moves her mouth over me and swallows me down.

My head falls forward as I release a groaning breath, and my hands find their way into her hair. She moves her mouth up and down my cock, her tongue twirling around the head with each pass. "That's so fucking good, baby," I moan as she takes me deeper each time.

Her mouth releases me and is replaced by her hand, gripping me firmly and twisting as she strokes me up and down. "I love your cock, babe," she breathes as her mouth moves back to it again. She flattens her tongue against the base of my shaft, running it all the way up the underside of it to the head, where she looks up at me through hooded eyes as she curls her tongue around me. It's a good fucking look. "I want you to come in my mouth," she says, taking me in again, hollowing her cheeks to suck hard, while she bobs her head. Overwhelmed by how incredibly good this feels, I can't help the moans that escape me. Hell, I'm surprised I'm not whimpering.

Her hand reaches to cup my balls, where she rolls and squeezes them as her mouth continues to work my cock. I look down and see a woman who is really into what she's doing, so much so, that my eyes follow the curve of her other arm when I realize that hand isn't on me. I look closer and see that her hand has snaked into the opening of her robe and is stroking her pussy. "Fuck," I grit out through clenched teeth as my hips surge up into her mouth when it comes down on me. The heat of her mouth and the feel of her throat surrounding me almost take me over the edge. As tempting as it is to shoot off in her mouth, I've missed her and I need more.

I grab her under her arms, picking her up and dragging her onto me as I lie back, and she whines in protest. "In your pussy," I pant, "I need to be in your pussy." I untie the sash of her robe and move my hands to her hips to rock her wet pussy over my cock.

She rises up on her knees, positioning my cock at her entrance, and then slowly slides herself down on me. The movement makes us both moan loudly. I grab her hair with my hand and pull her to me. Our mouths collide, which helps to keep the moaning down. She rides me hard and fast, gliding all the way up until just the tip is inside before she slams back down on me with a grind and twist of her hips.

My hands leave her hair to grip her hips, my fingertips digging into her flesh, our tongues still tangled with one another's.

I feel her hand moving between us, and I let go of her mouth to look at her. Her hair is sticking up all over the place from my rough hold on it, and her tits bounce each time she moves. Her eyes are half closed in bliss, but what makes my cock pulse inside of her is the sight of her hand between her legs.

She has one hand planted in the bed next to me while she strokes her clit with the other. "Fuck me," I groan right as I feel her pussy tighten around my cock.

"I'm coming," she whispers with a sexy little hitch in her voice as her eyes slide all the way closed and her hand continues to rub her clit furiously from side to side, never slowing her ride on my cock. When her orgasm winds down, she starts to slow her thrusts, but I don't let her. Instead, I tighten my grip on her hips and use them to move her up and down on my cock. Her clit and my dick glisten with her wetness, and my balls pull up tight at the sight.

"Give me one more, Lauren, and then I'm going to come." I continue to pound her down onto me by her hips.

"I can't," she says breathlessly, now moving with me to grind down against my pubic bone.

"You can and you will. I can feel your pussy getting tighter, wetter, hotter." I keep slamming into her. My balls are so tight with the need to come, it's almost painful. "Fingers to your clit. Now, Lauren," I command as I lean forward and bite her nipple. "Come on my cock like a good girl, and I'll come in your pussy." It seems that my woman likes a bossy, dirty mouth, because she whimpers at my words and her pussy clamps down even tighter on my cock.

I thrust up a few more times until she comes again. This time biting her lips to keep from screaming. It's the last straw for me. I pull her all the way down onto me and explode inside her. I see stars, hell, I may even black out a little as I come harder than I ever have in my life.

CHAPTER THIRTY-ONE

Lauren

The alarm starts to buzz, waking me up. I go to stretch, but I'm wrapped up tight in Austin's arms. Every morning, we set the alarm for five a.m., so he can leave before the kids get up.

It's been over two weeks since he made his declaration. In those two weeks, he's been here every single time I went to spin class to watch the kids. Proving how much he meant what he said, he sticks to our routine, following it to a T. It's crazy how well he just fits in. It's like he was always meant to be here.

We end every night by starting out on the couch before slowly making our way upstairs. Every single night, I fall asleep with a smile on my face, and every single morning, I wake up feeling happy. I'm happy.

He's about to get up and out of bed when Rachel comes running into the room and jumps onto the bed. "Momma, there's a monster under the bed," she whispers as she crawls in between Austin and me. My eyes are wide open as I take them in, trying to gauge both of their reactions to this surprise development. I know the kids are used to having Austin around now; it's just that we haven't done the whole sleepover thing yet. "Asstin, you the man, go kill it." Rachel gets under the covers with us. Thank god, we got dressed last night after we finished. When Austin doesn't move, Rachel looks back at him. "Are you scared, too? Momma, call Noah," she whispers, and it's then that Austin snaps.

"I'm going to go get that monster and kick him out." He walks out of the room, his basketball shorts hanging on his hips. Just one look at him, and my mouth waters. Another thing that has changed is that he has changes of clothes here. When he comes in after work, he changes into something more comfortable and always leaves those clothes here.

I hear some banging coming from Rachel's room and then a swoosh of something. Rachel curls up tightly into me, and I pull her into my arms to hold her. "Honey, there is nothing to be scared of."

"All gone." Austin comes back into the room scratching his side.

Rachel pulls the cover from her face watching Austin. "Are you sure?" she asks, while he nods yes.

She gets up and starts jumping on the bed till she jumps into his arms. "You killed the monster? For me?"

"Anything for you, princess," he replies with a kiss to her head.

"I love you, Asstin," she says, and my mouth just opens and closes as I stumble to formulate a response. But Austin doesn't skip a beat.

"Well, that's good, because I love you, too." He climbs back into bed with her held close to his chest.

"Are you going to do sleepovers like Ms. Camilla does with Dad?"

Austin looks over at me, as if to ask for the right words to say. When I just shrug my shoulders, he once again proves his words from two weeks ago when he does his own thing and tells her, "I would like that a lot, and maybe sometime we could have a sleepover at my house. Would you like that?"

"Are there monsters at your house?" she asks him with all the seriousness of a scared six-year-old little girl.

"Nope, none. I think Noah has some at his house, though." He smiles over her head at me.

"We are never sleeping at Noah's house, Mommy." She turns to me. "But maybe we could try sleeping at Asstin's?"

"Yes, baby." I kiss her head. "Maybe we can." I return his smile over her head.

"Do you love my mommy, Asstin?" Her question has my breath stopping in my chest. My heart is beating so fast and loud in my ears, I'm pretty sure that people on the moon can hear it, so obviously the two other people in this bed with me surely can, too.

"Rachel, honey, how about we make some pancakes?" I try to get out of bed in an attempt to forget the question, trying to bail Austin out from having been put on the spot. As I whip the covers off me and Rachel to get us out of bed, Austin's arm reaches out and latches around mine to halt my movements. I look at his hand on my arm, but I'm too afraid to look up at him.

I don't know if I want to know the answer. I mean, I do want to know, but I don't know if this is the way I want to learn it. What if he is feeling forced into telling me? What if he just doesn't want to say it?

"I love your mom more than you know," he answers her, and me as well. His words bring tears to my eyes. There's a softness, almost a reverence to his voice as if he's talking to me, only me, as if we were alone. "I've never loved anyone the way I love your mom." One tear slips out, landing on my arm and rolling onto his hand that grips me. "To the moon and back," he says, quoting one of the books he's read to Rachel when he was putting her to bed while I was out one night last week.

"That's a lot." Rachel stretches out her arms as wide as she can. "It's big, really big, like this, right?"

He squeezes my arm again. "Bigger."

"Do you want pancakes?" Rachel asks Austin, then whispers to him, "If you want, you can ask for chocolate and bananas. Those are the bestest ones that Mommy makes," she informs him as she climbs over him to get up. "Mommy puts chocolate spread on them and then she cuts bananas in a smile." She nods her head to convince him, as if it is something unbelievable. "Ask her."

"Will you make me pancakes, Lauren?" He's almost whispering.

I nod my head, the lump in my throat threatening to dislodge and let loose the sob it's holding back. "I need the washroom," I say, rushing into the bathroom and locking the door behind me. I slide down the door, listening to Austin tell Rachel that she could go downstairs and start taking out the bowls. Once I hear her running out of the room and then downstairs, I listen for Austin's steps.

I don't hear anything until there's a soft knock at the door. "Baby, open the door," he urges softly.

"Um, I'll meet you downstairs," I say, trying to get my voice to come out without cracking.

"Baby, open the door, please," he whispers into the crack of the door.

I get up and slowly unlock the door, opening it slightly. "I'm okay."

"I didn't want to tell you like that." He pushes the door open and grabs me around the waist to carry me over to the vanity, where he sets me down. He pushes the hair from around my face, tucking it behind my ears. "I wanted to tell you in some romantic way." He opens my legs, stepping in between them, while I put my hands on his waist. "But this is our normal now." He smirks at me. "And I wouldn't have it any other way. I love you. I love how much you love your children. I love how much you put up with from your sister, who is crazy, by the way." I smile at that comment, thinking of last week when she made tofu burgers and didn't tell him, and they were half raw inside. "I love how selfless you are, always putting everyone before yourself." He kisses my lips softly, his lips lingering on mine.

"I love you," I whisper. "I love how much you love my kids. I love how you took us all on. I love that you don't actually kill Kaleigh every day, even though I'm sure you want to." I smile. "But most of all, I love how you love me. I love how safe you make me feel. How you make me feel so sexy and, most of all, so loved that it's overwhelming." I give him a smile that I'm sure lights my eyes, because my heart is soaring and I feel like the happiest person in the world.

"Now, wasn't that romantic?" he whispers to me, and I can feel him smiling while he kisses my lips.

"Very. Much better than when you tried to woo me." I nip his lip.

"None of that now. We have Rachel searching for bowls." His hands cup my face. "Now, let's go make pancakes."

"You are totally getting the best blowjob of the year as soon as the kids go to school and I call in sick."

"Oh, and we're totally playing hooky today and having sex all day long," he informs me.

"That we are, Mr. Mackenzie, that we are," I agree as I get down from the vanity and walk out of the bathroom to head downstairs. Once there, I see that Rachel has started by getting the mixing bowl out as well as the box of pancake mix, which must have fallen on the floor, because there is powder all over the place with little footprints in it.

"I'm ready!" she shouts excitedly, standing on a chair that she pushed to the counter.

"What is all the noise for?" Gabe says, dragging his feet as he comes downstairs, rubbing the sleep from his eyes that are squinting as they adjust to the light.

"We are making pancakes with chocolate and bananas!" Rachel yells at him, far too loudly for this hour of the morning.

"Hey, Austin." He looks right at him. "You didn't leave yet?"

"Leave?" Austin questions him right back.

He smirks at him. "I know you sleep here and sneak out." He smiles at both of us. I'm too busy with my mouth hanging open to answer. "I got up early last week, and you guys were sleeping, but then he was gone in the morning."

"Um… ahh… well, um…" Austin stutters, not sure what to say.

"It's cool," Gabe says. "If Ms. Camilla can sleep over naked at Dad's, it's ok that you sleep here." He shrugs before going over to the refrigerator and grabbing the orange juice.

"Yeah, she's naked a lot," Rachel agrees from her chair at the counter.

"Rach," Gabe says to her in warning.

"And she says 'oh, God' a lot, too," Rachel continues. "I don't want to pray like that at night, Mommy. Once is good."

I look at Austin, who is trying to hide his smile, then I look at Gabe, who is pretending he doesn't hear anything.

"Let's make pancakes. How many do you want, Gabe?"

I mix the pancake batter while we change the subject and chat about what we should make for supper. By the time the kids leave for school, the conversations of the morning are long behind us.

I finally close the door and lock it. I look at Austin in the kitchen, putting the dishes in the dishwasher. "That is almost like watching porn," I tell him. "You doing stuff like washing dishes, vacuuming, homework with Gabe. It's mom porn."

His eyebrows shoot up. "Are you checking me out?" he questions with a smile.

"I'm doing more than checking you out. I'm undressing you in my mind," I tease him as I lean against the counter.

He shakes the water from his hands. "Really? Well, in that case, where the fuck is the vacuum?"

"How about we do that after. I believe I owe you a world-class blowjob." I turn around and head out of the kitchen. I turn my head to look at him over my shoulder. "You coming?"

I don't have to ask him twice. He storms over to me and lifts me up and over his shoulder with a slap to my ass. "Your mouth on my dick, and there's no doubt about it, I'll be coming, alright. Maybe all over you," he states as he walks us up the stairs and throws me onto the bed. "How long are they in school?" he asks, stripping his pants off.

"They get home at three." I watch him strip down, and his cock springs free.

"Good. We have all day." He fists his cock, giving it a few rough jerks.

"How will we fill the time?" I ask him, taking off my shirt now.

"Oh, we'll think of something." He meets me on the bed.

And do we ever. We find ways to fill the time in the bed, on the kitchen counter, on the kitchen table, and finally, in the shower.

The rest of the week goes off without a hitch. Austin runs home and brings back some suits, since he doesn't have to leave at five a.m. anymore.

Now, here we are on Sunday morning, getting ready for my parents to come over for brunch, when Kaleigh and Noah walk in.

Another thing that has changed is that she is never home anymore. She comes to get the kids off the bus in the afternoons, but when it's time for dinner, she leaves. I've never seen her looking happier. Except this morning, she looks a little pale, with circles under her eyes.

"Are you okay?" I ask her while readying the roast for the oven. I set the alarm to make sure we put it in on time.

"I just feel tired, and I think I caught a bug." She sits on the stool at the counter.

She is beautiful, her hair curled at the ends, in tight blue jeans and a pink long-sleeved sweater that's tight at the top and flares out at the bottom.

"She was up all night barfing. You know it's love when you get someone water while they are yacking," Noah says, grabbing a coffee cup and filling it up.

"That is really nice of you, pal," Austin comments from his side of the counter while he looks at them. Both Austin and Noah are dressed down in jeans and button-down shirts.

"I can do a lot of things. I just can't do the whole vomit thing. But I was proud of myself." He reaches over and rubs Kaleigh's head.

We don't have a chance to say anything before we hear my mother. "Knock, knock, knock!" she calls out before walking into the house.

"Mom, it defeats the purpose if you just walk in," Kaleigh says. "What if we were all naked?"

My mother gasps. "It's noon, why would you be naked at noon?"

"Oh, dear God," I say under my breath. The kids come barreling downstairs, yelling for grandma and grandpa.

"Hey, Austin," my father greets him, hitting him on the back. "How are you, son? Should we be expecting any penises today?" He laughs as he goes to Kaleigh to give her a side hug.

"Kaleigh, you look like death," my mother remarks while she comes to hug her and then me. "Austin, it's good to see you, without, you know." She motions her hands into the shape of a penis in the air.

"That was a fun time," Noah says into his cup, smiling, while Austin and I just glare at him.

"I don't feel good." Kaleigh gets up to go to the bathroom.

"What can I do to help?" My mother comes into the kitchen and opens the oven to check out the roast. "That looks delish."

"I made it," Noah pops up, winking at my mom while she blushes.

"Yeah, right," Austin says. "Come on and help me set the table." He orders Noah as he grabs the tablecloth and shows him where the plates are.

When they are out of the room, my mother and father both look at me, but it's my mother who speaks first. "He really knows his way around the house."

"Um, yeah, he usually stays for dinner." I don't make eye contact while I move around the kitchen, looking for nothing in particular.

"Does he do this every night?" my father asks, sitting down.

"Most nights, yes." I put the cloth that I have in my hands down. "I like him. A lot."

He nods his head, while my mother clasps her hands together. "You love him?"

"Um, yes. Yes, I do," I finally admit. "I'm happy. Like really happy. So, please, let's just drop the third degree."

"My lips are sealed." She pretends to zip her lips shut. "Is he good in bed?"

"Mom!" I exclaim at the same time my dad warns, "Dede."

She looks at both of us. "Oh, please, she is in the peak of her life. She should be having sex daily." She shrugs. "I read it in Cosmo."

"Oh, dear God," I say again just louder.

"There is a quiz you can take to show you what kind of lover Austin will be."

"What?" I ask the same time Austin and Noah come back into the kitchen.

"It asks you questions." She looks at Austin. "Are you a selfish lover?"

Noah snickers behind Austin, while Austin's face turns from white to red. "Um…"

"Don't answer that," I tell him.

"Do you wait for her to go first, or do you just think of yourself?" my mother continues, actually trying to recall the questions in the survey.

Austin just stands there like a deer caught in headlights. "Um…"

"Well, that isn't good if you have to think about it. I'll send you the quiz, too. You can both take it and see."

"Can you send it to me, too?" Noah asks, grabbing a grape from the fruit bowl. "Frank, did you take this quiz?" He turns to my father.

"Don't need to. I'm a bull in the sack," My father deadpans, fist pumping in the air.

"Gross, I think I'm going to be sick." I put my hand on my stomach.

"Maybe you caught Kaleigh's bug." My mother is not catching on.

"I think lunch is ready." Austin heads to the stove at the same time Kaleigh comes back into the room. "Kaleigh, we made you some tofu stuff that Lauren found in the freezer. I made sure to put it in another pan."

"Awww, so you forgive me for tricking you into drinking breast milk?" she asks him with a smile.

I grab the side dishes that have been warming in the oven with the roast, while Austin grabs the roast. My father grabs drinks from the fridge, and my mother calls the kids. Noah walks over to the wine fridge, grabbing two bottles.

We make our way to the dining room. Gabe runs in, while Austin puts the roast down. Rachel comes into the room banging two white things together. "Tap, tap, tap!" she shouts. "Click, click, click."

"What is that?" I look at the white sticks in her hand.

"They're drum sticks. I found them in the bathroom." She is still tapping them together. "Like a wand. Bippity boppity bo."

"Oh my God," I hear Kaleigh whisper as my mother grabs one of the sticks from Rachel's hand.

"Oh my god." She looks at me. "You're pregnant!" She sits down at the table.

My head snaps back and I grab the other stick from Rachel. Sure enough, it's another positive pregnancy test.

I look at Austin, who has gone paler than a ghost. "Lauren?" he questions, holding the table with one hand, while he looks like he is going to fall over.

"You have to marry her," my mother announces with tears in her eyes. "A child out of wedlock is a no-no." She shakes her head no over and over again

"Lauren," I hear Austin again, this time his voice quivering.

I look around the faces at the table. My heart beating fast in my ears, my throat going dry, my palms getting sweaty.

"It's mine," I hear from Kaleigh, who then looks at Noah. "I'm pregnant."

Noah places the bottles of wine on the table. "What do you mean?"

"I mean, I'm pregnant," Kaleigh repeats, throwing her hands in the air.

"But… but… but," Noah stutters.

"This is worse than Lauren being pregnant," My mother groans with tears running down her face.

"Mom," I snap at her, walking over to Kaleigh and hugging her. "It's going to be okay," I whisper in her ear.

"Holy shit," Austin breathes, finally sitting down.

Noah walks over to us, grabbing Kaleigh's face in both his hands. "I love you. So, so much. More than I love me." He smiles at her and rubs away the tears that are rolling down her cheeks. "Marry me? Be my wife?"

"Are you sure?" Kaleigh asks him while she puts her hands on his.

"More sure than anything I've ever done in my whole life." He pulls her close to him.

"Yes," she agrees right before her hands leave his and she throws them around his neck, kissing him.

"This is wonderful," my mother squeals. "Frank, we are planning a wedding."

"Great!" My father looks at Austin. "Open that wine."

"I'm getting married!" Kaleigh shouts.

"Um," Noah murmurs as we all turn to look at him. "I just need to get divorced first."

EPILOGUE

Lauren

My heels click on the cement pavement as I walk down the street. I'm going to meet Austin at his 'new adventure,' as he calls it. Kaleigh was supposed to come with me, but the baby is throwing up, so she opted out of it.

It's been over a year since he smashed into my car. One year of pure happiness, really; well, minus that week I kicked him out after he bought both kids a drum set. That they played together. We also made the decision that we should keep it at his house, for when we go there.

The cream peep-toe slingback shoes I'm wearing are starting to pinch my feet, but they were the only shoes I had that go with this outfit. I'm wearing a baby pink high-waisted pencil skirt that stops at the knee and a long-sleeved, lace turtleneck crop top to match. My hair is pinned up in a bun at the base of my neck. To show off the lace back, a gold zipper is holding it together.

I make my way up the stairs to the address he gave me. I check my phone and make sure I'm in the right place. Once I confirm that I am, I pull open the huge mahogany door.

Opening the door, I step inside and stop. The whole room is filled with white candles, accentuating the dark mahogany color of the interior. The thick bar sits in the middle of the room, open on both sides. Bouquets of white roses fill all four corners of it. Three crystal chandeliers hang above the bar. Shimmering pieces of crystal drip down from it, looking like diamonds falling.

The whole place has low tables, all with white roses in the center and candles around them. The flickering candlelight throughout the bar casts a dim yellow glow through the space. There, standing in the middle of the room, leaning against the bar, is my man. Dressed in one of his black suits, this one with a slight sheen to it. One arm cocked on the bar, with his feet crossed in front of him. "Hey there, beautiful," he says, coming to meet me.

"What is this?" I look around, noticing that no one else is here.

"You look fantastic." He moves down to kiss my neck.

"You look pretty fantastic yourself." I hold onto his jacket lapels. "What is this?"

"This," he tells me, "is my new adventure called Crazy Days. It's mine and John's and Noah's. God forbid, we leave him out."

"So, this is all yours?" I look around to see that it is very him. Dark mahogany everywhere, low tables, elegant.

"It's ours," he says as I see his hands fidget at his sides. "I sold my house." He rubs them together. "I'm never there. It was silly to keep it. But..." His voice trails off.

"But?" I walk to him and take his hand, which is cold in mine. "What is going on?" I kiss his hand to try and make him feel better.

"I want us to buy a house together. I want us to have something together that is just ours," he whispers and then lifts our hands to kiss mine.

"Okay," I tell him.

"Okay? Just like that, okay?" He is surprised by my answer.

"Honey, we live together. We haven't spent a night apart in a year." I smile at him, while he looks down at me. "I would like to stay in the same neighborhood for the kids and school, but yeah, just like that."

He smiles at me, his eyes lighting up. "That was easy." He drops to one knee in front of me. The hand that he isn't holding moves to cover my mouth, and the purse that was in it falls to the floor. "The day I ran into you changed my life. You came into the office with all that sass, and you almost killed me. Twice." He laughs, his eyes never leaving mine, while I smile at the memory.

"Oh, please, how was I to know you were allergic to that powder?" I roll my eyes at him. "I saw the pictures. It wasn't that bad."

He just glares at me, obviously disagreeing. "Needless to say, I fell in love with you. I fell in love with Gabe and Rachel, and even Kaleigh." continues, "I want us to be together forever. I want to wake up every morning and see my ring on your finger. I want to go out and hold your hand for everyone to know that you're mine." He shakes his head. "I know it sounds silly, but my ring on your finger, the world knowing that you're all mine, it's important to me."

The tear that I blinked back now makes its way down my cheek. "You want me to be yours?" I ask him as he nods his head yes. "Good, because I want you to be mine. I want to see *my* ring on your finger every morning. I want to see *my* ring glisten in the sun when you drink coffee at work. I want to see *my* ring on your finger when we go to hockey games and the other moms all drool over you." I smile at him. "So, I guess that would be a yes. Yes, I'll be yours. I'll be your wife. I'll be yours forever." I tell him and in one second, he is off his knee and twirling me in his arms. I laugh out loud while I wrap my arms around his neck, my head leaning against his. He stops and puts me down, taking a blue ring box from his pocket. When he opens the box, the round diamond solitaire sparkles in the candlelight. He grabs my left hand, slipping the ring on my finger. It is a perfect fit.

"She said yes!" he calls out, and I laugh at him before, seemingly out of nowhere, Gabe and Rachel run to us, followed by my mother and father. Noah, Kaleigh, Barbara, and all of our closest friends and family follow them.

I hear congratulations being shouted out while a waiter comes around with glasses of champagne. Austin makes his way back to me with Gabe next to him and Rachel holding his hand, and he raises his glass to toast. "Thank you, everyone, for coming. I would like to toast to my future wife, and to Gabe and Rachel for giving me their permission. Cheers."

"To tempting the boss," I say as I raise my glass with a smile for the man who started off as my boss and ended up being the man of my dreams. He leans down and kisses my lips, sealing the deal.

And they lived happily ever after.

ABOUT THE AUTHOR

When her nose isn't buried in a book, or her fingers flying across a keyboard writing, she's in the kitchen creating gourmet meals. You can find her, in four inch heels no less, in the car chauffeuring kids, or possibly with her husband scheduling his business trips. It's a good thing her characters do what she says, because even her Labrador doesn't listen to her...

Facebook
https://www.facebook.com/AuthorNatashaMadison/

Twitter
https://twitter.com/natashamauthor

Instagram
https://www.instagram.com/natashamauthor/

ReadersGroup
 https://www.facebook.com/groups/1152112081478827/

Goodreads
https://www.goodreads.com/author/show/15371222.Natasha_Madison

Amazon
https://www.amazon.com/Natasha-Madison/e/B01JFFMPP8/ref=ntt_dp_epwbk_0

OTHER TITLES FROM NATASHA MADISON

HELL AND BACK
SOMETHING SO RIGHT
PIECES OF HEAVEN

ACKNOWLEDGMENTS

Every single time I keep thinking it's going to be easy. It takes a village to help and I don't want to leave anyone out.

My family: Matteo, Michael, and Erica, Thank you for letting me do this. You encouraged me, you pushed me, you support me, and I am utterly and forever grateful for all of that. Well when you weren't complaining you want real home cooked food, which was often. Thank you for going on this journey with me.

My Husband: You share me with this hobby that has taken over our lives. Thank you for holding my hand and for coming up with words when I'm stuck.

Crystal: My hooker. What don't you do for me? You named this book! Thank you for holding my hand. Thank you for cheering me on even when I was overly dramatic. Just thank you for being you and loving me!

Rachel: You are my blurb bitch. Each time you do it without even reading this book and you rocked it. I'm really happy I bulldozed my way into your life.

Kendall: You have become a special part of me. The nice part, of course. You pumped me up when I get down, you pushed me to be better, and you made me cry. Your friendship is better than chocolate.

Lori: I don't know what I would do without you in my life. You take over and I don't even have to ask or worry because I know everything will be fine, because you're a rock star!

Beta girls: Teressa, Lisa, Natasha M, Lori, Sian, Yolanda, and Ashley. You girls made me not give up. You loved each and every single word and wrote and begged and pleaded for more.

Danielle Deraney Palumbo: See I told you, rainbow and glitter farts.

Madison Maniacs: This group is my go to, my safe place. You push me and get excited for me and I can't wait to watch us grow even bigger!

Mia: I'm so happy that Nanny threw out Archer's Voice and I needed to tell you because that snowballed to a friendship that is without a doubt the best ever!

Neda: You answer my question no matter how stupid they sound. Thank you for being you, thank you for everything!

Julia My Editor: Thank you for not tearing my book to shreds and for loving it with me.

BLOGGERS. THANK YOU FOR TAKING A CHANCE ON ME. EVEN WHEN I HAD NO COVER, NO BLURB, NO NOTHING! FOR SHARING MY BOOK, MY TEASERS, MY COVER, EVERYTHING. IT COULDN'T BE DONE WITHOUT YOU!

My Girls: Sabrina, Melanie, Marie-Eve, Lydia, Shelly, Stephanie, Marisa. Your support during this whole ride has been amazing. GUYS, HOLY SHIT, LOOK AT ME GO!

Made in the USA
Lexington, KY
27 July 2017